ONE WINTER ... ND

WINTER ROMANCE ...LECTION

❄

MELISSA HILL

Copyright © Little Blue Books 2024

The right of Melissa Hill to be identified as the Author of the Work has been asserted by her in accordance with the Copyright, Designs and Patents Act 1988.

All rights reserved. No part of this publication may be reproduced, stored in a retrieval system, or transmitted, in any form or by any means without the prior written permission of the author. You must not circulate this book in any format.

All characters in this publication are fictitious and any resemblance to real persons, living or dead is purely coincidental.

A WEEKEND IN VENICE

CHAPTER 1

"She is beautiful, no?"

"What?" Max shook himself out of his daze. He was huddled uncomfortably at the back of a Venetian water taxi, trying to ignore the swaying of the little boat and the lapping water of the canal only inches away.

"The city, Venice. She is beautiful?" The driver gestured with both hands to the wintry scenery around them, seemingly unperturbed about steering the vessel.

"Oh. Yes—of course."

The Italian man beamed and went back to zooming along the canal. Max tightened his grip on the wooden seat and tried not to show his extreme discomfort at being forced to ride in this treacherous little bucket.

Instead, he focused his attention on his wife Naomi, who was gazing around in pure delight.

If this makes her happy, then it will be worth it. Max tried to keep that thought in the forefront of his mind. It would be worth the long flight, the chilly December air, and yes even the endless network of canals, if only his wife enjoyed their trip.

It was a much-needed getaway for both of them. They hadn't

had a moment to themselves, let alone a whole weekend, since the birth of their daughter eight months before. Max loved baby Julia and adored being a father—he wouldn't trade it for anything in the world—but in truth, the craziness of having a newborn in the house was taking its toll on their marriage.

Julia had only just begun to sleep through the night, and Naomi's constant fussing over the baby was hard to take. She was reluctant to leave her alone with a babysitter for more than a few hours; the fact that he'd convinced her to leave her with her parents for a whole weekend was a minor miracle.

But she'd agreed—reluctantly, but even so—and Max had put together a romantic weekend getaway as an early Christmas present for her. He knew she'd dreamed of visiting Venice all her life.

As for himself, he had no love of the water, no taste for Italian food, and no knowledge whatsoever of the language or history of this odd little place. But if the break could help them reconnect as a couple—no demanding infant in the background, no baby paraphernalia to cart around everywhere—then it would be well worth the discomfort.

He snuck another glance at his wife. *So far, so good.*

She'd nearly had a change of heart at the last minute, fretting over how Julia would do on a full weekend without her. Luckily, Naomi's mother had all but shoved her out the door of their home. "You need a break." she'd said firmly. "You have a husband, remember? Spend some time with him. Try and remember what your relationship was like before the baby came along."

"But what if she misses me?" Naomi protested feebly, and her mother waved a hand in dismissal.

"There's such a thing as being too attached, darling. She'll be fine. She has to learn to spend a little time away from you sooner or later. What will you do when she goes to preschool? When she has friends and wants to go to a sleepover? Do you want her to be so attached to you that she can't function on her own?"

Naomi hadn't liked that very much, Max could tell, but she didn't really have a reply. And so, taking wheeled suitcases packed with warm clothing and rain gear—Max had read that Venice could be rainy this time of year—they took a taxi to Gatwick and set off for Italy, Naomi fretting about what she was leaving behind, and Max thinking warily about everything that lay ahead.

THEIR HOTEL WAS on the water—*right* on the water, as was everything in Venice, with guests stepping out of water taxis onto a dock with an awning and large double doors welcoming them into the lobby.

The concierge checked Max and Naomi in quickly and summoned another employee to help them carry their luggage up the stairs; apparently there was no lift in the building.

Their room was small but cosy, and there was a little kitchenette with a coffee maker and a microwave. The wooden headboard and dresser were ornately carved and there was a vase of perky fresh flowers on the nightstand.

Max stowed their suitcases and checked his watch; they'd arrived in the late afternoon, and there was still some weak winter sunshine outside as the sunset. "Well. We're here. Dominic we head out for a bite of dinner?" Travel always made him hungry.

But Naomi was already on the phone. "I'm just going to call Mum and Dad quickly and check in on Julia," she explained, covering the mouthpiece with one hand. "It'll only take a minute."

Max nodded and stifled a sigh. *She's going to be calling multiple times a day*, he thought gloomily. *I'm going to have to work hard to keep her distracted.*

Naomi was making cooing noises into the phone, talking to their daughter.

He could tell when her mother came back on the line because the cooing stopped and his wife said reluctantly: "Well, I know it's still early but I just wanted to—oh, the flight was fine. Did she sleep through her afternoon nap? Oh, that's good." Max thought his wife almost sounded a little disappointed to hear that Julia seemed to be doing fine without her.

When Naomi finally put down the phone he suggested brightly that they find a place to eat lunch but she still seemed worried and distracted.

"Mum says she slept this afternoon but I can't help worrying—I mean, we'll be gone for three nights, and what if she doesn't sleep through the night for any of them? Maybe a full weekend was too much too soon, Max. Maybe we should have stuck to just a night in London in case something goes wrong and she needs us..."

He stifled a groan and wrapped his wife in a hug. "Look, you're an amazing mother, and it's brilliant that you love our daughter so much. I do too. But your mum will take great care of her! I'm sure she's thrilled to get some grandma-granddaughter time in. In the meantime, let me spoil you, okay? A night in London is nothing out of the ordinary. You've always wanted to visit Venice and I want us to really make the most of this weekend."

"Well, okay." Naomi melted a little in his arms, returning his hug. She smelled like vanilla and pears—the perfume she'd worn since they first started dating over six years ago.

Max breathed deeply of her scent and promised himself that he would make sure she enjoyed herself with the most perfect, romantic vacation possible. *Even if we do have to go everywhere in a bloody boat.*

He couldn't actually understand why he feared the water so much. When people asked, he usually told them that as a toddler he fell off a dock into a deep lake while at a family reunion. Unable to swim, he would have drowned if an older cousin hadn't quickly pulled him out.

In truth, though, the story was a lie. Max had never fallen off a dock and never even come close to drowning; in fact, he'd taken swimming lessons and learned to swim perfectly well.

He just didn't like water, or boats or being piloted everywhere in one of these low-riding gondola things that Venetian tourists seemed to view as so romantic. All the same, there was no way to get from their hotel to the restaurant he'd selected from the guidebook unless they went via water, so again they climbed into a water taxi and set off.

The driver chatted to them in a mix of English and Italian. Max truly only grasped every other word the guy was saying, so he tried to smile and pretend he was too wrapped up in the city sights to talk.

Naomi leaned forward to talk to the driver, asking him about sights as they glided down the Grand Canal and asking him how to say basic words and phrases in Italian.

Finally, they reached the area of the restaurant and disembarked from the water taxi.

There were only a few other diners—apparently a Thursday evening in December was not the busiest time in Venice for tourists—and Max and Naomi were given a quiet table with a nice view of the canal.

Nice if you enjoyed looking at the water, Max thought bleakly and turned his attention to the menu.

Once again his lack of Italian was flustering him. He read through the dishes suspiciously. Culinary exploration was not one of his strong points; in fact, when he and Naomi had first started going out, it had been a bit of an inside joke between them.

After a while, though, it turned into a slight sore spot. Naomi loved ethnic foods, trying new recipes, and sampling new cuisine at new restaurants. For Max, the definition of "trying a new food" meant using a different brand of ketchup on his burger. He preferred good old English cooking—burgers, meat-and-potatoes dishes, that sort of thing—and tried new stuff only with the greatest of reluctance.

As far as Italian food, spaghetti and meatballs were about as familiar as he got with the cuisine. *Antipasto?* That sounded like something that would require an antacid later on. *Secondi?* He didn't know what it was, but it sounded like a side effect of a bad illness. *Brioches?* Were they made of shoe leather? There were plenty of other items on the menu that he couldn't even pronounce.

When the waiter finally appeared to take their order, Max explained haltingly his trouble with the choices. The waiter smiled and explained several of the dishes.

Finally, Max settled on polenta with grilled meat and vegetables. The way the waiter explained it, the polenta sounded like a kind of cornmeal porridge, which seemed like a weird choice for a dinner item, but he supposed it was better than pumpkin ravioli or calf liver and onions, both of which the waiter explained were Venetian specialities and seemed to think were very fine dishes.

Max ordered a bottle of red wine for the table while Naomi picked out her own meal—some type of fried sardine and onion dish, risotto, and vegetables. It didn't sound in the least bit appetising to Max, but he wasn't about to admit that.

The food arrived quickly and they dug in. Max decided the polenta wasn't half bad; at least there was a generous helping of meat to be had, though he couldn't help wishing for a bottle of ketchup to smother it in. He poked through the vegetables and wondered idly if Italian supermarkets sold anything like Heinz; he could buy a bottle and carry it around with him.

Dessert was at least a touch more familiar; Naomi ordered tiramisu, that strange, spongy creation which looked like cake but was soaked in espresso and a dark cocoa powder that made his nose feel itchy.

For himself, he managed to order, of all things, a small plate of fried doughnuts and a cup of coffee. The doughnuts were suspiciously filled with raisins and bits of orange, and the coffee was extremely strong, but at least it somewhat resembled something he might find back at home in England.

He was pleased at least to see that Naomi was enjoying the meal though. She'd *ooh*ed and *aah*ed at every dish the waiter presented and blissfully downed two glasses of wine.

They'd lingered over their meal for over two hours; now she seemed quite ready to return to the hotel for an early bedtime.

"Great food," Max exclaimed, more enthusiastically than he felt, as he paid the bill and then hailed yet another water taxi. *How many more of these meals will I have to eat? Not to mention get water taxis.... Let's see, tomorrow is Friday and our flight leaves Monday morning...*

The driver helped them into the boat and they sat down at the back, Max somewhat awkwardly, Naomi leaning her head on his shoulder.

"This was a good idea," she surprised him by saying. He put one arm around her shoulders and squeezed gently, forgetting momentarily the uncomfortable rocking of the boat.

The sun had set, leaving Venice dark and quiet for the night. City lights reflected on the canal and lent the scene a sort of peace that even Max could appreciate. Bright lights twinkled here and there; the city was getting ready for the Christmas season.

Back at the hotel they hung up their coats, scarves and gloves and turned down the bed. After the earlier flight and the heavy dinner, Max was ready for an early bedtime.

Naomi's hand wavered momentarily over the phone, and Max hesitated, holding a spare blanket. Then she let out a massive yawn, covering her mouth in surprise. "Oh my goodness! I don't know where that came from."

"I do," he said smiling. "You're just worn out from the journey and all the excitement of finally being here."

"I suppose that is it," she agreed.

Max duly spread the extra blanket over the bed for added warmth and watched with relief as Naomi switched off the lamp and curled up in bed, phone call forgotten.

He switched off his own bedside lamp and curled up next to her, breathing in her vanilla-pear perfume and stroking her hair as she snored softly.

Maybe Venice can work its magic on us yet, he thought sleepily, before he too drifted off to sleep.

CHAPTER 2

❄

*L*ucy stared forlornly out the window of the plane. They were descending into Venice and in the late afternoon sunshine, she could see the city laid out below her, full of promise.

But she didn't have eyes for the snow on the cobbled rooftops, or the maze of canals in the place of city streets. She was too wrapped up in her thoughts to notice any of those picturesque details.

She exited the plane with the other passengers and collected her luggage mechanically, moving through the airport terminal with a heavy heart. She flagged down a cab that would take her as far as the outskirts of the city, and from there she needed to get a water taxi to take her to the hotel for the night. After the flight from Dublin, she needed a hot bath, a simple meal and a long, deep sleep in a plush bed.

At the Piazzale Roma - the main transport hub of the city — her water taxi driver helped her load up her luggage and steered the little boat quietly along the canals of San Marco, sensing she wasn't in the mood for small talk.

Reaching the stop-off point to the hotel which was located a couple of blocks away from the Grand Canal, Lucy got out near Rialto bridge and dragged her single suitcase along the cobbled streets to the hotel.

She checked in and accepted her room key with a smile and a nod, trudging quietly up the stairs to her room and dropping the suitcase on the floor.

One year.

It seemed so much longer. Only one year had passed since she and Dominic had enjoyed the weekend of their dreams here in Venice.

Gliding along the canals, drinking too much wine in trattorias, taking in the theatres and the opera of the festive season—it had been a magical time, full of romance.

Then towards the end, they had capped it all by stealing away to a quiet corner of the city — a tiny bridge off a side street, away from the hustle and bustle of central San Marco.

There, on the picturesque wrought-iron bridge and above the inky black canal waters, they had marked their initials on a metal padlock and hung it from the rail of the bridge, sealing in a promise of their love in this most romantic of cities.

What a difference a year makes, Lucy thought forlornly. Maybe the trip had been *too* romantic, too perfect, because not long after they returned to Dublin everything seemed to start going downhill.

For starters, they'd got into a fight at a friend's party on New Year's Eve over a simple understanding made much worse by the copious amounts of drunken champagne. Then Lucy suffered from a cold on and off for the rest of the winter, and feeling rundown only made her more irritable, which led to more fighting.

Spring was supposed to be a breath of fresh air, but a promotion at work meant more hours away from home, which Dominic resented. Once summer came she thought they might get away for a mini-break to make up for all the stress, but then he was busy with family issues. By the time autumn arrived, there was barely a shred left of the relationship they had once had, and one day Dominic announced out of the blue that it was over.

He was moving on, and so should she.

In retrospect Lucy supposed she shouldn't be surprised. But she was still hurt. How could someone just walk away so easily, without putting up a fight? Surely everyone had a bad year now and then, and it was worth sorting through it all to save your relationship.

In any case, Dominic was gone, and Lucy was back in Venice alone.

She shrugged off her coat and scarf, hanging them over the back of a chair, and slipped her tired feet out of her boots. When she and Dominic had come here last year, she'd packed two suitcases full of clothes—gorgeous dresses, cashmere scarfs, plenty of jewellery, and of course silky negligees to wear underneath. Now she had a single suitcase with a few sweaters and pyjamas in it. What was the point in dressing up, when there was no one special to see it?

Lucy slowly got ready for bed, changing into cosy flannel pyjamas and brushing out the knots in her hair. *Once this weekend is over, I'll feel better,* she promised herself.

Eating Ben and Jerry's in front of the TV and crying on the phone with her friends wasn't helping her feel better about her break-up, so she was trying a more radical plan.

She would unlock the padlock from the bridge, thereby unsealing their promise of last year. Maybe then she could finally move on with her life and accept that Dominic was gone for good.

CHAPTER 3

In the morning Lucy located a café and sat down for a lonely breakfast. The skies were full of the promise of snow, much as they had been here this time last year.

She ordered a cappuccino and biscuits and gazed out the window of the café. San Marco was twinkling with holiday lights; festive greenery hung from balconies and decorated windows and shop fronts. All along the canals, glowing decorations were reflected in the water. Venice was well and truly ready for Christmas.

Other tourists were enjoying the morning, gliding down the canals in gondolas or hoofing it on one of the narrow cobblestone side streets. Some were shopping, enjoying an early morning cup of coffee, and others had their heads down, chatting on cell phones and planning out their day. Lucy watched idly as they passed her by. People were walking alone, but there were many couples or families out and about, too. It gave her a small pang to see so many carefree people happily striding by when she herself felt so down in the dumps.

She sipped her cappuccino and considered what she should do over the next two days. She truly adored Venice and would love nothing more than to spend more time exploring it, so she hadn't booked her return ticket until Monday morning.

That gave her plenty of time to hit the major sites—St. Mark's Square, perhaps a concert at the Basilica—and maybe just float around the city a bit on a gondola, looking at all of the lights and enjoying the gentle chatter of other tourists. It would be a nice, relaxing, and well-deserved weekend break.

Since the sun was peeking weakly through the clouds and the temperature seemed fairly moderate, Lucy decided to make her first stop at the Piazza San Marco—St. Mark's Square—for a refreshing stroll and some more people-watching. She didn't fancy lingering outdoors in the cold but as she was bundled up in a wool coat and cuddly scarf, she thought a little walking about wouldn't hurt. Besides, she wanted to get a closer look at the architecture of St. Mark's Basilica. She and Dominic had briefly visited it last year, but one visit was not enough.

Her memories of that visit with Dominic stabbed a bit. They had strolled through the square, surrounded by the cooing of pigeons and the lightly falling snow, admiring the cathedral but mostly admiring each other. *Well, this time I'll be alone, so maybe I'll get a better look at the details,* Lucy thought ruefully.

And the Basilica was magnificent, even if she had no one to share the view with. The murals on the outside and the gleaming domes were beautiful. She stood for a moment on the stones of the piazza, contemplating the work that must have gone into planning and building such a magnificent structure.

Other tourists nearby were talking about the cathedral and snapping pictures, and she amused herself by watching them, too.

One couple in particular caught her eye. Something about them reminded Lucy of Dominic and herself on their prior trip; something about their cosy posture that said clearly "We're head over heels in love".

The girl had red hair tumbling down under a knitted hat and was wearing a bright red pea coat that complimented rather than competed with her hair. The young man was clearly enamoured of her, though he also seemed a bit distracted. Lucy looked closer. Not distracted...nervous? Suddenly he slipped down to one knee in the crowd, and Lucy realised what he was about to do.

A proposal! The romance of it touched her as much as it hurt, and she turned away quickly, partly to give the young couple their privacy, and also to spare her own feelings. She wouldn't deny that when she and Dominic had visited the city, she'd secretly hoped it might lead to a proposal. Clearly, it wasn't meant to be.

Lucy decided to warm up a little by touring the inside of the Basilica. The interior was just as impressive; gleaming gold and bronze mosaics on the ceiling gave the cathedral a warm, shimmering appearance. Between the mosaics and the enormous paintings everywhere the eye could travel, Lucy had the feeling of being inside a Faberge egg. It was incredibly beautiful and a little overwhelming. She found a pew away from other groups of tourists and sat down to admire the interior of the cathedral.

She was still musing about Dominic when she had the oddest feeling of being watched. Turning, she glanced around the back of the pews, but it was so large and there were so many other groups of people that it was hard to tell if anyone in particular had been looking at her.

Nonsense, she thought sadly. *You're so lonely that now you're imagining you might bump into a friend, at least for the duration of your trip. Snap out of it!*

She looked back up to the religious paintings on the ceiling and resolved to put the feeling behind her. If someone could put so much effort into a project of this scale, I think I can manage the very tiny project of rebuilding my love life, she thought resolutely.

And with that notion, she decided to put Dominic out of her mind for the rest of her trip.

She would enjoy herself, unlock that padlock, and fly home again ready to start over fresh and enjoy her newly single life.

CHAPTER 4

*O*utside the cathedral Lucy had to make a decision about what tourist site to visit next. The Basilica tour guide had recommended the Doge's Palace, across the Square, but she wasn't altogether interested in another tour of rooms and historical artefacts.

Instead she decided to take a boat tour.

She'd heard that the slow-moving vaporetto on the Grand Canal offered a great water tour of the San Marco, and somehow she and Dominic had never gotten around to taking one last year. It would be nice to see the city during the daytime when she could really peer at the sights.

She bought a ticket and a hot chocolate and took her seat, with her guidebook at the ready. The views were pretty decent: she could see the bridges on the main canal and the side streets, including Rialto Bridge, which was decorated with festive lights for the season. Gradually she stopped thinking about everything she saw in the context of whether she and Dominic had seen it the year before; she was simply enjoying the colourful buildings and festive displays as they slid by, simply because they were beautiful—not because they evoked any particular memories.

The water bus ran around the city for about an hour. Finally, Lucy collected her guidebook and empty cup and stepped off to plan the next part of her day. She fancied going out to Murano Island to visit a glass-blowing studio, and since the next water bus wasn't leaving for nearly an hour, she decided to grab a quick bite of lunch first.

There were plenty of cafes and small restaurants offering both traditional Italian lunches and more standardised tourist offerings, like miniature pizzas. Lucy chose a hot sandwich and another frothy cappuccino and watched the tourists around her while she ate. She'd always enjoyed people-watching, and it helped to distract her from the fact that she was alone.

Finally, it was time to board the water bus and head out to Murano. Lucy was happy to see that there weren't quite as many tourists out here; the island was much quieter by comparison to San Marco, though there were still some tourists here and there exploring on foot. She wandered the streets until she found a quiet glass-blowing shop that appeared to be open, and ducked inside.

The man in the workshop was skilfully blowing and moulding glass before the delighted eyes of a few other tourists. Lucy watched with wonder as the man shaped the molten glass into a vase. The tourists broke into applause, and the man smiled. Lucy lingered on for a while to listen to him explain his craft, the history of glass-blowing in the city, and the time that went into crafting each piece.

In display cabinets there were glass vases, abstract sculptures and glassware for the kitchen; Lucy marvelled at the work that went into each piece. Ultimately she left without purchasing anything; she certainly didn't need anything for herself and she was terrified of something breaking in transit back to Dublin. *Maybe another time,* she thought wistfully, giving the colourful, fragile pieces one last look before exiting into the street.

Almost before she knew it the sun was setting over the island and it was time to take the water bus back to San Marco. By the time Lucy reached her hotel, she was famished, and she was happy to pop into a small trattoria down the street for her evening meal. *I don't think I'll ever tire of the food here,* she thought as she dug into a fragrant bowl of pasta and washed it down with a glass of wine.

By the time Lucy returned to her room and crawled into bed, it was fully dark in Venice, and the city was slowly quieting down as people returned to their homes or hotels for the night. Somewhere in the distance, Lucy thought she could hear Christmas carols playing in Italian.

"Goodnight, Venice," she mumbled sleepily, burrowing deeper into her blankets. For the first time in weeks, she was looking forward to the coming weekend.

CHAPTER 5

Scott checked the pocket of his coat for what seemed like the hundredth time.

Still there.

He patted his pocket and zipped up his coat, stepping out of the hotel lobby into the brisk December air.

Rachel was waiting for him outside. Her red hair was gleaming under a knit cap and she was wearing a red woollen pea coat that made her look as though she belonged on a Christmas postcard.

Scott stood back for a moment, silently admiring his girlfriend as she chatted to an older woman in fluent Italian. Rachel was obsessed with Italy—the language, the art, the food, everything—so of course when everyone else chose to study Spanish or French in high school, she picked Italian.

She'd even spent a college semester abroad in Italy as an exchange student. Her efforts were paying off now; she'd been eagerly chatting to everyone she met since they'd touched down from New York on Thursday night. She seemed to be having the time of her life.

Everything is going according to plan, Scott thought with relief.

After all, when your girlfriend is obsessed with all things Italian, what better place to whisk her away for a romantic vacation…and a Christmas proposal?

He'd spent nearly six months planning everything out. Step one: find the perfect ring, a combo of diamonds and emeralds that would appeal to Rachel's non-traditional tastes. Step two: book the perfect hotel in Venice, a five-star affair with a gorgeous view of the Grand Canal. He wanted their long weekend in the city to be one of utmost luxury; nothing less would do.

Step three: choose a romantic site for his proposal. Venice had such a reputation as a romantic city, he was sure he'd have no shortage of memorable spots to choose from, so he planned to take Rachel on an extended tour of the city and just wait until the mood felt right. They had plans to visit the Basilica, have a romantic dinner or two, and perhaps tour the canals, so he was confident the perfect magical setting for a proposal would present itself in no time.

But first, they needed to get breakfast. A small café near their hotel offered piping hot cappuccinos, pastries and more for a tasty Italian breakfast. They sat at a small table by the window, looking out at the festively decorated streets, sipping their coffee and chatting about their plans for the day.

"Where do you want to go first?" Scott asked, still absentmindedly fingering the ring box in his pocket.

"Oh, I don't know." Rachel nibbled at a pastry, her eyes alight with happiness. "There's so much to see! Did you have a preference?"

"I was thinking St. Mark's Square," he said casually. "It's pretty mild today, so it's a good day to be outside. And after that, we could tour the Basilica, since you did say you wanted to go there."

"Oh, I'd love that." Rachel gestured expressively with her hands when she was excited; just like an Italian, Scott thought. "We should go to the sung Mass there on Sunday. I hear it's amazing."

"We will," he promised. They finished breakfast and went outside to navigate their way to St Mark's Square. Scott hoped he was keeping his excitement under wraps; he didn't want Rachel to have a hint of the surprise that was waiting for her.

CHAPTER 6

They were able to zigzag their way to the Square on foot, crossing small canals via ancient stone bridges and finally emerging into the crowded piazza.

It was full of tourists and pigeons, exactly as it had looked in hundreds of postcard-worthy pictures that Scott had seen online.

Weak winter sunshine peeked through the clouds to illuminate the masses taking pictures of the Basilica or each other.

The Basilica was an impressive sight even to Scott, who knew little enough about the history of the place. The sheer size of the structure and the murals on the front of the building were enough to make anyone pause for a second look. Rachel was fairly glowing with excitement, rattling off a steady stream of facts about the architecture and construction of the cathedral. Scott looped an arm through hers as they walked, meandering slowly through the crowd. He loved her intelligence and enthusiasm for the world and was happy to listen to her talk.

Rachel trailed off and leaned her head on his shoulder, smiling. Scott gave her a quick kiss on the forehead. "What are you thinking about?"

She snuggled closer to him. "How nice it is to be here with you."

"Yeah?" He gave her an affectionate squeeze, and she grinned up at him.

"Yeah. I love it here. This is the best Christmas present ever." She stood up on tiptoe and kissed him.

He kissed her back, not caring about the crowds of tourists around them. For a moment it was as if everyone and everything else faded away, and it was only the two of them, arm in arm in this romantic city. Rachel's eyes sparkled as she turned away with a contented smile, gazing at the spires of the Basilica.

The perfect moment…

"Actually, there was something else…" Scott started to say, kneeling on the cobblestones and feeling for the ring box in his pocket.

Splat! Suddenly he felt something wet land on his head.

Horrified, he quickly stood up as Rachel turned back to him. He touched one hand to his hair and stared at the white smear on his fingers in disgust.

"Ew!" Rachel exclaimed, quickly pulling tissues out of her coat pocket. "Is that…"

"Stupid pigeons." Scott wiped at his head and looked around the square for the offending pigeon in question, but they were all busily cooing at tourists trying to get scraps of food.

"Come on," Rachel said, already tugging him toward a café on the edge of the piazza, "you can duck in the bathroom and get cleaned up, and I'll get us something hot to drink. It's kind of cold out here anyway."

"Okay," Scott said reluctantly, fingering the box in his pocket. He let her lead him across the crowded stones through even more flocks of pigeons. In the cafe, he popped upstairs to the tiny bathroom and quickly cleaned up, mortified and irritated in equal measure.

So much for that…

CHAPTER 7

When he emerged Rachel had ordered two hot coffees to go. They headed back out into the piazza, and Scott hopefully slipped an arm around her shoulders, but the earlier magic was lost.

It was late morning now, and St Mark's Square was filling up with winter tourists taking pictures and talking loudly in a mixture of languages. It was difficult to have an intimate conversation with all the noise and bustle, and Scott soon gave up trying.

When they had finished their coffees they entered the Basilica, and for a moment left the hustle and bustle of the outside masses behind. Stepping into the cathedral was an experience that Scott could only classify as otherworldly; the paintings stretched up the walls and all over the ceilings of the domes above, combined with swirling mosaics and inlays that made the entire interior seem to spring to life.

Rachel pointed out several of the paintings. "St. Mark's Basilica was constructed in the eleventh century," she whispered. "The paintings and mosaics were constructed and touched up over the centuries. Very little of the original mosaic tiling on the ceiling is left—probably only a third—due to restorations over the centuries.

If you look up to the roof you can see scenes depicting the life of Christ and the lives of the patron saints of Venice."

Scott checked out the scenes overhead. Every available nook and cranny of the walls and the ceiling was covered in some Biblical scene or another—some that he recognised, and some that he didn't. The press of tourists meant that they had to move fairly quickly through the church interior, and soon they were back out in the Square.

Rachel hooked her arm through Scott's and laced their fingers together. "So, where to next?"

"You're the tour guide," he said, and she grinned a little. "True. How about a tour of the clock tower? One should be starting soon. We can get a good view of San Marco from up there."

"Sounds good to me," Scott said, wondering if the clock tower would provide him with a good spot for a proposal. Surely a quiet spot overlooking all of the city would be romantic enough for that?

Unfortunately, the stairs were steep and crowded with tourists, and their tour guide kept up a brisk pace as he told them about the history of the construction of the piazza, the Basilica, Doge's Palace, and the clock tower itself.

"The clock tower, Torre dell'Orologio, was designed by Maurizio Codussi and took ten years to complete, beginning in 1496 and ending in 1506. The wings were added later on, perhaps by Pietro Lombardo. You can see the original workings of the clock, which was wound manually until 1998; now it runs off of electricity."

The tour ended on the roof, with a magnificent view of St Mark's Square. Scott didn't regret the tour for a second, but with all of the people, there was no way he could propose. Rachel was enjoying herself though, even if she was distracted by all of the chatter around her. She conversed for a moment in Italian with their tour guide and turned back to him. "He says that if we love the view here, we should go to the Campanile. It's the tallest building in the city."

"Off we go, then." Scott let Rachel lead the way as they

completed the tour and bounded away to the Campanile, where they climbed yet more steep stairs to reach the top. The view, however, was reward enough: at 325 feet tall, the bell tower offered them an amazing view of the city, even more so than what they had seen from the other one. All of Venice was visible from here, and even Rachel stopped talking long enough to be enchanted by the sight.

Snow dusted the rooftops of Venice like powdered sugar. Holiday decorations could be seen strung in streets and along canals; here and there a brightly lit Christmas tree was visible. From up so high the people of Venice looked like brightly coloured ants, rushing here and there in the streets. Scott's stomach rumbled, and he realised it must be dinner time; many of those people below were likely rushing off to eat.

With this in mind, he and Rachel descended the steep flights of stairs back to street level and set off in search of a restaurant.

It wasn't hard to find one, and once they were settled in and dining on appetisers of fried meatballs and calamari, waiting for their *Secondi* to appear, Scott started to relax. This day certainly hadn't lent itself to the perfect romantic moment, but it was only Friday afternoon; he had two more days to make it happen. He'd already sought out a charming restaurant and a gondola ride, both of which he imagined would be perfect settings for a proposal that would surprise and delight Rachel.

The waiter arrived with part of their order, and she chatted to him in Italian. Scott sipped contentedly at his wine. Rachel was having a blast, and he had to admit that he was having fun, too.

He just needed to be patient and wait for the right moment.

In a city so famed for romance, surely it couldn't be far away?

CHAPTER 8

❄

Naomi woke slowly, stretching languorously. The winter sunshine was barely peeking around the curtains of their hotel room, and she snuggled deeper under the fluffy duvet. Max was still sleeping, blissfully unaware of the world, and she smiled to herself.

Poor, dear Max.

She knew he was probably dreaming of being back at home in England, where he didn't have to travel by boat and where Frosted Flakes and bacon sandwiches were easy to come by.

The fact that he would go to such lengths to treat her to a dream holiday in Italy when he was so clearly out of his element spoke volumes about how he felt about her.

She stole a glance at the clock and bit her lip, feeling momentarily guilty for having not called before she went to bed for the night.

What if Julia fussed, or had trouble sleeping, or wasn't feeling well? What sort of mother didn't check up on these things?

Almost as if he could sense her consternation, Max woke beside her, stretching and groaning. Naomi smiled as she rolled over to face him. He always looked so rumpled when he woke up—hair sticking up in multiple directions, pillow creases on his face—and somehow she found it charming. He looked so relaxed and unassuming, much like he had in college when they had first started dating. She leaned over now and planted a quick kiss on his forehead. "Good morning, sleepyhead."

"Morning." He rubbed the sleep out of his eyes and looked around. "Mmm. What time is it?"

"Eight o'clock, aka time to rise and shine and get some breakfast." Naomi threw back the covers and raced to the bathroom for a hot shower. Max protested weakly from the bed, laughing. "Not fair. You had a head start."

Naomi laughed and pulled a fluffy towel down from the rack. Her guilt over not calling home was fading a little. Julia was in the most capable of hands, she reminded herself, and after all, she had to admit spending time alone with Max was a luxury she'd sorely missed.

She'd gotten so used to building her daily routine around the baby that she'd forgotten what it was like to spend a romantic evening with her husband and wake up slowly, on her own timetable, the next morning.

It was rather a lovely feeling.

Once they had both dressed for the day, in warm sweaters and coats, they set out to find breakfast. Naomi was thrilled to get a chance to experience a real Italian menu, though she could sense Max's trepidation.

To say he wasn't big on trying new foods would be putting it nicely, but luckily a traditional Continental breakfast didn't veer too far from what he was used to eating back home. At the café near their hotel, they ordered frothy cappuccinos and plates of flaky pastries filled with sweet cream or chocolate. There was fruit, yoghurt and muesli on the side and hot chocolate. Max seemed pleasantly surprised, and Naomi found herself relishing her breakfast without having to worry about feeding the baby.

CHAPTER 9

After breakfast they set out to see the sights.

Naomi had read plenty of guidebooks on Venice before they had left, taking meticulous notes in a small notebook to carry in her purse, but nothing could have prepared her for the reality of the city.

The narrow stone side streets felt almost like hidden passageways, beckoning to visitors with the promise that they might lead to some secret location. Even with the winter chill, the canals were a sight to see, with gondolas gliding past and colourfully attired gondoliers calling out to each other as they went. Everywhere there were strings of Christmas lights and oversized decorations for the upcoming festivities.

Wandering through the streets and over the stone bridges that crisscrossed the canals, Naomi felt like she was melting away into another time and place entirely. Shop windows with signs in Italian and English advertised blown glass, Venetian masks, and leather goods. They stopped to browse in a few shops and when Naomi admired a hand-blown glass Christmas ornament, Max promptly bought it for their tree back home. She eagerly pressed her face to the windows of other shops, admiring the handiwork within even though she couldn't decipher most of the signs.

There were plenty of other tourists about, but as she strolled hand in hand with her husband, Naomi was starting to feel like it was just the two of them. Max seemed happy to find plenty of streets that could be walked rather than toured by boat, and he was starting to relax.

Italian music drifted from shops and trattorias as tourists entered or exited, holding the doors open just long enough for the sounds and smells within to escape onto the street. There was an intoxicating blend of spices, perfumes, leather, food, and wine in the air, and it fueled Naomi's excitement at seeing the city.

According to her guidebooks, one of the must-see attractions in the city was the Piazza san Marco, or St. Mark's Square, which was bordered by several attractions: St. Mark's Basilica, the Doge's Palace, a historic clock tower, and a bell tower of impressive height, the tallest building in the city. Naomi had planned ahead and booked a multi-attraction ticket and tours, so they could take in all of the sights in one day.

She had no intention of missing out on anything so magnificent; after all, who knew when they might be able to take a trip like this again?

CHAPTER 10

*A*s it turned out, the tours were every bit as amazing as promised online.

The Square was packed with tourists and flocks of pigeons; Max snapped a few shots of Naomi trying to coax one onto her outstretched hand, laughing as it flew away, disgruntled, because it realised she didn't have a snack for it. They lined up with other tourists for the trip through the Basilica and were rewarded with hearty neck cramps from gawking at the mosaics and paintings inside.

"When we get back to the hotel, I'm wrapping a hot towel around my neck," Naomi said with a laugh. Max wrapped an arm around her as they moved leisurely across the Square to the clock tower, where their next tour awaited. "Maybe the front desk could recommend a spa or something? You know, one of those places that do couples' massages?"

"You'd be up for that?" Naomi looked at him in surprise. Normally any mention of a new activity would have him wrinkling his nose in suspicion. But he nodded. "You'd enjoy it. And I would…try to enjoy it!"

Naomi nestled closer to him as they joined the line for the

Doge's Palace. She couldn't even remember the last time they'd been able to do something like this—well over a year ago, she supposed, before the late stages of pregnancy and then the baby left her essentially housebound. She was startled to realise she was truly enjoying herself, not worrying about Julia. She snuck a glance at Max, who only smiled. She smiled back a little. Was he thinking the same thing—that they were long overdue for this kind of date? As if to answer her question, he pulled her close and gave her a quick kiss.

Their guide was enthusiastic about her subject and gave them a richly detailed rundown of the history of the Palazzo Ducale. Even Max looked interested as she explained that the Palace was the hub of political power in Venice from the ninth century onwards, and its proximity to the Basilica was no accident, but rather a result of the intertwining of church and state in Italy at that time. Gothic arches and an impressive array of sculptures, paintings and frescoes covered the inside of the palace. The tour wound through multiple floors, through staterooms, criminal courts, cells, cramped administrative offices, and finally outside to the Bridge of Sighs.

"Why is it called that?" asked one of the tourists, and the guide explained that the bridge connected the interrogation rooms of the Palace to the outside world. Built-in 1600, the bridge earned its name from Lord Byron centuries later based on the somewhat romantic notion that it offered convicts their last view of Venice before entering their cells; prompted by the beauty of the city, they would sigh over their city.

"Of course," she added, tapping on the stone bars on one of the bridge's tiny windows, "there wasn't a lot to back up that notion. By the time the bridge was built, there wasn't a lot of criminal traffic going in and out of the palace. And with the small windows and the roof, there wasn't much you could see of the outside city. But it makes for a very poetic name, in any case."

Following the tour of the palace Max and Naomi joined the line leading into the Torre dell'Orologio clock tower. The stairs inside the clock tower were steep, and Naomi marvelled at the idea that for years someone had actually climbed the tower regularly to wind it up. Thank goodness for the modern marvel of electricity.

If she thought that tower was steep, however, the Campanile bell tower was even more staggering. The guide explained the story of the tower's 1902 collapse and rebuilding and pointed out the view of the Dolomite mountains in the distance. Naomi sighed with delight as she leaned on the railing, surveying Venice below. It looked to her like one of those miniature Christmas towns that people assembled on their mantels in December, complete with tiny people, glowing shop windows, and snow-powdered rooftops. She could almost picture the spot where a tiny horse and carriage would travel, laden with packages to be delivered to homes in the city. Her mother loved to create such miniature cityscapes in her home every Christmas; she was probably setting one up now, or shopping for new pieces with baby Julia in tow.

The thought of her daughter made her start suddenly. She looked quickly at her phone. Time to call and check in!

She slipped the phone back into her bag and joined the crowd of tourists edging their way slowly down the steep stairs.

CHAPTER 11

❄

*N*ight was falling in Venice, and while another city might have quieted down with the dying light, San Marco seemed even more beautiful now as the Christmas lights blazed to life.

The Basilica was gloriously illuminated, and everywhere Naomi looked festive displays were being lit up in the darkness. The city looked like a romantic postcard at night.

Unfortunately, the dying daylight also meant the temperature was dropping, and Naomi and Max hastily moved on from the Square to find a restaurant. Naomi hadn't realised her stomach was growling; now she realised they had skipped lunch in the excitement of the tours. It didn't take long to find a little trattoria that wasn't too crowded and sit down to order their dinner.

Max let Naomi take the reins in ordering, and she found it hard to pick just a few dishes. There was calamari, a favourite of hers already; pumpkin risotto and seafood risotto; seafood dishes she'd never even heard of, including squid ink and cuttlefish; and of course plenty of tempting noodle and vegetable dishes, often with seafood in the mix. Max visibly paled at the mention of the squid ink but bravely ordered a tamer seafood dish with crab meat and vegetables. Naomi finally settled on her order and also asked for a bottle of wine for the table; the waiter produced one with a flourish, along with two very generously sized wine glasses.

The concept of lingering over a meal at a restaurant had always seemed a little odd back home since Julia, but somehow here in this ancient and magical city, it seemed that hurrying through the meal would be an affront to Venice itself.

Max and Naomi ate slowly, talking about everything they had seen during their tours. By the time dessert had been served, they drank the last of the wine, paid the bill and got ready to leave, they had been at the restaurant for nearly three hours.

It was only once they had returned to their hotel room that Naomi realised she hadn't called her parents to check in on Julia. While Max brushed his teeth in the bathroom, she guiltily dialled her mother's cell phone.

She answered after several rings. "Naomi! How is Venice?"

"Beautiful," she answered truthfully. "Amazing. We're seeing so much. And the food is incredible."

Her mother chuckled. "And how is Max coping?"

Naomi laughed a little, remembering her husband's face as they perused the menu at the restaurant. "Well, he's a little alarmed by some of it, and he doesn't like the boats. But he's having fun. How is Julia doing?"

"Oh, she's as perky as ever! We're out shopping for Christmas decorations now."

"You remembered to bundle her up?" Naomi immediately thought of a dozen other things to ask: *Did you pack her favourite stuffed animal? Do you have an extra soother in case she loses hers? What about a bottle? What about...did you...what if...*

But her mother seemed to anticipate the questions. "She's wearing her favourite teddy bear coat, I packed Mr. Hippo in her diaper bag, she has an extra soother and a bottle of formula, and she ate and got a clean nappy on before we left the house. And we'll be home in plenty of time for a little pre-dinner nap. Don't worry,

Naomi, she's doing fine! Concentrate on enjoying yourself. Your weekend will be over far too soon."

"I suppose you're right," Naomi said, giving her 'I love you's' and hanging up. Max emerged from the bathroom and collapsed onto the bed. "Oof. I'm worn out from all that walking. How's Julia?"

"She's doing great," Naomi said, fiddling with her phone. She felt torn—on the one hand, she was glad to hear that her daughter was doing well, but on the other, she still felt bad for being so far away. And yet, she'd truly enjoyed her day and knew this entire trip would have been impossible with a baby in tow. "You're still up for more sightseeing tomorrow?"

"Of course," he said quickly, trying to look alert and failing utterly. She leaned down and kissed him. "Get some rest. There will be plenty of time to make plans in the morning."

Max fell asleep almost immediately, and Naomi slipped under the blankets.

For a moment she debated leaving the phone on in case her mother tried to call, but then she resolutely turned the ringer to the "silent" mode. *Mum's right,* she thought sleepily, pulling the blankets up to her chin. *This weekend will be over in a heartbeat. I'm going to enjoy it while I can.* With thoughts of decadent desserts and twinkling lights still filling her head, she drifted off to sleep.

CHAPTER 12

Lucy woke on Saturday morning feeling strangely refreshed. She wasn't sure what had changed overnight, but somehow as she stretched and stood in front of her window, gazing down at the canal below, she somehow felt lighter, brighter, and full of excitement for the rest of the weekend.

She chalked it up in part to the delightfully fluffy mound of blankets and pillows on her bed—a good night's rest always made her feel so much better about things—and partly to her visits to the Basilica and Murano the day before. She couldn't exactly explain why, but seeing something so magnificent made her feel a little better about her own small problems. Even if her relationship had crashed and burned, there was still so much beauty to enjoy in the world, so why should she mope? She felt ready to get out and enjoy herself.

She hummed a little to herself as she dressed, pulling on warm black pants and a black turtleneck sweater with her boots and coat. She slightly regretted not bringing anything more colourful with her; she'd been in a bit of a funk when she packed. She pulled her blonde hair up into a French twist and added her everyday diamond stud earrings. On impulse, she popped down to the front desk and asked for the nearest chemist.

Twenty minutes later, she stood in front of the glass window of the shop, surveying her reflection as she applied red lipstick from a freshly purchased tube. She looked over her appearance with a small amount of satisfaction. The lipstick seemed to make all the difference in the world. She no longer saw a sad post-breakup woman in the mirror; now she saw a sassy single gal out to have a fun holiday weekend in a foreign city. Just this thought excited her.

She had a new sway in her step as she popped into a small coffee shop for a frothy hot coffee and biscotti. The only Italian she knew was *'grazie'* but she grinned nonetheless as she thanked the girl at the counter for her food. Sipping the coffee and munching on the crunchy-sweet biscotti, she set off down the street to the nearest dock to catch a vaporetto.

Lucy made it a point to visit museums and art galleries in any city she visited, and her main destination today was the Gallerie dell'Accademia—an amazing collection of artwork that spanned back over centuries, and included work by the sixteenth-century Venetian painter Titian—followed closely by a trip to the Peggy Guggenheim collection, which boasted a dazzling array of more modern art by American and European artists alike, including Picasso and Jackson Pollack. She was certain the museums would hold her for most of the day. After that, she could spend her Sunday doing a bit of leisurely souvenir shopping—what better Christmas gifts to bring home than genuine Italian stuff from Venice? Then, she thought sadly, she would return to the bridge and do what she came here to do.

The Gallerie proved every bit as involved as her guidebook had promised, and the hours flew by as she toured the various rooms. The tour was guided, but the group that day was fairly small, so she was able to linger and enjoy the various pieces of art. At one point she thought she saw a man who reminded her of Dominic in one of the adjoining rooms, and for a moment she wished he could be there to share the tour with her, but she quickly pushed that thought aside. *Today is for me to enjoy the present, not linger on the past.*

In one of the rooms, surveying Giorgione's *Tempest*, Lucy found herself near an English couple. She commented casually on the artwork and hearing her Irish accent, they immediately introduced themselves, and the trio quickly fell into small chat about all they'd seen in the city.

"We're here as an early Christmas present to ourselves," the man who was called Max explained, beaming at his wife. "It's our first outing since our daughter was born."

"Oh! You have a daughter?" Lucy had always loved the idea of having a little girl. "How old?"

"Eight months." His wife, Naomi was clearly a proud mum, pulling up pictures on her smartphone to show off. Lucy made appropriate compliments on the little girl's cute looks and wide smile. "Is it hard to be away from her?"

Naomi hesitated for a moment. "A little," she confessed. Max looked like he wanted to say something but wisely didn't, and Lucy guessed that it was harder than the mother wanted to admit. She tactfully changed the subject. "What's been your favourite sight in Venice so far?"

"I think the bell tower at St. Mark's Square," Naomi said dreamily. "The view makes you feel like you're looking at a postcard. It's such a romantic city."

Yes, it is, Lucy thought with a pang. She couldn't help envying the couple a bit for their romantic trip. It was clear they were relishing the time spent together, without the demands of parenthood interrupting their time together. She supposed that *was* one perk to the single life—no worries about other people imposing on your routine, especially "people" of the nappy-and-bottle variety.

Naomi was asking Lucy about her own trip to the city, and she struggled for a moment to explain what she was doing there. She finally settled on the generic half-truth "It's a gift to myself" rather than explaining that she was there to forget about love lost. It seemed like too sad a tale to share with strangers, especially those celebrating their own happy romance.

CHAPTER 13

❄

She had a bit of time in between tours to grab lunch and found herself munching on a hot panini and coffee at a tiny cafe.

Afterwards, she joined the tour through the Guggenheim collection and quickly lost herself in room after room of art. The variety presented made it impossible to get bored, and the tour almost seemed to end too quickly.

Outside the weak afternoon light signalled the close of day. Tourists were moving in groups to find dinner, attend an evening mass at one of the city's cathedrals, or rent a gondola for a private cruise up and down the canals to view the holiday lights.

Not quite yet ready to move on to dinner so early, Lucy opted to hire a gondolier and relax on the canals.

She was glad she'd bundled up warmly because the air off the water was freezing. However, the view of San Marco at night by boat was worth the chill. One of Lucy's favourite childhood memories was that of piling into the family car with her parents and siblings and driving around their hometown to look at the Christmas light displays on homes and businesses. Lucy and her sisters had given imaginary ratings to the displays as they passed and debated seriously about the merits of each display, awarding scores to the decorations based on imagination, colourfulness, and sheer size of the displays.

Some of their favourite houses went all out, with all of the trees in the front gardens ablaze in ropes of lights and lighted figures across the driveway and even on the roof. As a child Lucy had found it delightful; now she thought about how much work those displays must have entailed.

The displays in Venice evoked a similar feeling of awe.

Large lighted stars hung above her, seemingly suspended in thin air. Strings of lights outlined windows and doorways or encircled trees on balconies. Here and there a business had a brightly lit nativity or other display in their shop windows. Most of the bridges, too, were brightly lit for night, and the cathedrals all featured lighting of their own. Christmas music floated down the canals from nearby businesses; though most of it was in Italian, Lucy recognised the tunes and hummed along.

Her good-natured gondolier hummed too and occasionally sang along to the tunes.

By the end of her forty-minute boat ride, Lucy had pretty well lost the feeling in her nose and fingertips, but her heart and soul felt warmer. She asked the gondolier for a nearby restaurant recommendation and thanked him warmly, rubbing her hands together as she walked down the street. The joyful Christmas spirit combined with the obvious magic of the city was improving her mood more and more with every passing hour.

She ducked into a trattoria playing an Italian rotation of sacred festive music; Lucy recognised the tunes of "Silent Night" and several other hymns that had played on heavy rotation during her childhood. She smiled at the thought of how she had squirmed through Mass services at church while thinking ahead to opening presents!

The waiter brought appetisers and wine and soon returned to the table with a hearty order of seafood risotto, crusty bread and marinated anchovies. Lucy ate her fill and lingered at the table afterwards, enjoying a strong cup of espresso despite the late hour. She nibbled her tiramisu and asked the waiter to add an extra bottle of wine to her order; she could take that back to one of her sisters in Dublin as a Christmas gift.

Satisfied and laden down with a bag containing her wine, Lucy strolled down the street, lost in thought. She felt almost giddy from the fun of the day and of course, the delicious food. She was so lost in thought (and more than a little tipsy) that for a moment, she imagined Dominic standing at the corner of the narrow streets, waiting for her.

She sighed to herself and continued walking.

My imagination is just not going to let me be, she thought ruefully. *Now I know what unrequited love means.*

Even a full day of great fun and good food can't get a person out of your head. You still see them everywhere you go.

CHAPTER 14

Back at the hotel Lucy tucked the wine safely in her suitcase, and drew a hot bath scented with plenty of lavender and chamomile.

Soaking blissfully in the bubbles, she considered what to do the following day.

First, a lazy breakfast. Second, shopping; she was already compiling a mental list of things to look for in the little shops: a leather-bound journal for Dad, some blown-glass trinket for Mum (maybe a Venetian mask or a paperweight)?, perhaps a knitted scarf for her younger sister.

And of course, if I find some little things for myself, too, that wouldn't be half bad.

Her eyes fell on her smartphone, sitting on the bathroom counter. It was tempting—oh so tempting—to call Dominic's number, just to see what he was doing. They hadn't spoken since the breakup, but that didn't mean she couldn't call just to say hi. She might get his voicemail, and then that would solve a lot of the awkwardness of having an actual conversation. And wouldn't he be surprised when he heard she was calling from Venice?

She composed a message in her head:

Hi, Dominic, I'm in Venice and I was just thinking of you—remembering all the fun we had here last year. God, no—that was far too needy. Maybe: *Hey Dominic, was just thinking of you and wanted to wish you a Merry Christmas.*

Too casual? What about: *Hi Dominic, hope you're doing well. Maybe we could grab a coffee sometime and catch up?*

She half reached out for the phone before she pulled her arm back. *Nope. Don't do it.*

This trip was about getting over heartbreak, not inviting it back in. Besides, she wasn't sure what might be worse—having to talk to Dominic and dealing with a stilted conversation, or leaving a message that he might not return.

After all, it was possible he didn't want to speak to her at all, and calling him might just confirm that for good—something she'd rather not deal with, in all honesty.

Or, he might return her call with some news about a new girlfriend—something she *definitely* didn't want to hear about. At least if she didn't call, she didn't have to face the complications of a conversation. Dominic could stay safely tucked away in her memories and one day he would be just that—a memory.

Lucy finally drained the bathtub and wrapped herself up in a fluffy robe before settling down in bed with a magazine. She was drowsy from the wine and the warm water, and it was easy to put Dominic out of mind and curl up for bed.

She dreamed that night of standing on the bridge last winter with Dominic in the snow, hand in hand as they locked the padlock.

But in the morning she didn't remember her dreams, and she whistled cheerily to herself as she got ready for another day.

CHAPTER 15

Saturday morning dawned colder than the previous day, but Scott wasn't daunted in the least.

He'd already bounced back from the disappointment of his failed proposal at St. Mark's Square, and moved on to an even better idea: a romantic candlelit dinner near Rialto Bridge followed by a stroll along some of the quieter streets nearby.

There under a starry sky, away from all the hustle and bustle of the tourist crowds, he would get down on one knee and propose to the love of his life. He could already picture the scene in his head; he'd replayed it a dozen times since he got out of bed that morning.

But first, the day ahead promised plenty more sightseeing in the historic city. Rachel, enamoured of Italian art, was eager to tour the Gallerie dell'Accademia, which boasted centuries' worth of Italian paintings, frescoes, sculptures and more. For his part Scott didn't know the difference between the various periods and styles of painting, nor did he understand the political significance of some of the pieces, but Rachel was having fun and for her sake, he made an effort to have fun, too. It was hard to concentrate on the tour, though, when he kept thinking forward to the table he'd booked for the evening.

Even as they sat at lunch, he was only half-listening to Rachel as she chattered on eagerly about the art they'd seen. Inside he was playing out the proposal as he intended it to happen:

First, they would go to the restaurant. Scott had found one near the impressive Rialto bridge; if you sat near windows you had an excellent view of the bridge, and for the festive season the bridge was lit up much like the rest of the Grand Canal.

They would enjoy a lovely dinner, then take a walk across the bridge and enjoy the sight of the holiday lights across the Grand Canal. Perhaps, if the mood struck them, they would take a gondola down the canal and marvel at the lights from the water.

Then, they would take a quiet walk through the less-populated city streets. Then, on a quiet bridge, away from the crowds, Scott would get down on one knee, pull out the ring, and…

"Earth to Scott." He snapped out of his reverie to see that Rachel was staring at him, looking slightly bemused. He realised she must have asked a question, and he felt his ears reddening a little. "Sorry, babe, I was lost in thought. What were you saying?"

She smiled and said, "I was suggesting we do a little shopping today. Instead of hitting another museum. I could tell you were a bit bored with the last one."

Scott winced a little. "Was it that obvious?"

She laughed out loud. "It's okay. I know I'm the one who's crazy about Italy; I know you're not as big of a fan."

"We can do whatever you want today," he promised, and meant it. He wanted her to enjoy herself, and more importantly, he wanted her to be in good spirits for their dinner date. He patted his coat pocket once more and followed her out of the cafe and through the city streets.

Shopping proved to be a bit of an interesting experience. Rachel was enjoying chatting with the shopkeepers in Italian, and she found several small items that she wanted to purchase: a leather bag, a cashmere scarf with a gossamer texture and a price tag to match, and some beautiful tiny glass birds, which were wrapped carefully and placed in a sturdy box for safekeeping.

CHAPTER 16

By the time they had finished touring the shops and returned Rachel's purchases to the hotel, it was time to get ready for dinner. As usual, Scott was astounded by how a few simple changes could turn Rachel from a daytime tourist into an evening beauty.

She emerged from the bathroom with her hair swept back up from her face, showing off a pair of diamond earrings he had bought her for her birthday. She'd added a little makeup but not much—she didn't need it—and swapped out her sweater for a silky, low-cut black top. She'd kept the warm black pants and boots, though, and bundled up in a thick scarf, gloves and coat.

"It's freezing out here!" she exclaimed, as their water taxi took them to the restaurant. "I'm so glad we're not going on a gondola tour tonight."

"Yeah, me too," Scott echoed, privately disappointed. *Well, there's always tomorrow...*

As promised, the Rialto Bridge was aglow with lights that changed colour as festive tunes played over the water. Scott and Rachel *ooh*ed appreciatively at the sight and hurried into the restaurant to their table.

The waiter frowned when Scott mentioned his reservation. "We seem to have had some issues with our booking, sir," he said, and Scott's heart sank. "Somehow there are mixups with the seating. That table is not available this evening."

His expression made it clear he wasn't going to offer any further explanations or help, so Scott tried politely, "Could you find us another table then? I promised my girlfriend a romantic dinner tonight."

The man looked irritated at this request, as though the endless romantic trials of visiting tourists were of no concern to him. However, he consulted his book and grouchily conceded that he did have an available table.

"This way," he said, marching off briskly without a backward glance, and Scott and Rachel glanced at each other in concern. Nonetheless, Scott was determined to make the most of the night, and they hurried after the man to the table he indicated.

Scott thought that it was almost as if the guy had deliberately selected the worst table in the restaurant. Tucked into a dark corner, it offered no view of the bridge whatsoever, but a very good earful of the clamour from the kitchen.

He reached under the table and squeezed Rachel's hand in apology. "I'm so sorry, I didn't know this would happen. Do you want to go somewhere else?"

"No, this is fine." She busied herself studying the menu. Scott also buried himself in the menu, and when a waiter appeared to take their order, they decided to start with a round of appetisers. This waiter also seemed a little on the surly side, but Scott decided it could just be the busy evening—the restaurant was packed—and tried to brush it off.

Wine appeared on the table in short order, and Scott and Rachel tried to strike up a conversation. It was difficult to chat quietly with the din of their fellow diners and the noise from the kitchen, and after a while, they fell silent. Some time passed before it occurred to Scott that their appetisers had yet to appear. He finally caught the attention of their waiter and inquired about their order, only to be met with a terse, "I'll check" before the man disappeared without a second look.

Scott glanced at Rachel, but she was carefully studying the other diners, trying not to let on that she was disappointed. After what seemed like forever, the waiter finally returned with a plate of bread and olive oil and fried meatballs—all rather lukewarm, now, after what Scott suspected was a long period sitting on a side counter waiting to be served. They picked halfheartedly at the food and waited for their Secondi to be served.

The second round of the meal came out with decidedly more speed, but when the waiter set Rachel's dish down in front of her, she said something haltingly in Italian. The waiter did a double-take and apologised curtly, whisking the dish away. Scott didn't need a translation to know that whatever the man had brought was definitely *not* the risotto dish she'd ordered.

Next, the waiter brought out another dish, but after a couple of bites, she had to signal him back. "Sorry," she said, "it's just that this has cuttlefish in it, and I asked for the chicken."

This time the waiter was duly embarrassed, and muttered several apologies as he took away her plate. In the meantime another order had arrived—polenta with porcini and sausage—and Rachel nibbled a bit at it while they waited. She urged Scott to go ahead and eat his, but he felt bad eating when she was having so many issues with her own order.

Finally, the waiter brought out fresh risotto with chicken, and Rachel dug in. By now Scott's food was growing cold, but he ate as much of it as he could anyway. When Rachel finished eating he leaned across the table and whispered, "Do you want to order dessert?"

"No thanks!" She shook her head and glanced at the kitchen, as though expecting to see the waiter again. "No, this was terrible. Let's just go."

They paid and left, Rachel shivering in the cold. Scott quickly abandoned the idea of either a gondola ride or a walk; he guessed she wouldn't enjoy either, and after their disastrous meal, he felt terrible that he hadn't planned out better entertainment for the night.

BACK AT THE HOTEL, he scrolled through Internet listings of local late-night happenings while Rachel warmed up with a hot shower. When she emerged, wrapped up in a cosy robe, he queried, "Would you want to go out again? We could catch a late-night movie, maybe, or go to one of the local bars for a drink?"

Rachel made a face as she crawled into bed. "Ugh, I don't think so. I'm so worn out, and it's so cold. Let's just stay in for the rest of the night, okay?"

"Okay." Scott closed his laptop and decided to take a quick shower to warm up, too; Rachel was right about the temperature outside. By the time he emerged ten minutes later, however, soft snores could be heard coming from Rachel's side of the bed. Stifling a sigh of disappointment, he switched off her bedside lamp and crawled in beside her.

The ring box was still waiting in his coat pocket. Scott thought sadly of his ruined evening and wondered if the following day would provide any better chances for the proposal he wanted to make.

Come on, Venice, he thought desperately, *show me a little romantic magic before we go home.*

CHAPTER 17

Saturday morning, Max and Naomi got off to a sluggish start.

He noticed happily that she was relaxing more with each passing day; today she slept much later than usual, and seemed happy to cuddle in bed rather than rushing to get up and out the door. He took it as a good sign that the beauty of the city was working its magic.

He didn't want to say it out loud and spoil the mood, but he missed mornings like this—just the two of them, cuddled up in bed, then perhaps picking out an activity for the day. No baby needing to be fed, clothed, changed and coddled; no schedule that included mandatory feedings and naps. Just he and Naomi, the way it used to be.

Part of him felt so guilty for even thinking that though. Of course, he loved Julia—until she was born, he hadn't quite understood how people fell head over heels in love with infants, but one look into her serious green eyes and he was a goner.

He adored his daughter, loved playing with her, napping with her on his chest, dancing around in the living room holding her and listening to her laugh. He looked forward to many years of firsts—first day of school, first pet, first date, first car—and to many father-daughter chats. He was thrilled with his daughter and thrilled with what a wonderful mother Naomi was to their baby.

He just missed having his wife around, too.

He sat in bed and watched her put on makeup in the bathroom mirror. It seemed like so much of her energy these days went into the baby, not into herself. It wasn't just their relationship that had been put on the back burner; he realised that now, a bit belatedly.

Little things like putting on mascara in the mornings, or picking up a novel she wanted to read—they had gone out the window in favour of feedings, changings and caring for Julia. Max realised a bit guiltily that his wife didn't have a lot of time for her own interests anymore and he wondered if maybe he should be chipping in a lot more than he was. Either way, he wanted to do something to help make it up to her.

So, while she was busy getting ready for the day, he popped down to the hotel reception desk and asked the manager on duty to help him find a good couple's massage therapist in the city. "I don't speak Italian, so perhaps you could set something up for us? Preferably with someone who speaks a little English?"

The manager seemed only too happy to help and promised to have something lined up for the afternoon, after they came back from their museum tour but before dinner. That treat all taken care of, Max went back upstairs to collect his wife and whisk her off to tour the art galleries.

The first one was full of classical Italian art from the past several centuries, and Max looked around with amazement at the extensive collection. He didn't necessarily know anything about the artists featured—none of the names jumped out at him—but even so, it was hard not to be impressed with the huge collection. Their tour guide was fairly chatty but also let them have plenty of time to study the pictures on their own.

In one of the rooms, he and Naomi struck up a conversation with an Irish girl visiting the city—from Dublin, as it turned out.

"Oh, we're from Newcastle," Naomi explained. "So we're used to this cold!"

The woman laughed. "At least the city isn't flooded," she said. "It happens from time to time. I've been lucky though; both times I've visited it's been dry."

They chatted for a while about everything they'd seen so far, and Naomi asked if Lucy was travelling solo or with a partner. For a moment the woman looked sad, but she laughed. "No romantic trip for me, I'm afraid. I'm just taking a little break as a Christmas gift to myself."

After the galleries, Max and Naomi found a nearby café where they ordered miniature pizzas and drinks for lunch.

Naomi checked her phone, scrolling across the screen to check the time. Max could see that she was calculating the time difference and whether it was too early yet to call home, and he said quickly, "I have a surprise for you."

"Oh?" Naomi was distracted enough to put the phone back in her bag. He nodded, encouraged. "Remember I mentioned that massage yesterday? Well, I asked the hotel manager to book us one. I've got the paper in my coat pocket with the address; we can have a water taxi take us straight there. Our appointment is at two o'clock."

"Really?" He'd expected her to be excited, but he hadn't realised she would light up so much at the idea. She quickly checked the time. "Oh, we should leave now! We don't want to be late."

At her insistence, Max hurried through the rest of his pizza. *That wasn't even half-bad,* he thought reluctantly. *Maybe Italian food is growing on me.*

CHAPTER 18

The directions were clear enough to follow, and the water-taxi easily deposited them outside a luxurious looking day spa.

To Max's relief, the masseuses who were handling their appointment both spoke fluent English, so at least he didn't have to feel awkward about *that* part of things.

If Max tolerated the treatments—he thought they were a little frilly, to be honest—he could tell Naomi was beside herself. They started with a foot bath and moved through a series of massages and body treatments, rubbing in fragrant oils that Max supposed were relaxing or calming. Naomi certainly looked relaxed, and he settled down onto his treatment table, feeling a touch better himself.

By the time their hour session was up, Naomi was practically radiant, and Max could definitely feel that the kinks in his neck were long gone.

She was beaming as they glided back down a canal to another restaurant for dinner. "Have you ever felt so relaxed before?" she said dreamily, and he couldn't help but grin. He supposed he hadn't, but better than that was seeing how relaxed she was. It was like her old self was coming back—the one who wasn't constantly stressed and fussing over the baby.

Dinner was the usual mix of terrifying choices, but somehow Max didn't care so much. He discovered that he could order pasta with a tomato and meat sauce, and did so without caring if it looked too English. He didn't even know the names of the dishes Naomi ordered, though he could smell seafood in at least one of them. When dessert came around he even tried a bite of her tiramisu, even though he still thought the espresso and chocolate were too strong.

They finally left the restaurant late and went to hail a boat to take them back to their hotel. Max noticed all the gondoliers lining up outside nearby and on impulse said, "Shall we take a detour?"

Naomi was snuggled up tightly against him. She followed his gaze, looking delighted. "Are you sure? I know you don't like being so close to the water..."

"I can put up with it." *I think.*

Max asked the gondolier to take them on a short tour of the canals, and off they went, poling out into the Grand Canal and taking in the sights of San Marco by night.

Naomi sighed contentedly. The lights strung up along buildings and over bridges reflected on the lapping waters of the canals, leaving the whole city aglow. It was hard to not feel festive gliding under lit snowflakes and stars and listening to classic Christmas hymns sung in Italian playing through loudspeakers on Rialto Bridge and in shops closing up for the night.

Max tried carefully to avoid looking down at the water as they glided along. He found that if he just kept his eyes on the level, looking at the colourful paint of the buildings or the lights overhead, he could almost forget they were in a glorified canoe.

Naomi seemed perfectly content. Out of the blue, the gondolier gently sang something Italian in a baritone voice, and although Max couldn't understand a word, he thought he could sense some of the joy in the man's voice.

Their gondolier ended their tour right at the dock of their hotel, and Max released a breath as he climbed out of the shallow boat. A dock wasn't solid ground, but it sure beat a gondola for stability.

Upstairs he shrugged out of his heavy clothes into pyjamas and listened as Naomi drew a bath and changed into nightclothes. To his surprise and delight, she emerged from the bathroom smelling like her perfume and wearing a silky black slip that was not intended for sleeping in. Apparently, she'd forgotten all about calling home promptly each evening, and once she'd climbed into bed he forgot all about it too.

Later that night he woke up for no reason, startled out of a dream, or maybe hearing some noise outside the hotel. He got up quietly and went to the bathroom to get a drink of water, and when he came back he lay propped up on one elbow, studying his wife.

For the first time in over a year, she seemed totally at peace, breathing softly, her hair spread out over the pillow.

It was a good idea to come here, he thought, satisfied, as he curled up next to his wife. They hadn't had so much quality time together since the baby came, and he thought it was worth every moment spent in those darn boats.

A feeling of extreme contentment spread through him as he listened to Naomi's soft breathing, and he eased himself carefully back under the blankets to cuddle up next to her, drifting away to sleep.

CHAPTER 19

When Sunday morning dawned cold and overcast, with a chance of snow, Scott knew at once that his chances of getting Rachel to take a scenic gondola ride were probably low.

After the crowds, the disastrous dinner, and now with the cold, it was obvious her excitement at visiting Venice was waning. She was already talking about what they might do the next weekend at home, discussing the possibility of a movie and drinks with friends, and his heart sank.

Was he never going to get a chance to propose here?

But when he asked if she was game for a gondola tour on the Grand Canal, to his surprise, she agreed. "It'll be cold," he added, almost as an afterthought, expecting her to change her mind. But she just shrugged and said that she would wear an extra layer of clothing.

They attended the late morning Mass at St. Mark's Basilica, as he'd promised they would, and they were not disappointed. The sacred chorale was sung in Italian, and echoing off the gilded domes of the cathedral it sounded otherworldly.

Scott didn't know much about Catholicism or how Mass progressed, but he was able to appreciate the obvious meaning behind the service. They emerged onto the steps of the Basilica to light snow, oversized fluffy flakes drifting down to the stones like tiny down feathers.

He was more than happy to spend a quiet afternoon at the hotel, and when they left for their evening gondola ride, he made sure Rachel had bundled up in extra thermals and a warm sweater. He didn't want anything to ruin the night; this was his last big chance to propose before the weekend was over, and nothing would mess it up if he could help it.

But the line for gondola rides was long, and the gondoliers themselves seemed jaded and in a less-than-cheerful mood. Scott tried to put a positive face on things; Rachel remained silent. The minutes in the queue dragged by, and soon it became apparent that they were going nowhere fast if they intended to go in a gondola.

After nearly an hour, they finally secured a free gondola, and Scott sat down next to Rachel with relief. At last, they were underway!

Rachel tried chatting a bit with the gondolier, switching from English to Italian, but he seemed dismissive and uninterested in making tourist small talk. Finally, she gave up, sitting back and snuggling up against Scott to take in the sights.

The view of the Grand Canal was even more impressive from this vantage point, with views of the buildings and also the side canals and bridges that led off to smaller businesses and homes.

However, after just a few minutes floating along, their boat came to a halt. The large number of vessels out on the canal for the night had led to a water-locked traffic jam, and now boat traffic was nearly at a standstill as gondoliers and water taxi drivers shouted and argued with each other.

Beside him, Rachel was shivering. Scott hugged her a little tighter. *This was a terrible idea,* he realised, listening to their gondolier mutter to himself in his native language. English or Italian, the tone was the same with a complaint, and it was clear to Scott that the man was not having a good night.

The ride was supposed to last about forty minutes, though Scott knew he could pay for a longer period if he wanted.

However, by the time the forty minutes were up, it felt as though they'd been in the boat for hours. As soon as the gondolier pulled up at a dock, Rachel nearly bolted out of the boat, and Scott hastily paid the man and followed her.

From the set of her shoulders and the way she walked, Scott could tell his girlfriend was dejected. He could also tell she was freezing, and when she ducked into a small café and ordered hot chocolate he asked the waiter to make it two and followed her to a quiet corner table.

They sat in silence for a moment, warming their hands on the cups and sipping their drinks without speaking. Scott finally reached out to touch Rachel's hand. "Babe, I'm so sorry for how this weekend's been going. It seems to have just got worse and worse as it went on."

"It's not your fault," she said gently, wrapping her hands more tightly around the cup to steal its warmth. "I guess I thought Venice would be so much more ... magical I guess."

"We've just had some bad luck, that's all." Timidly he asked, "Do you want to try and find something else to do for the evening... maybe sit by that cafe orchestra in Piazza San Marco?"

Rachel shook her head firmly and she looked sad. "No. The city was fun at first, but like I said I'm a little ...disenchanted by now," she admitted. "It's cold, people are in a bad mood, and there are so many tourists. It just isn't the romantic getaway I thought it would be."

"Yeah, I guess I'm bummed too," he admitted. *For more reasons than one.*

Rachel drained the last of her hot chocolate. "So while it's been fun, I think I'm ready to go home."

"Me too," he agreed halfheartedly, even though he didn't feel the same way. He quickly finished his hot chocolate and they returned to their hotel by the quickest route possible, avoiding the packed Grand Canal.

CHAPTER 20

*In the lobby, Christmas music was playing softly, and Scott took a moment to admire the nativity scene by the front desk. He hadn't paid it much mind before, but now he thought wistfully of the romantic Christmas break he'd planned and how things had run downhill so fast. There didn't seem to be much for it but to admit defeat and head back home.

Maybe I can arrange a more romantic proposal back home, he conceded. *It won't be as good as Venice, but it will be better than nothing.*

Scott climbed into bed as quietly as possible, thinking Rachel was already asleep, but to his surprise, she rolled over to face him and said quietly, "Remember our first date?"

Scott was surprised by the question. "How could I forget?" he said, snuggling up to her. He had planned the day for nearly two weeks, down to the restaurant reservation, tickets to a movie starring her favourite actor, and dessert at a local hotspot he knew she'd been dying to try.

It had taken no small shortage of planning and a considerable chunk of his wallet, but he'd managed to pull off the best first date he could imagine, and Rachel had been delighted.

Now she rested her head on his arm, closing her eyes. "And

remember when you put together that surprise birthday party for me at that new nightclub, and I had no idea you'd invited my best friends because they were all sworn to secrecy?"

"It wouldn't be a surprise otherwise," he protested, and she smiled.

"You always go to such lengths to make things perfect," she said sleepily. "But I'm happy just spending time with you. Isn't that enough?"

"I guess," he said reluctantly, nuzzling her cheek.

She opened her eyes and gave him a wry look. "It's not, though."

"It's not that," Scott sputtered, trying to put his feelings into words. "It's just that…well, I feel like you deserve the best of everything. And I know how much you love Italy, and Venice is supposed to be such a romantic city…and I wanted you to have the time of your life on this trip. That's all."

"I did have a lot of fun," Rachel said, rolling over to tuck her back against him. He curled around her, enjoying the softness of her skin. "But I've had fun because I was here with you. It wouldn't have mattered if it was a five-star trip if I was alone. Everything—the dinners, the bell tower, touring the Basilica—it was all amazing because I was sharing it with you."

Scott buried a sigh in her hair. "I've had an amazing time with you, too. I just wish I could have created more perfect romantic surprises for you. That was part of the whole point of coming here."

"Well," Rachel said, sounding suspiciously less sleepy, "I have a little romantic surprise of my own …"

"What's that?" Scott ran a hand down her side, lingering on her hip, and was surprised when she suddenly pulled his hand around to rest on her stomach.

"I was going to wait to tell you until we got home. I was surprised you didn't say something about me skipping the wine and the seafood."

For a moment Scott could only stare down at her in shock, and she rolled onto her back, peering up at him in concern. "Babe? Say something. You're worrying me."

Scott racked his brain, thinking of the perfect most romantic thing to say. Instead, all he could blurt out was, "I can't believe you climbed all those stairs in the tower yesterday!" and Rachel started laughing and pulled him down for a kiss.

CHAPTER 21

❄

On Sunday morning Max and Naomi decided to attend the late morning Mass at St. Mark's.

Max had attended a few Masses as a child and Naomi had attended more than her share throughout her childhood and teens, but there was something different about standing in a cathedral, listening to a carol sung in a foreign language. It gave a person chills, and yet at the same time it was beautiful. The voices of the choir echoed off the domed roofs and filtered back over the assembled worshippers in the pews.

After the Mass, they walked slowly through St. Mark's Square, under a cloud of softly falling snow. There were fewer tourists out today, and fewer pigeons due to the weather. Max noticed a young couple of tourists also walking through the Square and pointed them out to Naomi. "Don't they kind of remind you of us, before we got married and had Julia?"

Naomi looked at the pair and smiled. The girl was bundled up against the cold and clearly not enjoying it; she pulled her hood up over her red hair in a bid to stay warm. The boyfriend kept one arm protectively around her. "We were always glued at the hip," she mused. "Whatever happened to us?"

"We got busy," Max conceded. They stopped at a café for coffee and took a quiet table where they could watch the falling snow and talk. Naomi wrapped her hands around her coffee mug and studied the scene outside without speaking.

"Sometimes I think you don't worry about Julia like I do," she said suddenly, and almost immediately her cheeks reddened, as though she hadn't meant to speak out loud and was embarrassed that she'd done so.

Max was a little startled, but he thought guiltily of how often he wished they could have more time apart from the baby. "It's not that," he began. "It's just that I miss you—I miss *us* before we got so wrapped up in real life—and now you're so wrapped up in being a mum, it feels like we don't get much time together. And I don't like that. I miss my wife."

To his utter bewilderment, Naomi suddenly started to cry. Alarmed, Max patted her arm and fished in her bag for tissues, unsure of how to react.

She dabbed at her eyes, trying to wipe away the tears without disturbing her makeup. "I just get so worried about her! I'm afraid to be a bad mother. I'm constantly thinking, what if something happens, and I'm not there? What if she needs me, and I'm busy doing something else? It feels so—so selfish to have fun!"

Max blinked, still unsure of how to respond to this sudden outburst. "But I am having fun, and now I feel terrible for it!" she continued, sniffling. "I'm enjoying spending time together, just the two of us. I enjoy going out for dinner and sleeping without listening for a baby monitor. I like getting dressed up and going out, instead of packing a nappy bag. This whole weekend, it's been —"She flailed her arms a bit as she tried to find the words. "It's been brilliant, and I don't want it to end. But I feel like a bad mum because I'm not checking in on my daughter every few hours."

"I don't think that makes you a bad mum," Max said cautiously. He still wasn't sure if this was his cue to say something, or if he should let her keep talking. She didn't respond though, only sniffled, so he kept going. "I think you're an amazing mum to Julia. And I love you for it. I wouldn't want you any other way. But you need to take care of yourself, too. And I don't want us to be so wrapped up in being parents that we forget about each other. That was the whole point of this trip—for us to reconnect." He grabbed her hands in his own and gave her a pleading look. "Please don't feel bad for that. I don't want you to feel bad, I want you to be happy."

Naomi sniffled and nodded. "I am happy," she admitted. "This whole trip has been so lovely. I just…I'm torn. I feel guilty for not missing Julia more, and I feel guilty for being away from her, and I feel guilty for ignoring you…"

"You can be all those things. It's normal, I promise. I feel them too."

"Really?" Naomi looked doubtful, but Max nodded. "I miss her, and then I feel bad for not missing her enough. And I feel bad because I don't think about how you're feeling sometimes."

Naomi wiped her eyes and drained her mug of cappuccino nearly in one swallow. She set her mug down with a sigh. "Today I woke up glad that I'll see my daughter tomorrow, and then I felt sad that it's our last day in Venice."

"Then we should enjoy it," Max said firmly. "Tuck the phone away in your bag. You know your mum is perfectly capable of handling anything that comes up."

"I know but…"

"So let's get going. We can tour the city, eat as much Italian food as we can, and go home tomorrow happy and contented. How does that sound for a plan? C'mon. We might only get this one chance to explore the city. Let's make the most of it."

Naomi seemed to finally make up her mind. "OK," she said, tucking the phone in her bag. She gave Max an apologetic look. "Just don't get upset if I check it now and then throughout the day."

"Promise," he said, grabbing her hand. "C'mon. I know you have a notebook full of destinations and notes tucked away in your bag; tell me where we're going today."

CHAPTER 22

They started with a map of the city and no real destination. It was cold out, but they were dressed warmly and there were plenty of cafes dotting the streets where they could buy hot coffee, hot chocolate or a snack to eat while they warmed up.

The snow was falling only lightly, drifting past them without a whisper. They started out from their hotel and began wandering across the map, exploring tiny side streets and playing a sort of treasure hunt game. Could they find the narrowest lane in the city, Calle Varisco? Could they find the house labelled "1"? They also looked for street addresses that reflected their birth years and anniversary years. All of this was marked down with a pen on the map.

When they had crisscrossed the city, they ended up near Rialto Bridge. Naomi's notebook listed the Rialto food market as an interesting place to linger, and while Max had no interest in the actual food on offer (lots and lots of seafood), he did find it interesting to see the cultural side of the markets. He hadn't put a lot of thought into the lack of farmland available or how most Venetians got their food, and a look at the market gave him a greater appreciation of the many types of seafood up for grabs at local restaurants. *I still want English fish and chips when I get home,* he thought with amusement as a vendor showed off fresh squid.

After that, tired of walking, they decided to hop a water bus and cruise the Grand Canal for a daylight look at the city. The snow had stopped by now, and they had a nice view of the hotels and other businesses lining the water, along with glimpses of some of the side streets and canals. It was nearly dusk now, and the Rialto Bridge was well lit up for the night. Further down they spotted the Bridge of Sighs—somehow less impressive now that they had heard the story of its name—as well as a myriad smaller bridges, quiet and deserted in the gathering dusk.

Rising above all they spotted the bell tower and clock tower in St. Mark's Square, and the spires on the cathedral. Max checked his watch. "If we're ready, we can get through a quick meal and make the late Mass. You up for it?"

"Definitely." Naomi's eyes were sparkling.

They grabbed food at a small takeaway cafe nearby—more pizza for Max and a panini for Naomi—and then headed into the Basilica with the other tourists and worshippers who were joining the Mass.

They were in for a treat. They'd been expecting a regular service, but tonight there was a visiting choir who would be singing the Mass. The voices that rose up to the gilded domes filled the cathedral with the same spine-tingling sound they'd heard that morning, yet somehow it seemed even more impressive at night.

Outside, the Basilica was flooded with light for the nighttime hours, and Max and Naomi took a moment to admire it as they stood in the piazza. Finally, the cold got the better of them, and they all but ran back to the hotel, laughing at their attempts to hurry without slipping on the fresh snow.

Back at the hotel, Naomi made a quick check of her phone. "No calls," she said happily, and stayed it away again.

Max plumped up a pillow and handed it to her. "Aren't you going to call and check in?"

She thought about that for a moment. "I don't think so — not today," she said at last. "It's our last day and I'll let my mom do what I asked her to do—watch Julia. And I'll enjoy us for one more night before we go home."

"Speaking of the night— look at this." Max turned off the lamps and opened the curtains, gesturing out the window. Naomi joined him and gasped a little. They could just see down the canal to Rialto Bridge, and it was still lit up with an ever-changing rainbow of Christmas lights, even at this late hour. Very faintly, they could hear the stream of a jazzy-sounding Christmas carol drifting down the water.

"It's magical," said Naomi. "Like something you see in a movie. And we were lucky enough to see it in person."

They stood in the window for a while longer, holding each other and not speaking. Sometimes, they both realised, you didn't need words to express a feeling.

Just being in the moment and sharing it was enough.

CHAPTER 23

On her last full day in Venice, Lucy slept late.

She indulged a little, ordering room service so she could linger in bed a while longer, watching a local English-language morning news program and nibbling on a croissant. Finally, she took a hot shower and dressed for the day.

She made sure to pick out the nicest outfit she had and tied a scarf around her neck. She wanted to see the morning Mass at the Basilica, and afterwards, she would do a bit more sightseeing in the city, and go to dinner.

Then return to the bridge, do what she came here to do and go home.

After the late Mass she found a café where she could get a quick snack—more coffee and croissants sounded just about right—and then set off to do her shopping. She wandered through the Rialto food market and was fascinated by the variety of items available for purchase, but declined the vendors' inquiring nods regretfully. Unfortunately, she had no way to take home fresh squid or crab meat in her suitcase, however delicious they might be. She would have to settle for one more evening of stuffing herself with local delicacies before heading home.

After the food market, she spent some time admiring Rialto Bridge from the windows of a local café, where she snacked on deep-fried meatballs, olives and bread drizzled with plenty of olive oil and herbs.

The waiter who dished up her antipasti had plenty of suggestions for where to shop on her last day, along with a warning that if something seemed cheap, it probably was: "Many shops import goods from China," he explained, "so stay away from the cheap stuff. Real Italian quality, it will cost you. But it's worth it!"

Lucy kept his warning in mind when she caught a water bus out to the island of Burano. She wanted to take a peek into the Church of San Martino, which looked positively rustic after the decadence of the Basilica, and the Oblique Bell Tower.

She also hoped to see the school of lace-making, where she was told a few dedicated Venetians hung onto the craft of making fine lace by hand. She was impressed by the number of hours that went into the craft; for herself, she'd never had the patience for fine handicrafts, so she couldn't imagine spending hours and hours on one tiny piece.

Besides the church and the lace-making museum and school, Burano boasted rows of colourful houses along the main canals that looked even prettier with a dusting of snow on the roofs. They reminded Lucy of colourful cupcakes with icing on top. Too soon it was time to board the bus back to San Marco, and she looked one more time at the colourful waterfront as they sailed away.

Back in the city, it didn't take long to find all manner of shops with tempting goods that she knew her family and friends would love. Leather goods, Venetian masks, handmade chocolate and more—it was hard to pick out just a few things.

Finally, she settled on a tooled leather journal for her dad, one which she knew he would enjoy writing in and would look lovely sitting out on his desk. He prided himself on keeping a neat study and this journal would fit right in. There were lovely cashmere scarves and tiny blown-glass paperweights for her mother and sisters.

She picked up an extra blown-glass necklace charm for herself—a souvenir of her trip—and finally returned to her hotel as dusk fell and the shops began to close up for the day. In the distance, she could hear the bell tower chiming out the hour, and she knew it was time to find something to eat—her stomach was rumbling even louder than the chatter of passing tourists.

CHAPTER 24

She tucked her bags safely away in her room and went down the street to a cosy restaurant that was just gearing up for the dinner rush. There were lots of other tourists out and about at this hour too, but Lucy had no trouble getting a small corner table and her dinner arrived quickly.

She had a little trouble choosing what to order—there were so many delicious things to choose from, and this would be her last dinner in Venice—but finally, she picked out fried crab and pasta with an anchovy and onion sauce. Fried doughnuts and strong coffee for dessert prepared her for the walk ahead of her, to find that cursed bridge.

Unfortunately, there was one small detail Lucy had overlooked in her planning: she couldn't remember where, exactly, the bridge was located.

She had a map of Venice and she thought she knew the name of the area, but now she realised that she was somewhat off on the name. It hadn't seemed important at the time—why would it be? She wasn't planning on going back there—but now she belatedly realised that she had a bit of a search ahead of her.

It took the better part of an hour, but eventually, she had circled several possible bridges on the map and was methodically setting out to each one.

The first bridge was a bust; not only did it not bear any locks at all, it was made of solid stone whereas the one she wanted was wrought iron. Another had some padlocks on it, but it was so close to the busier tourist districts that Lucy was almost certain it couldn't be the right one. Nonetheless, she checked each of the padlocks, wanting to be certain.

It was getting late now, and it was getting cold too. Lucy was discouraged, and she muttered under her breath as she marched to her last location. *Stupid romantic ideas, stupid lock, stupid bridge in the middle of this stupid city...* She thought she might start crying if she got mad enough, and she took a deep breath to calm down. It was just a symbolic thing, after all. Nothing to get all worked up about.

When she turned onto another street, suddenly she knew she was in the right spot. She walked to the middle of the bridge and gazed out over the quiet water. If she closed her eyes, she could picture it all: she and Dominic standing her under a snowy sky, their breath coming out in puffs, writing their initials on a lock and then locking it around one of the metal rails on the bridge. What a silly, romantic, yet lovely thing to do.

She opened her eyes and knelt in the fresh snow, feeling for the lock. There were a few on the bridge, and her fingers were getting cold when she found theirs. Feeling in her pocket for the key, she was about to unlock it when she heard footsteps crunching in the snow.

Lucy dropped the lock and stood up. A man was standing at the foot of the bridge, hesitating.

"Hello?" she called out cautiously.

"Lucy?"

Lucy froze to the spot. *It can't be! There's no way...*

But even while her brain was denying it, her eyes confirmed

that Dominic was, indeed, standing in front of her now. He walked hesitantly onto the bridge, shoulders hunched up in his coat against the cold.

CHAPTER 25

❄

They stood looking at each other for a long moment, neither sure of what they should say next.

Then they both started speaking at once. "What are you doing here?" she blurted out, even as he started to say, "I was hoping I'd catch you…"

Embarrassed, they both stopped. "You go first."

"No, you go ahead," she said quickly, and he shuffled his feet in the snow.

"Maybe we could go somewhere warmer to talk? There are a few places around the piazza open late."

"What are you doing here Dominic?" she demanded, remembering her original question.

In answer, he took a key out of his pocket. "I was hoping to persuade you to not use this."

She stared at his key for a moment, then took her hand out of her own coat pocket and opened it to reveal a matching key. They stood silently, looking at each other and at the tiny keys that had once meant so much.

Lucy closed her hand and thrust the key back into her pocket.

"Why are you here?" she repeated defiantly. "You broke up with me, remember?"

"I do. But I made a mistake."

"And now what? You fly halfway around the world to stop me from unlocking our old padlock?"

"That sort of thing usually works in the movies," Dominic said, looking desperate. She snorted, and he burst out suddenly, "Look, the real reason I flew here was that I was too stubborn to call you and admit I made a mistake. I thought you'd laugh or hang up on me, and I hoped eventually you'd be the one to call, and then I wouldn't have to hurt my stupid pride by begging you to take me back. But obviously, that didn't work, and when I found out you were coming here—well, I knew what you were planning, or thought I did, and I hoped I would catch you in time to stop you. And to tell you that I still love you, and I want to give us a second chance."

She stared at him for a moment. "I almost called you," she said finally. "I've missed you. I thought unlocking the padlock was the best way to let go of our past together and move on."

"I don't want to let go of our past," Dominic said, moving closer to her.

There was just enough moonlight peeking out of the clouds to show the blue of his eyes and the gleam of his hair. He took Lucy's hands in his own and drew her close. "I made the biggest mistake of my life when I let you go. But I want you back if you'll have me. I think we can give that promise a second chance."

Her heart soaring, Lucy looked down at the padlock on the bridge, and then up at Dominic. Around them, the snow had started again, softly.

"I think so too," she whispered, leaning into him. His lips brushed hers, and for a moment she forgot all about the cold.

Only for a moment, though.

"I think you're right," she said, leaning back from him. "We should definitely go somewhere warmer to talk about this. Preferably somewhere serving hot chocolate."

"I know just the place." Dominic tucked his arm through hers and pulled her closer as they walked slowly over the bridge, their bridge.

She leaned in to him and as the snow fell, touched the key in her pocket once more.

I think I'll hang on to this, she thought, *but not to unlock the padlock.*

I'm going to tuck it away somewhere to remind me that even when it seems impossible, miracles can still happen.

CHAPTER 26

*D*ominic and Lucy spent the next hour sitting in a small café, drinking hot chocolate and mostly ignoring the plate of fried doughnuts that they'd ordered.

What started as awkward small talk quickly turned into rapid-fire chatter about everything that had been going on in their lives since the split.

And more pertinently, how Dominic had come to find her in Venice.

Lucy had been on his mind ever since that disastrous night when he said he wanted to break up. Okay, so he *had* wanted to at the time—they'd had a terrible stretch of months, and it seemed like they fought more than they enjoyed each other's company. There was the nasty blow-up at Mick and Jenny's party and then a general period of friction that he honestly couldn't put down to any single thing. It was as if they had just stopped "clicking".

Oh, and that ridiculous summer barbecue at his parent's house. Even now Dominic cringed. He shouldn't have badgered her to go. He still wished she would make more of an effort to get along with his parents, and he did *not* think his mother was overbearing—well maybe a little bit, but not enough to warrant a fight—but he had to admit that if he hadn't pushed Lucy to go when she would rather stay home…

Weeks of rehashing all their arguments from the past year only seemed to bring him back to the same conclusion, time and time again: they didn't have any major problems, they just happened to make very big mountains out of totally manageable molehills. They were both strong-willed—something Dominic loved in Lucy, as much as it often irritated him—and neither was willing to back down when they thought they were in the right. They'd had too many complications thrown at them too quickly, and they just weren't good at working through them. But breaking up? That had been a stupid move, too impulsive and too unthinking. And afterwards, he couldn't figure out how to talk to her without admitting he felt like an idiot.

So he said nothing. His friends assured him she would reach out first: "Women can't help it," his best mate Tom said reassuringly, while they were out drinking and playing pool one night in a bid to help Dominic get over his misery. "She'll want you back, but she'll try to play it casual. She'll call and act like she just wants to say hello, or she'll make up an excuse to come to your place—she'll say she left a jumper there or something. And here's your chance to charm her and show her that you want her back. Seriously, everything will come together."

But how wrong his friend had been. Lucy didn't call, and she didn't turn up unannounced at his apartment. Dominic had spent a night hopefully going through drawers and wardrobes, thinking maybe he could find a wayward jumper or a lipstick and use it as an excuse to call her, but none surfaced. For a moment he was even tempted to head to the shops and buy something just so he could pretend it was hers, but he knew instantly that she would see through him, and then he would look like an idiot *and* a fool. That combo was too much for his pride.

But as the weeks went by and Dominic got more desperate, he finally decided to casually mention her to some other mutual friends—just to see how she was doing, he told himself.

Instead, he got the shock of his life.

"Lucy? She's great. Going to Italy next week, I heard," Mick said when they met up to watch the football last Saturday. Dominic felt his mouth go dry. He didn't need to ask what part of Italy; he knew Lucy well enough to know exactly where she was going: Venice, where this time last year they had pledged to love each other forever.

If he knew Lucy's mind—and he thought he did quite well—she wouldn't be content to just move on from a breakup. She would need to get rid of any romantic symbols that lingered on as a reminder of their relationship. It seemed extreme, but somehow he wasn't surprised by the realisation that she intended to unlock the padlock in Venice and throw it into a canal to sink into oblivion. It was just the sort of strong-willed thing she would do.

It took only a little prying to get more details on the dates she intended to be gone—Mick and Jenny typically kept an eye on her flat whenever she was away, watering the plants and feeding her fish—and within mere hours Dominic had in his possession a ticket to Venice.

En route, his nerves were jangling. He supposed he could have just *called* her, but what if she didn't want to talk to him? No, if ever there was a time to pull out all the stops with a big romantic gesture, this was it. And if flying to a foreign city to declare your love for someone didn't count as a big romantic gesture, then Dominic honestly didn't know what did.

It was a gamble of course, that he wouldn't catch up to her in the city, but he was pretty sure he knew how she would plot out her trip. According to Jenny she was flying in on Thursday night and leaving again on Monday morning.

Dominic guessed she would spend Friday sightseeing, probably catching up on the major attractions. She'd been particularly impressed by St. Mark's Basilica last time, he remembered, so it was almost certain she'd go there. She also loved art and he remembered regretfully that they hadn't made time to visit the museums during their trip, so she would likely spend Saturday touring the art galleries and culture hotspots.

He had a hunch she would wait to retrieve the padlock until the last day. It would be her farewell to the city and to that chapter in her life. In Lucy's mind, it would be the final touch to her trip, so it made sense that she would save it for the very end.

Dominic wasn't senseless enough to try to catch Lucy anywhere on Thursday night; he knew she was flying in too late to hit any tourist destinations. Instead, he set out on Friday morning, trying to put himself in her shoes and guess where she'd go first.

It was impossible to find her among the tourists in St. Mark's Square. He thought he caught a glimpse of her inside the Basilica and quickly shrank back behind a pillar. He wasn't ready to talk to her just yet, and by the time he got up his courage and looked for her again in the crowd, she was gone.

The next day he bought tickets to a couple of art gallery tours in the city. Browsing through one long collection of classical art, he again thought he caught a glimpse of Lucy, chatting with a couple. Was it possible she came with friends? He wondered. Then she parted ways with the couple, and he decided she must be alone.

Dominic almost decided to approach her outside of the museum, but he lost his nerve. For a moment his impulsive trip began to look like a bad idea. What, exactly, was he supposed to say to her when he materialised out of thin air? *Hi, I've been semi-stalking you around Venice in hopes of persuading you to get back together with me...* Probably not the best opening line.

And so he had decided that the best possible place would be their bridge.

Thank goodness, he thought now, sipping his coffee and staring at his beloved, it had worked.

. . .

Lucy was telling him that she had stepped down from her newly awarded position at work. "I thought I liked it," she confessed, "but the hours were terrible and the extra stress wasn't worth the pay. I wasn't seeing my family and friends as much as I wanted to. So I kicked myself back down a level."

"I'm sorry," Dominic said and meant it. He knew how much the promotion had meant to her when she got it.

But Lucy shrugged. "You know, I was annoyed for a while. And then I started thinking about it, and I realised I didn't care that much about the job itself. I just wanted the extra cash, and I realised I valued my free time more than the money. Lesson learned, I guess."

Dominic told her about his endless struggle to find a way to get in touch with her and reconnect, and Tom's terrible advice. Lucy laughed and told him about the night she'd nearly phoned him from her bathtub. "To think I was going to tell you I was in Venice just to see what you would do," she said, giggling, "and you were here, too!"

Eventually, the café owner made it clear he was ready to close up shop, and Dominic and Lucy left, strolling hand in hand through the quiet streets of San Marco. Even the gondoliers had mostly disappeared, leaving any late-night wanderers to find their own way around on foot.

They weren't really walking in any particular direction, but soon Dominic and Lucy wound up in a deserted St. Mark's Square. If the piazza was picturesque in the daylight, it was beautiful at night. Deserted save for one or two other hardy souls braving the cold—and devoid of the flocks of pigeons that called it home during the day—the Square now had a romantic ambience, like a piece of the city carved out of ancient times and deposited into modern Venice. It was well-lit, even at night, along with St. Mark's Basilica and the towers at the edge.

"When we were here last year," Dominic said, "remember the café orchestras that played here in the evenings?" Though the cafes in question, situated right on the edge of the square were long closed by now. "We danced in the piazza. Remember?"

Lucy nodded. They were surrounded by tourists, but it felt like they were the only two people there.

Dominic took her hand and gently led her out into the square, and they began slowly waltzing in place to an imaginary orchestra. "I think we should have a tradition," he whispered in her ear. "We should come back here every winter, or as many winters as we can manage. And we should visit our padlock on the bridge, and dance here in the square, and eat fried doughnuts until we burst."

"That sounds good to me," Lucy said dreamily, snuggling into his coat. She suppressed a yawn, and Dominic hugged her. "Aw, you're tired. I'll take you back to your hotel."

"I'm not that tired," Lucy started to protest, but a jaw-cracking yawn cut her off, and she admitted sheepishly that she was ready to drop.

Back at the hotel, Dominic sat gingerly on the foot of her bed. "How soon are you flying home?"

"I'm supposed to go tomorrow," she said, shucking her boots and coat.

"Do you think you could change the flight?"

"I'd imagine so. Why?"

He got to his feet, a slow grin spreading across his face. "Because I have a few days off, and we're here in the most romantic city in the world, and I think we should make the most of it."

"I like the sound of that." Lucy looked at him speculatively. "Are you going to stay? Here, tonight, I mean?"

"Are you inviting me?"

In response, she smiled and scooped up her pyjamas from her open suitcase.

"Tell me if I need these," she asked coquettishly.

Without another word, Dominic took them from her hands and dropped them back into the suitcase, pulling her down on the bed next to him.

"I guess that would be a no then," Lucy said, smiling as she kissed him, and reached to flick off the lamp.

CHAPTER 27

When morning dawned Lucy went online and rescheduled her return flight.

Dominic left to gather his things and check out of his hotel and returned an hour later, scrubbed up and ready for the day.

He still wouldn't tell Lucy what he had in mind for the day, though he insisted she check out at the front desk and bring her suitcase.

Then they boarded a water bus out to an island close by.

To Lucy's surprise and delight, Dominic had taken the liberty of calling ahead to the island's lone but massively exclusive hotel, the Cipriani and making a reservation for the two of them.

At this time of the year, the luxurious hotel was well decorated for Christmas but luckily was not brimming with guests, with most people opting to stay in the busier and less expensive hotels in San Marco.

As the older woman at the front desk explained, most of the island was now a dedicated nature reserve, with some hiking available to tourists. Obviously in this weather walking all over the island wasn't high on most visitors' priorities but from the wink

Dominic gave her, Lucy guessed he didn't intend for them to spend a lot of time out and about anyway.

The windswept little island seemed almost bleak in the December light, yet there was a sort of peacefulness to it. She could easily imagine returning here for a future getaway, though perhaps in a warmer month.

"Do you really think we'll spend every winter in Venice?" Lucy asked, snuggling closer to him.

Dominic shrugged. "I hope so. But I don't think superstitions should change our fate, though. I think it's up to us to decide our future." He stopped and looked down at her, tracing her chin with his thumb. "And I for one, am very serious about our future. I want to make sure our love stays locked in place forever."

"I want that too," Lucy whispered. He tipped her chin up for a kiss, and she melted into him, forgetting all about the cold.

THE FLIGHT from Venice back to England had to be rerouted due to weather, and when Max and Naomi finally arrived home late that night they were exhausted.

Max was thrilled to be home, but he would be most thrilled once he was tucked into his bed.

Naomi's parents were up waiting for them, but baby Julia was tucked safely in bed, sleeping. Naomi beamed down at her daughter despite her fatigue. "She's such a good sleeper," she whispered proudly to Max, who smiled and rubbed her back.

Naomi's mother poked her head into the bedroom. "You know," she said, a hint of a smile on her lips, "she's done so well this weekend. Why don't you leave her here one more night? That way you can get some solid sleep after your flight, and unpack at your leisure tomorrow."

One more night without the baby in tow sounded heavenly, but Max could see Naomi wavering. He held back, waiting to see what she would say.

To his surprise, she tiptoed out of the bedroom with a reticent—but exhausted—smile on her face. "You're sure you don't mind?"

"Absolutely not," her mother said, looking as surprised as Max felt.

Naomi gave her a quick hug. "Thank you! We'll come over tomorrow afternoon to pick her up."

They collected their coats and went back out to the cab, waiting for them at the curb. *Did I really just hear "tomorrow afternoon" from my wife?* Max wondered.

As if reading his thoughts, Naomi grinned sleepily at him. "I hope Mum is up for a lot of babysitting. I'm getting kind of used to these baby-free nights."

"I'm assuming that is the jet lag talking," Max said in amazement, and she laughed and leaned against him, snoring almost before the cab pulled out of the driveway.

CHAPTER 28

Monday morning, Scott was reluctant to drag himself out of bed. He was still beaming with the news of Rachel's pregnancy, and now he noticed that she had an extra glow to her as well.

He rubbed her stomach affectionately as she lay in bed. "Good morning to you too," he whispered, and she laughed as his breath tickled her skin. "Are you a he or a she? Either way, I hope you get your mom's brains because your dad doesn't have a lot going for you in that category."

They dressed and ate breakfast in their hotel room, with Scott springing down to a café for a large bag that included everything from pastries to muesli.

"You're eating for two now," he reminded Rachel, and finally she laughingly told him to stop hovering over her while she ate.

"Finish packing. I can feed myself just fine," she said, planting a kiss on his cheek. He quickly turned his head to plant a deeper one on her lips. "Are you sure you're fine? You don't need anything else? Is the baby moving yet?"

"Goodness no, I'm only eight weeks along." Rachel tucked herself up into a comfortable cross-legged position on the sofa.

"Eat, and pack. We want plenty of time to get to the airport. I imagine it will be busy today."

Soon enough they were packed and checked out of the hotel.

Scott bundled Rachel gently into a water taxi, fussing about the weather until they were safely on dry land and bundled into a cab. She leaned into him in the back seat with a contented sigh. "Venice was lovely. But I think home sounds even lovelier."

"Actually, I agree with you." He wouldn't have thought it twenty-four hours ago, but now Scott couldn't think of anywhere in the world more appealing than their cosy apartment back in New York. He was already thinking ahead to everything they would have to do to get ready for the baby. He supposed this meant cleaning out the spare bedroom so Rachel could turn it into a nursery.

Maybe that can wait until after Christmas.

There wasn't too much traffic on the roads, and soon enough they were unloading their suitcases at the airport. Scott checked everything in and they moved through the security lines to board their flight.

Scott kept one hand tucked firmly in Rachel's, and the other he jammed absentmindedly into his coat pocket.

His fingers touched the ring box and he froze. In all the excitement of Rachel's announcement, he'd completely forgotten about the original reason for their trip. Now they were mere minutes away from going through the metal detectors, and the box was still sitting unopened in his pocket.

A bored-looking official was checking passports at the top of the line.

He took Scott's passport and studied it with a glazed expression. "Anything liquids/metals or anything to declare?"

Scott stood stock-still for a moment, the man staring blankly at him. "Yes," he said, his voice sounding foreign to his own ears. "Yes, I do have something to declare."

He turned around to face Rachel. Other passengers in the line were staring, some curious, some irritated at the holdup, but he ignored them all.

Rachel was staring at him, puzzled, as he took her hands. "Rachel, you are the best thing that has ever happened to me. You're beautiful, intelligent, funny, and have a gentle soul. You're everything I could want in a partner, and now I'm blessed enough to learn that you'll be all that and more as the mother of my child.

I brought you to Venice because I thought there was no more romantic place in the world to ask you to marry me. Obviously, that didn't work out the way I'd planned, but I'm not about to leave before at least giving it my best shot. So with that in mind…" Scott heard audible gasps as he dropped to one knee and pulled the ring box from his coat pocket. "Rachel, will you marry me?"

A woman in line let out an excited squeal, and Rachel burst into tears.

He quickly stood up and caught her as she grabbed him in a hug, nodding and trying to wipe her tears away with her coat sleeve. He pulled a wad of tissues from her coat pocket and handed them to her, to the happy clapping and cheers of the passengers in line behind him.

CHAPTER 29

Rachel slept through most of the flight home, and when they landed at JFK, Scott quickly collected their luggage and hailed a cab, settling her in the backseat where she dozed off again.

When they got home he made sure she was settled on the couch with a hot cup of cider and dumped the suitcases in a corner. They could unpack tomorrow or the next day. He didn't see any reason to rush.

Their Christmas tree was all set up in the corner of the living room, and he plugged in the lights, bathing the living room in a soft glow. Scott sat down next to Rachel, and she snuggled into him. She was still admiring the way the stones in her ring sparkled, and he laced his fingers through hers, admiring the stones too. "Do you like it?"

"It's perfect," she whispered, leaning back into him. They sat still for a moment, admiring the tree.

Finally, Rachel broke the silence. "Are you hoping for a girl or a boy?"

"I don't care," Scott said after a moment's thought. "You?"

She shook her head. "I'm happy with either one," she said. Then after another moment, she said, "Promise me something."

"Anything."

"When we're getting ready for the baby—fixing the nursery, whatever…"

"Yeah?"

"Don't try to make it perfect, okay?" She rubbed her stomach, smiling a little. "Let's just enjoy these moments together and not worry about how they happen."

"You got it." Scott kissed her. "Merry Christmas, my amazing wife-to-be, who wishes for imperfect but totally real and romantic moments."

Rachel smiled. "Merry Christmas, my amazing husband-to-be who will never stop trying."

After a few moments, Scott could tell by her breathing that she'd fallen asleep. Gently he pried the cider mug out of her hands and placed it on the coffee table, then picked her up and carried her into the bedroom, tucking her gently under the blankets. She twitched and sighed in her sleep, smiling a little to herself.

"Merry Christmas," he said softly, pulling the blankets up over her shoulders. "Here's to years of imperfectly wonderful Christmases ahead."

And here's to the romance of Venice, he thought as he went back to the living room to unplug the tree lights. He smiled a little to himself as he tiptoed back into the bedroom. *I guess the best romantic moments happen when you stop looking for them.*

With Christmas hymns sung in Italian still echoing in his head, Scott snuggled up to his fiancée and drifted off to sleep.

A WEEKEND IN PARIS

CHAPTER 1

❄

A room full of Thompson & Jonas Associates cheered as they raised their glasses to toast the chairman's yuletide address.

It was the yearly Christmas party and everyone was dressed in festive finery as they ate the best catered food and wine the advertising agency would spring for.

It was the cheeriest time of the year, and Emily Richardson absolutely loved it.

"Merry Christmas, Tom," she said to her colleague and friend, who was already three sheets to the wind - his arm draped around his wife Bernice.

"Merry Christmas Em!" they both chorused back, silly grins on their faces.

"So what are you doing over the holidays? You're more than welcome to join us again, if you'd like," Bernice offered kindly. "Was great having you at ours last year. My brother in particular took a right fancy to you. I'm sure he'd love to see you again," she added with a wink.

"Ah you're both very kind, but believe it or not, I've got plans this year," Emily informed with a grin of her own. "I'm off to Paris."

"Paris? But you won't know anyone," Tom countered gruffly. "Don't you think this time of year should be spent with friends and family?"

"Of course, but this year, with Nan gone, I have no family in London anymore. And as much fun as I have with you guys, I'm a bit tired of being the odd one out at a table full of couples and families."

"I hear you," Tom commented, sipping on his beer.

"Oh, you shouldn't let a thing like that bother you: one of these years *you'll* be the one with a boyfriend, or who knows, maybe even a husband to accompany you," Bernice reassured her. "Though I must admit, I'm actually envious now - Christmas in Paris sounds divine."

"I've always wanted to see the city, and what better time?" Emily smiled. "The Eiffel Tower, Champs-Élysée and all the festive lights… It's going to be glorious."

"When are you leaving?"

"Friday morning," Emily raised her glass of champagne and took a long sip.

"Well, we'll miss you at ours this year, but I expect you'll have a ball on your adventures," Tom said, hiccuping a little.

"You never know what those adventures will bring either," Bernice chimed in with a wink. "Paris is the City of Love after all…"

CHAPTER 2

"*Must* you go?" Her best friend Sarah's voice was ringing in her ears as Emily packed her suitcase. "The boys'll really miss you."

"*You'll* miss your on-call babysitter, you mean," she countered, folding her favourite red cashmere jumper and placing it gently on top of her other stuff.

"Well that too, but seriously no one can handle my boys like you can."

The two childhood friends, who were only a year apart in age, were often mistaken for twins.

They were both average height with honey blonde hair and slender figures. Sarah had put on a little more weight after having four children, but Emily thought it suited her, and gave her more curves from her formerly athletic build.

Emily herself still had had some semblance of the swimmer's tone she'd had in her school days, though she'd softened out quite a bit since giving up the gruelling training schedule.

"Sorry but you, Jeff and the boys are just going to have to do your best without me," she joked.

"I'm really going to miss you at Christmas, though" Sarah got up from her reclined position on Emily's bed and held out her arms for a hug.

"I won't be gone *that* long," she replied, wrapping her arms around her friend and pulling her into a tight embrace. "But I *need* this trip. I need to get out of London. Explore what else is out there," she added as she released her friend and turned back to her packing.

"It's because of Nan, isn't it?" Sarah stated.

Emily's green eyes focused on the clothes that were already in her case, as she thought of her Nan.

Andrea Sutton had been ninety years old when she'd died earlier in the year.

While most didn't think she'd live that long, Emily knew she would. Her grandmother had a resilient spirit like none she'd ever encountered and one she hoped she'd passed on to her only grandchild.

"Yes," she admitted. "It is because of Nan," She took a seat on the bed, an unfolded garment still in her hands.

"I knew this trip was very spur of the moment, considering it's not long since you got the money."

Emily sighed. "I suppose I just felt the need to do *something* with the inheritance, something special to honour Nan. She always lived life to the fullest." Her gaze met Sarah's. "She was everything to me, you know?"

"I know," her friend replied with a smile.

"That's why I need to go. Nan did so much for me, but the things *she* wanted to do in life she never got to. She wanted to see Paris. She raised me on those old Gene Kelly movies, and it was her dream to go to the places she saw in movies but never got to. I feel like I owe it to her now to see every place she wanted to. It's the best way to celebrate her life that I can think of."

Sarah smiled. "Then you should go. Honour Nan," she said, pulling her friend into another hug. "I'm sure this trip will be everything she would have wanted for you, and more."

CHAPTER 3

Charles de Gaulle Airport was bustling with tourists and travellers who were headed out to visit family and friends over the holiday period.

Snow was falling as Emily stepped out of the terminal and into the chilly air.

She shivered slightly at the change in temperature, but the feeling was invigorating and the smile on her face reflected her enthusiasm as she searched for a taxi.

"Madame, you take my card?" a driver encouraged in heavily accented English, handing her a small white card.

"Thank you," she said reading his name, "Monsieur Babin."

"Maurice," he corrected cheerfully as they drove away in his cab. "I show you all the sights of Paris. You just call me, and I will be there," he said with a snap of his fingers.

"You're a tour guide too?" she mused smiling.

"In Paris, all taxi drivers are also tour guides. Didn't you know?"

"No I didn't, but thanks for telling me."

"You are staying at a lovely hotel, Madame."

"Emily."

"That's a pretty name," he replied pleasantly. "The hotel - my wife and I stayed there for our honeymoon. It's excellent, *très excellente*," he emphasised with a theatrical kiss of his fingers.

It made Emily giggle. Nan would have loved this. "Thanks for letting me know I made a good choice."

"My pleasure."

The drive to the hotel was faster than Emily had expected, though she believed Maurice may have had some car racing experience in his past, given the way he drove his taxi.

He pointed out the locations of the Air and Space Museum and the George-Valbon State Park as they drove. Maybe she'd visit them on another trip, but this time round she only wanted to see the city's more picturesque and romantic spots.

They arrived at the hotel, and Emily was delighted to find it even more magnificent in real life than it had been in the online pictures.

The white building, with gold and green accents and a planter box on every window and balcony, was dusted in patches of snow. It was like something from a film set, and the perfect place to spend Christmas week.

The lobby was just as picturesque as the exterior, and decorated in rich purple and gold, it radiated opulence and reminded her of a scene from a classic movie, where everything was so vibrant and alive and reminiscent of times gone by.

An attractive brunette greeted Emily at reception as she approached the front desk. "My name is Angelique and I'm your concierge. How may I assist you today?"

"Emily Richardson, I have a reservation," she stated as Angelique checked her computer.

"Ah yes, Miss Richardson, I see this is your first time in Paris," Angelique replied. "And you have reserved one of our finest suites. The views are spectacular," she assured. "Martin, will take your bags up," she added, indicating to the porter who was standing nearby.

"Follow me Madame," he said with a smile, taking the keys from Angelique and heading towards the elevator.

Emily followed, admiring the décor as she went. The hotel again made her feel as if she were in a movie, and the decor of the lobby extended throughout the building. It was like stepping back into a more regal time, with statues and fine art adorning every corner.

Her suite was located on the top floor. She'd wanted the best view and the suite she'd been given didn't fail. The colour scheme was gold and white, with an elegant but simply designed sitting room and a bedroom to the left. The entire suite was carpeted, and the bed visible from the living room. Emily was excited to find that it looked exactly how she'd seen it online, with the wall canopy adorning the head of the bed.

Martin deposited her bags in her room before wishing her a good day. The moment he was gone Emily walked out onto the balcony to see the view.

Even better than she'd anticipated.

The Eiffel tower stood regally ahead, the Arc de Triomphe to her right and somewhere in between was the Champs-Élysées, her intended first stop.

"I should unpack first," she mused, but knew in her heart she wasn't going to. She wanted to get out into the city and see everything. It felt as if she had waited a long time for this trip, and she wasn't about to waste a second of it.

"I'm here Nan - in Paris," she whispered, wishing her grandmother was in the room with her right now. "I hope you can see this. Isn't it beautiful?"

She turned back into the bedroom, closing the balcony door behind her as she grabbed a few things and headed out.

This was one of the few times of the year when Emily got to shake off the stress of her job and simply enjoy every day.

Her Nan had always said she needed to do better at enjoying life, so maybe it was time she started.

CHAPTER 4

❄

The falling snow made the air crisp and hearty and brought a smile to Emily's face as she looked up and down the busy street.

She was really here. She'd really come to Paris!

She strolled to her right, her hands stuffed into the front pockets of her red padded coat. She didn't need to rush, she planned to savour every moment of just being in such a beautiful city.

She smiled to herself as she watched couples walking arm-in-arm along the avenue, some in a rush and some like her, taking it easy.

It was only a short walk, no more than a few minutes, before Emily found herself at Place Charles de Gaulle, the Arch de Triomphe standing at the centre.

It was even more breath-taking in reality than in photos or in movies, even with all the cars rushing around it. It really was beautiful but she'd have to take a better look later, because right now she had an appointment one avenue over, on the Champs-Élysées.

Trees lined both sides of the street as Emily began her stroll. It wasn't quite like what she'd seen in the movies, more familiar shops and chain stores had moved in since, replacing stylish cafés with American brandnames.

She chuckled. "I guess that American in Paris left more than he expected …" she mused, walking away from McDonalds. She had no interest in fast food - in this city, she wanted something much more authentic.

The Renault restaurant was just that. Located along the avenue it was both modern and contemporary within a warm and welcoming atmosphere that made Emily indifferent to the fact that she was eating alone. She rarely did so, but this was a new day and she was ready for new experiences.

She was seated on one of the upstairs tiers, where all the chairs were yellow-coloured. The place had such a fun and irreverent feel, that she was sure children must love it. She decided there and then to treat herself; who cared about a few extra pounds at this time of year?

She started with avocado and shrimp tartare, followed by Milanese veal cutlet with linguine pesto, and topped everything off with a vanilla crème brûlée and two glasses of sauvignon blanc.

The meal was amazing, and she made a mental note to come there again during her trip if she had the time.

Looking down from her perch on the first floor, Emily watched other diners down below.

Some had large bags draped over chairs, no doubt full of festive trinkets to take home to decorate, or gifts ready to be wrapped. She wondered what would be the best places to find toys for the boys and gifts for Sarah and Jeff, plus maybe a little something for herself to commemorate her trip.

She was enjoying the view, slowly draining her final glass of wine, when she thought she spotted someone familiar down below.

She squinted, trying to see the face properly, but from this angle it was difficult and there were so many people.

Finally she shook her head; she was being silly. It couldn't possibly be *him*, could it?

After all, it had been at least ten years, would she still even recognise him now?

"Don't let your eyes play tricks on you," she admonished herself, draining her glass.

There was no way Patrick Wilde could be in Paris.

CHAPTER 5

The Champs-Élysées had so much to offer that Emily could hardly keep track of it all. There was so much to see on the main avenue, but also the side streets as well.

There was no way she was going to be able to take everything in on one day. The designer stores alone left her wanting more, and she hadn't even been to half of them. This was a shopper's paradise, and for the first time she was going to allow herself to enjoy it.

"I guess I'm going to have to make a repeat visit," she mused, as she looked into a boutique window. The handbags were fantastic and the designs so quintessentially French. She was *definitely* coming back to get one of those, maybe even two.

"See something you like?" a male voice said from over her shoulder.

Emily looked up, but hadn't the chance to turn around, before the speaker's reflection in the glass caught her gaze. He was tall, with carefully coiffed black hair, hazel eyes with dark rimmed glasses seated on a straight nose.

Then there was the smile, one she'd know anywhere, but still Emily couldn't believe he could actually be there.

"Patrick?" she said in disbelief, forcing herself to turn around and see for sure.

"Hello there," he replied, with the same grin. "This is a surprise."

Emily could hardly speak she was so shocked. "Yes, it is." She needed to catch her breath. "I really can't believe it's you. Were you in the Renault a little while ago too? I thought I saw someone who looked like you, but convinced myself it couldn't be."

"That was me," he chuckled. "When I saw you from up the street I wasn't sure it was you either, but I decided to take a chance. When I got closer I absolutely knew it was. You still bite your lip when you're thinking about something."

"Oh," she replied, raising a hand to her mouth unconsciously. "I suppose I do still do that."

"Glad to see everything hasn't changed," he laughed.

"But some things have. You look great! I would hardly have recognised you. You've become a real ... man," she mumbled, still a bit tongue-tied.

"Are you saying I wasn't when we were together?" he teased with a raised brow.

"Ah we were both children," she defended quickly.

"We were eighteen. I'd hardly call us children," Patrick corrected, before adding wickedly. "And we certainly didn't act like it."

Emily's cheeks blushed at the inference. He was the first boy she ever really loved, and the first she'd slept with too, both reasons to never forget him.

And she hadn't, even though life had pulled them in different directions.

"Do you have time to get a coffee?" he asked, inclining his head.

"Only if I get to pick the place."

He laughed. "Typical Emily. You always liked to run the show."

She smiled. "As you said, some things haven't changed."

CHAPTER 6

❄

This had to be a dream. She couldn't *really* be standing in a Ladurée café with Patrick Wilde. And in Paris of all places.

Every person had 'one who got away', or so she was always told. Though Patrick wasn't quite that because he hadn't gotten away as such - the choice to end their two year relationship had been mutual.

Emily had gone to university in London, and Patrick had no desire to leave their little home hamlet of Kingham in Oxfordshire.

He had a family inn and restaurant to tend to, and an ailing mother who needed his help. They'd wanted to stay together, but Patrick believed it selfish of him to ask Emily to stay when she'd been accepted to her first choice university. It was a once in a lifetime opportunity he didn't want her to give up or postpone. He wanted her success and she wanted his, but for that time his future was in their hometown.

They'd tried to stay in touch, but the hectic schedule of her life in London and his responsibilities, soon saw their communications dwindle into nothing.

A year or so later, it was over. Then Emily met someone new and started dating, and she presumed he'd done the same.

Their paths had never crossed again since, and though there had been times when she'd thought of him in fond memory, that was all that was left. Sometimes she'd wondered what might have happened if she'd made another choice, but it was something she could never know.

Yet now Patrick Wilde was there, right in front of her - in Paris - and she could hardly believe the change in him.

He had once been an athletic, broad shouldered swimmer who wore terribly thick glasses and stuttered when he was nervous, but none of that bothered her.

She found his shyness endearing and his swimming prowess formidable. Then there was his temperament. Patrick was always polite, helpful and willing to offer an encouraging word to anyone, and a lending hand.

He wasn't all shyness however; there had been a time, when they were around sixteen, when he'd got into a terrible fight with one of their schoolmates. He left the boy with a black eye and a bloody lip, but he'd deserved it in Emily's mind, having dared to speak ill of Patrick's unwell mother.

Though Emily never condoned fighting, she was very proud of him that day, and the way he'd stood up for his mother, a woman who had always treated her well.

Staring was rude, but now Emily couldn't help herself. Patrick stood at the elaborate counter, which was adorned with all manner of sweet macarons and colourful boxes that reminded her more of an elegant perfumery of times past than a delicatessen.

"Here we go," he said, as he approached her. "Something to go with our coffees. Shall we go find some place to sit?"

"Lead the way," Emily offered. "You seem to know your way around quite well."

"I should," he said with a laugh. "I've lived in the city for five years now."

Emily halted. Had she heard him right? "You *live* here - in Paris?"

"Yes," he confirmed, pushing the door open to the street and allowing her to go ahead of him. "I have a place in Gros Caillou, near Champ-de-Mars."

"I can't believe it," Emily replied, wide-eyed. "You never seemed interested in even leaving Kingham, far less crossing the Channel to move to Paris. What happened?"

"A couple of years after you left, my mother died," Patrick informed her, his expression growing momentarily sad.

"I'm so sorry to hear that. I hope …" Emily began, but the words were useless. There was no point in saying them.

"It's alright. She went peacefully in the end, which was all anyone could hope for," he continued as they walked. "After she was gone, my uncle thought it best to take me in. He didn't think I should have been left with the bills and the burden. So I sold the inn then moved to Bristol with my uncle's family. Eventually I enrolled in school and won a scholarship to study business here in Paris. Looks like those French lessons we took in school were of some use," he mused.

"You got the scholarship because you knew French?"

"And because I was in the top percentile in my class," he added mischievously.

"Then what happened?" she asked.

"My year here landed me a job with a company I interned with, and as they say the rest is history," he said with a shrug. "They put me in an apartment, gave me a car and well, that's it."

"I always knew you'd be successful," Emily said with a smile. "I'm so proud of you."

"And what of you? What have you been up to?"

"Well, after I moved to London, it was a bit of an adjustment for me," she admitted, biting her lip. "Being on my own wasn't something I was used to, and having Nan so far away was a little worrying, but she called me all the time and I called her, so it made things easier. I gave up competitive swimming for my studies, though. I just do it for exercise now."

"You - giving up the pool?"

"I could say the same of you," she countered.

"I guess we both knew we weren't going to be Olympians, so it made sense to give it up for things that would take us further."

"True."

"Where are you working in London?" he asked.

"An advertising firm, Thompson & Jonas. I've been there since graduation," she informed him. "I'm Creative Director."

"So soon?" he questioned, surprise lacing his words.

"Yes. Don't you think I could be good enough for the post?" she questioned, folding her arms across her chest.

"Of course you could. You could do anything you set your mind to Emily," he replied, giving her a familiar look.

CHAPTER 7

"You'd better believe it," she countered. "I worked my ass off interning with them from my second year, and by the time I'd graduated, they had a place for me in their Creative Department. Since then I've given up holidays, some weekends, and whatever I had to in order to get the job done. Thankfully, the company is a place that recognises you for your effort, and I was promoted a year after I started as a full-time employee. Since then I've continued to pull my weight so my bosses have given me more responsibility."

"Sounds wonderful, though very busy I'd imagine. What time do you have for your personal life?"

"Not much," Emily replied with a laugh. "I work and on the occasion when I do have time, I spend it with Sarah and her family. You remember Sarah don't you?"

"Sarah Marsh?"

"She's Sarah Cartwright now," Emily informed him. "She's been married seven years and has four boys now, all under the age of five. They live in London too."

"She must be busy," Patrick said in surprise.

"I do my best to help. When she and Jeff, her husband, need some time alone, I'm godmother and babysitter."

"And what does your boyfriend have to say about that?" Patrick questioned, taking Emily slightly by surprise, as they crossed into the park.

The snow, which had since ceased, began to fall again lightly, speckling Patrick's dark hair in white flecks.

"I don't have a boyfriend," she admitted, sipping her coffee and plunging her hand into the bag of treats he'd procured. "What's this?"

"*Noisette Chocolat,*" Patrick said in the most beautiful French she'd ever heard. "Chocolate and hazelnut macaron," he added, realising she was still lost.

"Thanks," she said, taking a bite.

"Someone hasn't been practicing their French," he teased, taking a long gulp of his coffee.

"Haven't had the chance to be honest," she admitted, between chews of the delicious morsel. It was so good it made her hum in satisfaction.

"I see you're enjoying that," Patrick mused.

"It's delicious."

"So back to this no boyfriend. Do you have a husband then?" he continued his questioning, as they began to stroll beneath the trees. A few seconds later they'd found a bench and deposited themselves upon it, while Emily enjoyed her second macaron.

"No husband," she once again confirmed. "What about you?"

"None of the above either," he admitted, shaking his head.

"But why?" He was handsome, successful, and if he had the same disposition he had when they were young, then his personality was stellar. And best of all he lived in Paris, the city of love! What woman wouldn't want him?

"Thanks, my ego need a little rubbing," he replied. He took another long drink of his coffee, then shrugged. "I suppose the women I've met have all been missing something," he divulged.

"Like what?" Emily asked, intrigued.

"Like I said just ... something," he replied, his eyes meeting hers and making her heart leap. What did he mean by that? Could he be referring to her?

No, she admonished. It wasn't possible. Patrick couldn't still have feelings for her.

Could he?

Their hands met in the bag, each gripping a side of the last macaron. Patrick tugged on one end teasingly, while she made a face, his words still tumbling in her mind.

"Take it," he said, releasing the morsel.

"Thank you," she replied, promptly sinking her teeth into the delicate chocolate flavoured confection. She could feel Patrick's eyes on her, and the flush that was creeping up her chest under his scrutiny.

She was being silly, she told herself again. It couldn't be possible.

But as Emily's gaze met his full on, she found herself wondering something she hadn't in years.

What might have been...

CHAPTER 8

Had it all been a wonderful dream? Emily questioned as she rolled over in bed the following morning.

The sun was shining in through the hotel window, letting her know that the morning was now well into the day.

Had her meeting with Patrick Wilde been real?

She reached over to the bedside table for her phone, a small card slipping out from within the case as she opened it. There in stylised black writing, was Patrick's name, office information and mobile number, and on the back his home number.

It *had* been real.

She clutched the tiny piece of card in her hand and held it to her chest, as a flood of emotions swept through her. Could it be that she was getting a second chance with her first love? Was Tom's wife right and had the City of Love, brought love to her?

"I should call him," she said to herself, springing up in bed. "No, it would be too soon. You'd look desperate," she countered then, putting the card on her lap and looking down at it. She'd wait at least another day, which was enough time to remove any sign of desperation on her part.

It was a respectable time frame, she told herself as she hoped out of bed and headed to the bathroom to get ready for the day. Paris had lots more to offer, and she wasn't going to see it from her suite.

HALF AN HOUR later she was headed downstairs. She'd slept in so late that breakfast was more than likely over, which meant she'd have to find someplace else to eat.

She wasn't ready for lunch yet, and she had a craving for croissants or even a crêpe. She had just collected her coat when the in-room phone rang.

"Hello?" she answered, and was greeted by Angelique's distinct cadence, informing her that there was someone downstairs waiting for her, a Mr. Wilde.

Patrick - here - now?

Emily's heart felt as if it would leap from her chest the moment she heard his name. She couldn't help but think of what his presence at her hotel meant, when she'd been scolding herself for potentially acting desperate by calling him.

Her step was just a little quicker as she left her room for the elevator, informing Angelique to ensure that Patrick knew she'd be right down.

CHAPTER 9

"I just took a chance seeing if you'd be here," Patrick informed her, when she reached him. "I thought with all the sight-seeing you'd planned you may have been out and about already."

"I had intended to," she admitted with an embarrassed laugh. "Unfortunately it seems my bed was more persuasive this morning."

"I get that," he chuckled. "Perhaps I can make up for it by giving you a personal tour around the city?"

"Don't you have better things to do? I know you're on holiday too, but you must've had other plans before you met me," she queried.

There was a twinkle in his eye. "Plans can change. Besides, I think this will be lots more fun."

Emily grinned and nodded.

"That's settled then. Let's go," he stated, offering her an arm. Emily took it and they headed out of the hotel.

After a few minutes she recognised the route. "We're headed to the Arc de Triomphe?"

"I thought it the best place to start our tour."

"Great, I had it on my list of places to see because I only got a glimpse yesterday," she informed him. "But do you mind stopping on the way? I'm a little hungry."

"Why didn't you say so? I know the perfect place to grab brunch," he replied, turning them back around and heading in the opposite direction.

"Where are we going now?"

"You'll see," he informed her intriguingly.

The eclectic café Patrick took her to was a sight to behold. The furniture was reminiscent of the regency era, some chairs covered in a plush velvety blue, while others in leopard print. There were white monkey statues with lightbulbs in them and a large mirror adorned half of one wall. Emily would have loved to eat outside and enjoy the alfresco dining, but it was far too chilly, so she'd have to live that dream another day.

"Pick whatever you want - my treat," Patrick stated as the menus were placed before them.

"I couldn't," Emily replied. "You're already being my free tour guide. You should get something out of all this. I'll buy this time."

He touched her hand gently. "Who said I wasn't getting something from this," he said, his soft gaze set on hers and it made Emily's stomach flip.

"OK," she acquiesced softly. "Your treat."

Was all the food so good in Paris? she wondered a few minutes later. With no breakfast she was famished and pumpkin soup was just what she needed on a chilly day, especially with delicious French roast.

"Now that you're fed and watered, we can start our tour," Patrick joked as he paid the bill.

CHAPTER 10

A few minutes later they were once again headed in the direction of the Arc de Triomphe, chatting animatedly as they went.

It must have been the conversation, because before Emily knew it they were at Place Charles de Gaulle and crossing the street to the monument.

"Its spectacular," she said, a little dazed as she stood at the foot of the structure. The memorial torch was unlit, much to her disappointment. "I thought the flame would be burning," she mumbled as she walked around the memorial, which was decorated with fresh flowers though barred by a low black chain.

"They rekindle it at six-thirty," Patrick informed her. "One of the associations of the La Flamme sous l'Arc de Triomphe veterans do it."

She looked at him in wonder. "You do seem to know a lot about this city."

He shrugged. "When I first moved here I did everything a tourist would do. Saw every sight. Then when it became home, I wanted to know more," Patrick continued, turning to look at her. "This place is a part of me now, as much as England was."

Emily went back to his side and hooked her arm in his. "It makes me a little sad," she said referring to the monument. "They don't even know his name, the man whose life they commemorate here. Makes you wonder how many more were lost and never found. Whose families never knew what happened to them, or returned with no name to mark their graves."

"War is a terrible thing but one that mankind keeps repeating," Patrick replied, laying a gentle hand on top of hers.

"Do you think we'll ever change? That there will ever be a world without fighting?"

"I doubt it. Most people gauge their happiness against the prosperity of others. When one set of people think the other has something they should, they fight for it. They fight for what they think is right. The only problem is we *all* think we're right."

Emily looked up at him quizzically.

"As long as we keep fighting over who's right and who's wrong, there will never be a world without war. All we can do is create something beautiful to help ease the pain of those wars, and celebrate the people who were lost to them."

The notion pained Emily. Her Nan was unknown to the world, important to no one but her. There was no special place to mark her life, only a headstone in a graveyard back home.

"We really need to celebrate people while they're alive," she said softy.

"I agree."

"Show me something cheerier now?" she suggested, still holding his gaze.

"It would be my pleasure," Patrick stated, taking one last look at the monument, before leading her away.

CHAPTER 11

❄

How did Patrick know just where to take her to make her smile?

The Palais Galleria, the museum of fashion, was every woman's dream. Filled with temporary collections showcasing well-known, slightly known and forgotten designers from around the world.

The exterior was inspired by Palladian architecture but known for its Beaux-Arts style. It reminded Emily of something you'd expect to find in Italy, perhaps in Rome, the preserved remnant of some ancient colonnade.

Here you could see designs that were hand-drawn by some of the most distinct and memorable designers, see their clothing draped elegantly on mannequins, or photographed in timeless memorial to the stars who'd made or worn some of the best clothing the world had ever seen.

It was a stark contrast to the Arc de Triomphe, which had left Emily a bit melancholy. Now she felt invigorated.

"Did I choose right?" Patrick asked from behind her. He was standing by a far wall watching her with some amusement.

"You absolutely did," she replied in delight, turning back to the display of Mariano Fortuny's famous Delphos gown, which was designed in 1909.

The designer was considered a liberator of the female form, and the dress before Emily was the epitome of it. Made of plain silk, and so finely pleated that it didn't even wrinkle after being rolled in a ball, it was spectacular. Emily could only imagine herself in a dress like it. She'd feel like an heiress in it.

"That would look great on you," Patrick commented, his arms folded casually over his chest.

"I'd have to win the lottery first," Emily joked.

"You always liked fashion didn't you? Even when you couldn't afford it," he commented, running his finger under the collar of her cashmere coat. "But I can see that has changed."

"I have a few nice pieces," she replied. It was true; she adored fashion; it didn't matter what, clothes, shoes or bags. She may not have had much of a social life, but she certainly dressed like someone who did.

"Let's go someplace you enjoy now," she said to Patrick, taking him by the hand and pulling him towards the exit.

"We better get a taxi if we're going where I'd like to go," he joked. "It's not exactly walking distance."

"I'm intrigued. Where to?"

"You'll see," he smiled, as they walked out to find a taxi.

CHAPTER 12

"When did you become so cultured?" Emily asked, as she stood before the Louvre Palace, home of the famed museum.

It was a formidable building, which had originally been built as a fortress. Then there was the iconic modern glass pyramids which marked the main entrance.

"I *have* to get a photo of this," she commented, slightly in awe.

Patrick waylaid a passerby, the gist of the conversation Emily was just able to get. They spoke so quickly in French it was hard to get to grips with what he was saying, but she figured he was asking the gentleman to take their photograph.

He took her phone and passed it to the other man, before coming to stand behind Emily and hugging her from behind. It was strange having his arms wrapped around her again, but so warm and familiar too. He lowered his cheek beside hers and she dared a glance, marking the hue along his jaw. Suddenly she heard a snap, and realised the man had taken the photo.

"Another," Patrick requested in French, as he turned to meet her eyes. He smiled at her, a wide smile she knew matched her own, as she folded her arms over his and kept his gaze.

"Did I tell you how beautiful you look today?" he asked, as the phone snapped again.

"No," Emily replied softly.

His smile grew, his eyes boring deep into hers. "You look beautiful, Emily." He tucked her hair behind her ear as the phone snapped again.

Then the man moved to hand back the phone and just like that the spell was broken and Emily was brought, heart racing back to her surroundings.

When Patrick returned to her side she was still trying to get her heart to slow. "Shall we go in?" she asked, eager to distract herself from the thundering in her chest.

"Of course," he said, handing her phone back to her.

They started their tour in Egyptian Antiquities, where she took several shots beside the Great Sphinx of Tanis,

"It's like I've gone to Paris and Egypt all in one day," she commented as she admired the beautifully crafted sculpture, which like its Giza counterpart was missing a nose. "Could you imagine that anyone could craft such a thing?" she continued in wonder, a soft chuckle drawing her attention. "What?" she asked, turning to Patrick, who was blocking his mouth with his hand as he laughed.

"The look on your face," he replied. "You're like a child on a first trip to DisneyLand."

"Is that a bad thing?"

"Not in my book."

"Then shall we continue?"

"Lead the way," Patrick encouraged, falling in step behind her, making her stomach flip once more. She knew he was watching her, she could feel his gaze upon her and had to fight the urge to look back at him.

Her efforts failed however, and when she dared to half turn to see if she was right, she was met by those beautiful hazel eyes, staring intently at her with a mischievous smile on his face.

"See something you like?" she mustered the courage to ask.

"You know I do," he replied coolly. "The real question is, do you?"

CHAPTER 13

*E*mily suddenly felt weak all over. She didn't want to be obvious, but it was clear there was something still between them.

But what?

Was it just their reminiscing unearthing the remnants of emotions past?

Or was this something entirely new?

"Perhaps," she replied playfully, as she turned around and continued into the next room.

Here, she saw ancient jewellery and art, papyrus scrolls, more ancient artefacts and mummies. It was more than she had ever expected, and it was only the contents of one of the many rooms within the Louvre.

"Had enough yet?" Patrick asked as they existed the last exhibit.

"How does anyone ever have enough of Paris?" she replied awestruck. "I don't think I have enough room in my brain to hold everything I've seen today, and we haven't even toured the art museum yet."

"We can always come back here," he suggested. "But it's near dinnertime now and I'm hungry."

"Is it? I hadn't realised it was so late, I was so taken by everything."

"Then we can come again tomorrow, but right now I need feeding," he said, then added jokingly. "I'd hate for you to faint from hunger either."

"That happened only once!" she protested laughing. "I'd had swimming practice that day and woke up too late to get breakfast."

"I didn't say anything …" Patrick teased, eyes twinkling and Emily had to laugh at the memory. He still remembered stuff about their past that to her was long-forgotten. Or had been at least.

"Where shall we eat then?" she asked.

"The best place in town."

"Where's that?" she queried, wondering what fancy local restaurant he was about to wow her with.

He smiled enigmatically. "You'll find out when we get there."

CHAPTER 14

*E*mily stood before a vista looking out at a city twinkling in snow and lights.

It was breath-taking, almost surreal.

Paris lay at her feet, or so it seemed she thought as she gazed out from the second floor vantage point of none other than the Eiffel tower. The Jules Verne restaurant was one of five places to dine in the tower, but equally spectacular as all the others.

Every table had a great view, but the table that Patrick requested was situated beside one of the large glass walls overlooking the city.

Emily couldn't bring herself to sit just yet though. "It's like you can see all of France from here," she commented, as Patrick stood beside her.

"Not France, but definitely all of Paris," he chuckled. "I'm so glad you like it."

"Like it? I love it! I can't believe they were able to accommodate us at such short notice, especially so close to Christmas."

"Usually you'd have to wait sometimes as long as two weeks for a reservation," Patrick informed her, "but my company uses this place for business lunches a lot, so they usually find some way to accommodate us."

"So you're a man about town too?" she mused, causing him to blush slightly.

"I'm no man about town, Emily, I just happen to know the right people. *They're* the ones who are the men about town. I just work for them."

She sighed. "Could you ever have imagined that us two kids from Oxfordshire would wind up in big cities like we are now?"

"Never in a million years," he said. "I thought I'd stay in Kingham all my life, but it wasn't meant to be." He turned to her. "But I'm glad for it."

"You are?"

"I got to see you again, didn't I? All those years in England and we never saw each other. A day in Paris and here we are."

The look on his face was indescribable, and so sweet, it made her remember all the half glances and smiles across the classroom when they were in school. Were those feelings alive again? How long would they last this time? She was only going to be in the city for a long weekend, then she had to go home.

"We better take our table before they give it away," he joked then.

Emily nodded, and allowed him to escort her to their table, where he pulled out her seat and made sure she was settled before taking his.

Their meal was superb, the best eight courses she'd ever had in her life, and the first time for it.

"That was so delicious. I wish I could rewind the night and do it all again," she mused, sipping her glass of wine.

"It was good, wasn't it?" Patrick agreed. His eyes had hovered between her and his plate the entire night, except for the moments when Emily had pulled his attention to the sights below.

She'd attempted to identify what she was seeing, and had done miserably at it. Patrick on the other hand, seemed to have all parts of the city committed to memory.

"What're you doing tomorrow night?" he asked, leaning on his elbows as he spoke.

"Nothing, actually. I suppose I'll wander around a bit more and then eat at the hotel. Why?"

"Would you like to come over to my place for dinner?"

Her heart gave a little flip. "I'd love that. Thank you."

"Not to sound like a song, but what about the day after? You'll still be here, yes?"

"Yes, but nothing planned either," she said with a smile, guessing that another invitation was imminent.

"My boss has a special Christmas party every year for us who don't have family in the city," he informed. "It's at his house in La Muette. I go by myself usually," he informed her. "And I'd rather not this year. Go by myself I mean."

"You asking me to go with you?" Emily asked, her surprise clear.

"Would you?"

"I don't know Patrick, it's a big business party with everyone you know, and your boss. What would they think if you showed up with me?" she questioned.

"They'd think that you're someone special to me," he countered. "And they'd be right."

CHAPTER 15

"Oh," she began, but he silenced her with the gentle squeeze of her hand.

"I watched you walk away from me ten years ago Emily, and it almost killed me. Did you know that?"

"No," she replied, shaking her head. "You said you were fine, that you wanted the best for me."

"I did, but I also wanted you to stay. I knew if you left and saw what was out there beyond our little town you wouldn't come back. And I was right. You didn't."

"I thought you'd moved on too …"

"I tried, but every woman I met just wasn't enough. They weren't enough, because they weren't you."

Patrick's words were so sincere that they tore at the fibres of her heart. Back then, she'd wanted to believe what he'd said when he wished her well all those years ago, but somewhere deep inside, she'd known he was lying. She'd wanted to go to London so badly that she'd ignored it.

Even when she convinced herself he'd move on, it was because she knew *she* needed to. If left to herself, Emily would have loved Patrick forever.

Perhaps that was why her other relationships had never worked out either; like him, she was looking for someone else while in the arms of another.

"When I saw you yesterday, I thought I'd finally been given my chance," he continued. "That somehow fate had returned you to me in the most unexpected of ways," he confessed. "Once I knew it really was you, I didn't hesitate this time. I was too afraid if I did you might turn away and I'd lose you again."

"Patrick..."

"Let me say this, please. I don't know by what means we found each other again here or why, but I do want to find out. I took a step towards you yesterday Emily, but now I need you to step towards me, if you're as curious and confused about this as I am."

His eyes were urging her response, but Emily wasn't sure what to say. This was unexpected.

Wonderful, but unexpected.

"I don't know if I can take that step," she admitted finally. "Your life is here, in this beautiful city," she began, turning her eyes to the twinkling lights beneath before returning them to his face. "Mine's in London, remember?"

"It's only a train journey away," he countered seriously.

Emily considered his words. "You're right, it is only a train journey away, but how long can we live with that?"

"What do you mean?"

"I mean, how long could we realistically go with a sea between us, having to trudge from one country to the other? How many times a month should we do it? Should I come to you or you to me? Only on special days, or when work will allow us? We both have demanding jobs that take up our time and energy, Patrick. How much time do you think either of us would have to dedicate to a long distance relationship?"

She could tell her questions were deflating his hopes, but she had to look at the reality of the situation.

They weren't teenagers anymore. She had a job where people

depended on her, and a position she'd worked years and sleepless nights to achieve. He'd done the same. How could she ask him to leave it? How could he ask her?

"You're saying you don't feel anything for me then?" he questioned, his tone low.

"That's not it," she countered. "I do. I think I always have, but I can't ignore where we both are either."

"Can't we just see what happens?" he asked.

"I really don't know if I can do that."

"Why not?"

"Because I don't want to get my hopes up, get more attached to you, and have one of us walk away again. I know I couldn't go through that again. Could you?"

Patrick looked at her for the longest time, his silence increasing her anxiety. Finally he spoke. "No, I don't think I could either," he replied, clearly disheartened.

"Do you still want to have me over for dinner tomorrow night?" she asked unsure.

"Emily, I'd rather be with you than anyone else," Patrick said, brightening a little. "I'll pick you up at seven."

"I'll be waiting," she said smiling, but inside she wasn't sure.

Had she done the right thing?

CHAPTER 16

The next day, Emily was seriously considering cancelling their dinner to hide under the covers and order room service, but Patrick had called to confirm he'd be picking her up, and she knew she wouldn't - *couldn't* - do it, the moment she heard his voice.

The drive to his apartment was a quiet one.

They were both obviously feeling the tension from their heart to heart the night before, and Emily had no idea how to remedy it.

She couldn't take her words back, and she couldn't change the facts either. The sooner they accepted that the better, wasn't it?

Patrick's apartment was modern and fresh, the walls and cupboards all painted white, with dark wooden floors throughout. The fixtures were modern stylish, and very contemporary.

"Did you decorate this place yourself?" Emily couldn't help questioning, as she saw the colourful decorative cushions on the couch. It really was the quintessential bachelor pad.

"No," Patrick said with a chuckle. "It came already decorated when I moved in. Part of the company package."

"I wish I had such a company package," she replied, as she continued to look around, albeit somewhat furtively.

"Feel free to take a tour. I have nothing to hide," Patrick offered, as he opened a bottle of red wine and left it to breathe.

"You sure the ghosts of girlfriends past won't come out to get me?"

He chuckled. "I'm pretty sure I had those demons exorcised a long time ago."

Emily wandered around his apartment slowly, taking in every nook and cranny. He kept it exceptionally neat, which was a surprise, considering how messy his childhood bedroom used to be.

"Maybe he has a maid," she mused.

"Yep. She comes in on Mondays," his voice chimed from behind her, making her jump.

"You almost scared me to death," she admitted, with a hand to her chest.

"I wouldn't want that," he stated, stepping closer. "I'm still planning on convincing you that you and I can work."

Her heart danced a little. "Patrick, I thought I already explained —"

"Yes, you explained why you thought we couldn't work, but you haven't yet heard the reasons I think we can."

How she wanted him to be right, that there was some way they could do this, but something told her it was impossible.

Couldn't he just enjoy the time they had together here now and not worry about anything afterwards?

"I let you go too easily before. I'm going to make it difficult for you this time," he said, stepping towards her and closing the space between them.

Every synapse in Emily's brain began to fire as Patrick's hands sought her arms gently, his thumbs stroking her exposed skin as a gentle tug drew her closer.

She shouldn't let this happen. She should push him away and leave, go back to the hotel and not answer any of his calls.

There was only one problem with that though. She didn't want to, couldn't resist. Despite her protests, Emily knew she wanted what was about to happen.

His face drew closer and her heart quickened even more, until all she could hear was the sound of it drumming in her ears.

She licked her lips involuntarily in anticipation of the moment when his would meet hers, yet still she was nervous. She hadn't kissed a man in a couple of years. She hadn't kissed Patrick in over ten.

Could you forget how? Emily didn't have long to wonder though, as seconds later, she felt Patrick's mouth on hers.

His lips were gentle, asking, not demanding and Emily willingly gave in. She returned his kiss with equal tentativeness, allowing herself to relearn the feel of him after all these years.

CHAPTER 17

*H*is technique had changed, grown better.

He no longer had the excited anticipation of a teenager, eager to explore and claim. Patrick's kisses had matured just like he had, and Emily found that even more irresistible.

When their lips finally parted she was breathless, and her knees just a little shaky. Thankfully he hadn't released his grip on her so the fear of falling was eliminated, though the smile on his face didn't help the situation.

"Shall we eat?" he asked then, as if nothing at all had happened.

Compose yourself Emily. It wasn't that good of a kiss.

Who was she kidding? Yes it was.

"Sure," she mumbled, stepping round him and heading back to the living room.

Sitting at the table, she discovered something else new and improved about Patrick. He could cook.

The table was laid tastefully, with matching dinnerware and cutlery. "Did this come with the flat too?"

"No, this bit is all my doing," Patrick replied. "You seem to forget that our family owned a restaurant," he reminded her.

"Touché. So what are we eating?"

He practically beamed with pride as he began to uncover the festive meal he'd prepared, course by course.

They started with the amuse bouche, a bite-sized puffed pastry filled with ham, cheese and chives, followed by pheasant wrapped in bacon with chestnut stuffing, roasted mushrooms and vegetables.

Afterwards, as was fitting in Paris, Patrick served a cheese platter with small salad, and then topped it all off with a Yule Log.

"I can believe you made everything but the log," Emily challenged, as she dabbed the corners of her mouth and set her napkin aside.

"Guilty as charged."

Emily smirked at him.

"What? I'm not a baker. I cook," he stated matter-of-factly, as he began to clear the table.

"Do you want a hand with that?"

"No, you just go and take a seat on the couch, and I'll be right with you," Patrick ordered.

"If you say so," she replied, taking her glass and walking over the couch, a spring in her step.

She made herself comfortable as she watched him continue to clear the table, before pushing up his sleeves and beginning to wash up.

It was strange, but there was something so cosy and domestic about the whole situation that she couldn't take her eyes away. When he finally settled on the couch beside her, he looked tired but was smiling.

"I did ask if you wanted help," she teased.

"I know, but you're my guest. I wasn't about to ask you to work for your dinner."

"Fair enough," she replied. "Now what?"

"Now," he said, picking up the TV remote. "We watch *Miracle on Thirty-Fourth Street,* and we fall asleep on the couch."

"Is that so?"

He grinned. "I had it all planned." He turned on the TV, the opening scene for the movie immediately appearing.

"You did plan this ..." she giggled.

"Yes I did. It's one of the things I really missed after you were gone. Not having you for our traditional Christmas week movie-watching sessions."

"Well then," Emily replied, settling in alongside him and resting her head on his shoulder, as the movie began. "We need to make up for that."

She'd missed this too - all of it - and it felt so amazing to have it back again.

CHAPTER 18

❄

*H*er stay rolled by so quickly, *too* quickly. Emily could hardly keep it all straight.

They'd spent a lot of time together at Patrick's place, watching movies and just enjoying getting to know one another again.

He'd made her entire trip to Paris a dream, but as the time came closer to ending, Emily began to dread the inevitable moment when they'd have to say goodbye.

He had done his best in the meantime to convince her that things could work, if only she'd give them a chance.

His persuasions were convincing, but not enough to surmount Emily's fears. What if they pursued a relationship and it ended, like all of her relationships before?

What if this entire thing was just the effects of the most romantic city in the world? Or worse, the lingering memories of a past they hadn't fully let go of?

"Stop thinking so much," Patrick demanded, tugging on her hand as they left her hotel. I'm not going to let you mope for your last day in Paris."

She looked at him sadly. Their last day together. It all kept coming back to the one fact. "Where're we off to now?" she asked, dismissing her own melancholy.

"Somewhere suitably Christmassy."

PARIS TRULY DID LOOK incredible at Christmastime.

The Champs-Élysée had been transformed for the season, and from the Grand Palais to the Concorde Palace the avenue was lit from top to bottom, each of the two hundred trees that lined the road bedecked in twinkling fairly lights, creating a wonderland.

"They outdo themselves every year," Patrick commented, looking down the avenue to where the Christmas markets were set up.

Emily felt like a child again, as she walked beneath the lights alongside Parisians hooked arm-in-arm, some kissing affectionately, others admiring the Christmas fair.

There were stalls in abundance, each offering their own take on festive specialities, from handmade crafts, to freshly made crêpes and sweets.

"Can we go there?" Emily asked, turning her gaze to the Ferris wheel that marked the end of the Concorde Palace.

"If you want," Patrick replied. "It's the biggest in the world, outdoes your London one even."

"Really? Actually, it does look bigger than the London Eye, even at this distance," she replied.

"You always did like going on those things," he commented.

"What can I say, I like looking at the world from a different perspective sometimes."

"That's good then, because I'm hoping you might change your view on a couple of things," he prodded gently.

"Stop it," she replied, giving him a playful shove.

"I'm not giving up. Not until you walk away."

"Can't we just enjoy now? It's my last day after all."

"That's why I'm trying so hard," he replied. "Because I don't want this to be *our* last day."

CHAPTER 19

❄

*H*e was wearing her down. The closer the time for her to return home, and the more time she spent with him, the less she wanted to leave.

Could it really work? Was this really their second chance? Maybe their last?

"You owe me a gift," Patrick stated out of the blue.

"What?"

"A thank you gift for showing you around the city. Come on."

They weaved through the crowd, their direction the Concorde Palace, but suddenly Patrick swerved to the right and led her down a side street.

Emily barely caught the name, Avenue Montaigne.

Like where they'd left, the avenue was illuminated in lights of all sorts of shapes, and in front of a Dior boutique was a giant chandelier. The trees were also dressed in their finest, decorated with so many lights that they seemed to be made entirely of them.

Still, she was baffled as to what Patrick could possibly want from there.

Then they stopped.

"What?" she asked, confused.

"Look up," he said, pointing up the ball of lights above their heads, some mistletoe hanging from it. Emily laughed instantly.

"Is that it - your gift?"

"It's enough, for now," Patrick replied, but didn't move.

Emily knew what he was saying, even without words.

Step towards me. Take a leap of faith. I'm right here.

Her eyes focused on the snow around their boots, and the way Patrick - her childhood sweetheart - held her fingers in his, each hooked into the other.

They'd always been bound together. In a small place like Kingham everyone knew everyone. They'd gone through every stage of school together, but only realised they loved one another when they were in their teens.

Now standing before him, in a city hundreds of miles away from all that, Emily had to make a choice.

She couldn't keep wanting him near, yet pushing him away with her words.

She stepped forward and sure enough, Patrick was waiting for her.

CHAPTER 20

The moment she moved, he pulled her in, enveloping her within the warmth of his body as his lips pressed against hers.

This kiss wasn't the gentle one from his apartment, it was a statement of everything he felt.

Love. Passion. Faithfulness. Endurance.

It was the kind of kiss that some women waited their entire lives to get and often never did.

When they parted, Emily was in tears.

"What's the matter?" he asked gently, brushing her cheek with his gloved hand. The soft fabric was like down against her skin.

"I'm happy, but so scared, all at the same time," she admitted, wrapping her arms around his waist, her head against his chest. She felt his hand against her head, stroking her hair.

"There's no need to be afraid. I'm right here, and I'm not going anywhere. I'm not letting you go, not ever again."

"What does this mean though?" she asked, through tearful smiles.

"It means some love is meant to be. Doesn't matter how many years you have to wait for it. When it's right, the time comes and everything falls into place. Just like it is for us now. Now we just have to write the rest of the story."

"Where will it lead?" she questioned.

"To a happy ending, I hope," Patrick teased softly before kissing her again.

CHAPTER 21

❄

The following morning it was time to go home.

She'd had an amazing trip, one she would never forget.

"I don't want to leave, Nan," Emily whispered, staring off her balcony, her eyes shifting between the Eiffel tower and the Arc de Triomphe.

Paris truly was the City of Love and second chances. This weekend it had given her both.

Live your life.

The thought entered her mind without summons, a fragment of words spoken by Nan the day Emily had told her she wanted to study in London, but was afraid to leave. It was that simple to her grandmother. Live your life.

Was she living her life? Was the life she had the life she wanted? If she'd been asked the question a few days ago she would have said yes, immediately.

Now, she wasn't so sure.

The knock on the door told her it was time to check out, the porter had come for her bags and Patrick was due to pick her up out front at any moment.

"*Au revoir*, Paris," she said, turning from her window and headed towards the door.

PATRICK WAS on time as usual, and within minutes of her arrival in the lobby and the customary procedures to leave, she was seated beside him in his car, holding hands as they drove towards the airport.

The silence was unusual between them, but for some reason on this occasion, it wasn't uncomfortable, but companionable.

Emily didn't want to speak and Patrick didn't seem to feel the need to either. They were content just to be with each other.

Charles de Gaulle came into view far sooner than expected. Patrick pulled her suitcase from the boot and sent her on ahead to get checked in. She'd protested, but he'd insisted and in the end he won.

She was almost to the counter when he appeared with three bags. She looked at him curiously. "That one isn't mine."

"No," Patrick said, a small smile creeping across his face. "It's mine."

If he'd meant to shock her he'd succeeded, and she was almost too stunned to speak as excitement began bubbling inside.

"Does this mean you're coming with me ... to London?" she asked slowly, trying to keep her joy under control.

"It's only days till Christmas. I haven't taken a holiday outside of the usual in years. I told my boss there was a very special someone I needed to spend more time with, and he gave me an additional stint off."

Her smile could no longer be contained. "You have a very understanding boss."

"He was once a man in love too. He understood where I was coming from." Patrick's gaze lingered on her face as he reached for her hand. She squeezed it tightly.

She too had made a decision she had yet to tell him, and there was no better time than now.

CHAPTER 22

"Well, he won't need to lose you for too long."
"Why is that?"
"Because you won't have to come to London from now on to see your 'special someone'," she smiled.

Patrick looked completely lost, and it was a look that amused her tremendously.

They stepped up to the counter.

"I'm still waiting for you to explain," he stated as he handed over his ticket and hers.

Emily turned to him. "I made a decision."

"OK…"

"I'm going to live my life, the life I want," she said, touching her palm to his face. "That life is with you. I'm moving to be with you - in Paris."

One moment she was standing at the desk, the next she was being spun round and lifted up in Patrick's arms, as confused passengers looked on.

"You won't regret this. I promise. I swear, you'll never regret this," he was saying as he peppered her face with kisses. "Emily, I have loved you all my life and - "

"*Excusez-moi?*" the clerk droned, in an attempt to get their attention.

A flush filled Emily's face as Patrick apologised and set her down, returning to the counter. He collected their boarding passes and apologised to the passengers waiting impatiently, albeit good-humouredly, behind them.

She wouldn't let go of his hand as they moved towards the departures hall.

"So how are we going to do this?" he babbled as they walked. "What should we do first?"

"Well, first you come to London with me for Christmas. I'll have to speak to my boss when I get back after the holidays, give notice and all that. Then I'll have to see about giving up the lease on my place and finding somewhere in Paris."

"You don't have to worry about that," Patrick replied. "I know a great place you can stay," he assured her, a bright smile on his face.

She smiled, delighted. "I thought you might."

Taking a seat in front of the large circular window that framed the sky and the runway below, Emily and Patrick continued to talk excitedly about what would happen next.

All of a sudden, anything seemed possible. Everything. There was nothing they couldn't do together.

She rested her head on his shoulder. "Patrick?"

"Yes, Emily."

"Say it now," she asked, a smile tickling her lips.

"Say what?"

"That thing you started to say back at the check-in desk."

He pulled her closer. "Emily Richardson, I have loved you all my life and will love you for the rest of it. We belong together you and I; always have."

She squeezed his arm and closed her eyes, savouring the sound of his words.

"So I guess we did find our happy ending after all," she said softly. "Right here in the City of Love."

Patrick smiled. *"Absolument."*

A NEW YORK CHRISTMAS

CHAPTER 1

A New York Christmas; a lifelong dream come true.
I'd always wanted to visit the famed city, especially around Christmastime, so when the opportunity came up to visit my cousin Sarah, an estate agent who lived in Manhattan, I jumped on it immediately.

Plus the perfect opportunity to get out of Dublin for a while and nurse my broken heart.

Don, my boyfriend of two years had cheated on me just weeks before, and the fact that it happened so close to Christmas seemed to make it even harder.

Since the split I'd felt numb and broken, so a trip to New York seemed like the ideal distraction and a perfect getaway.

It would be a reset button of sorts and while the festive atmosphere might well underscore my pain, I longed to see the legendary twinkling Christmas décor.

I wanted to feel snow crunch beneath my feet while I walked along the streets of the world-famous city.

My imagination was already alive with scenes of mesmerising department store windows and sparkling Christmas trees, Central

Park, ice rinks and softly falling slow, reflecting some of my favourite Christmas movies.

To put it simply, I wanted to experience a classic New York Christmas.

Now, I sat on the sofa of Sarah's thirty-fourth-floor apartment waiting for her to come home.

She had a tall, fat Christmas tree, a real spruce. It made the entire apartment smell of fresh pine needles. Simply decorated in silver and gold, all the ornaments were replicas of antiques. Tiny red, white and black nutcracker soldiers hung from the branches with red ribbon and silver tinsel dangled, giving it a wilder aesthetic.

It was perfectly placed next to an enormous window overlooking the city streets below.

Just then my cousin burst through the front door with piles of paperwork and two laptop cases.

She was definitely one of those typical New Yorkers you hear about; the ones who always seemed to be in a hurry even when they had all the time in the world. Rushing around like they were in some sort of imaginary race.

A complete contrast to my comparatively slower-paced Dublin lifestyle.

Sarah piled her stuff on the table and then turned to me with an apologetic expression.

"Let me guess, you have to work?" I asked.

I'd only just arrived last night. I went straight to Sarah's where we had dinner - Chinese takeout — and did some catching up. That had been the extent of my New York adventures so far, but today she had promised to show me around the city and have dinner at the Russian Tea Rooms.

"Maddie I'm so sorry. If I don't get to this property right now I could lose it. Potentially a million-dollar deal or more and with Christmas only a week away I'm on a deadline. Do you hate me?" she asked.

I feigned a narrowing of my eyes but then laughed.

"Of course not. Obviously, I don't expect you to stop your life just because I'm here. Do what you would normally do. Just give me a little guidance so that I can get out and explore on my own. I'm a big girl and I can handle the Big Apple on my own. Can't I?"

Half an hour later I looked at myself in the mirror.

I took hot rollers out of my hair and brushed out the soft shoulder-length curls. Now it was thick and bouncy. My hair was a dark auburn brown and my skin was pale, typically Irish.

I put on a nice matte shade of red lipstick, not something I would normally wear but it was Christmas after all, and I was in a festive mood.

It stood out against my hair and dark lashes. I was petite at only five foot three, so I tried to always wear at least one thing that made me stand out.

It added a nice touch to my otherwise basic outfit of blue jeans and a red woollen sweater. I tugged on black calf-length leather boots, added a grey cashmere hat and saying goodbye to Sarah, headed out the door and into the bustling city.

CHAPTER 2

❄

My first stop had to be Central Park. I ambled down the street, taking it all in. The big city buzz was apparent but a lot was missing from my classic New York Christmas expectations.

For starters it was daytime, so none of the twinkling lights were on and the city had not yet been hit by its first snowfall.

It all seemed disappointingly *non*-festive so far.

Soon I came upon a massive building right across from the park. The steps were full of people sitting around eating and talking.

There were two large fir trees on either side of the entrance decorated in red velvet bows, and matching red and gold Christmas baubles, with a large gold star on top of both. Huge classical stone columns were wrapped with green ribbon that spiralled down the entire length of each.

I looked with interest at the inscription above them that read the *American Museum of Natural History.*

Of course... This place was a New York icon.

I went to a nearby street vendor and bought a piping cup of coffee and a pretzel, then joined everyone else sitting on the steps.

I was thoroughly enjoying my buttery salty snack when I got the feeling that someone was staring at me.

Before I took another bite I looked around and there, only a few feet away, was the most gorgeous man I had ever seen.

Our eyes locked and instantly I was hypnotised. I couldn't look away. He was wearing a dark wool pea coat and a well-fitted suit underneath.

His eyes were a piercing grey that changed to blue in the light. His dark hair was a bit messy, almost like the way a student would keep it and he had a layer of rugged stubble on his chin. He smiled a little at me and lifted his coffee cup in a "cheers" sort of motion. It was then that I realised I was still in a frozen state with my pretzel in the air, halfway to my mouth.

I snapped out of it and raised my cup back to him in the same manner, suddenly feeling like a messy child with butter and salt all over my mouth.

Still, he must have seen my greeting as an invite because he stood up.

He walked over and my heart immediately began to pound. Surely he would be able to hear it if he got any closer.

"Is that good?" he asked pointing to the pretzel.

"Yes, it is," I replied.

"May I?" He gestured at the space next to me on the steps.

"OK." I was completely confused. I thought New Yorkers were supposed to be impolite and unapproachable.

"Seems like it must be. The way you were eating it; it looked like you were really enjoying it."

"You were watching me eat?"

"Well, yes," he said with a grin that was childlike and made me feel like I was playing some coy game. "So how long are you in town?"

"What? How do you know I'm visiting?" I asked, with my mouth wide open.

"The way you stood in front of the building staring at it. Only folks who aren't from around here can look at it and still be in awe. The locals are so used to it that they tend to take it for granted."

"Well, it is beautiful. And yes, I am visiting. To be honest I came here for a classic Christmas with snow and festive decorations and all that. But so far this is the only building I've seen that is decorated. I haven't been here very long though," I stopped suddenly, feeling like I was rambling on.

Why was I even telling this handsome stranger my every thought?

"Well, maybe you just need someone to show you around. A classic New York Christmas is out there; you just have to know where to go," he added gently. "Happy to point you in the right direction if you'd like."

There was a long pause. I stared at him. Looking into his sparkling grey eyes and then at his soft lips.

"I think I would - like that, I mean."

"Great. I'm Blake by the way." He reached a hand out to shake mine.

'Madeleine.'

CHAPTER 3

"Shall we get started then? There's something inside I want to show you," Blake said as he stood up.

I followed him up the steps to the museum and threw away the last of my pretzel and empty cup into a nearby bin.

He led me inside the lobby, and there right in the middle of the huge open space was one of the quirkiest Christmas trees I had ever seen. It was full of paper ornaments. Origami ornaments.

"This is how we kick off the holiday season at the museum. It's been going on for almost thirty years now. "

"It's beautiful," I said as I went in for a closer look. There were all sorts of animal decorations, from turtles to zebras ... all made of the most delicate paper. Some were shiny and others were matte, but they were all expertly done.

"There must be hundreds," I said in awe.

"About five hundred in all," he said, and then added. "So you like it?"

"Like? I love it."

"Good. Then I am off to a good start," he grinned. "Next up my office," he said as he walked off further into the museum.

"Office?"

"Yes, I work here."

Now the messy mad scientist hair and wool pea coat made sense. He definitely looked the part. I scurried after him to catch up.

Soon we arrived at a door labeled 'museum staff only.' Blake used a key card to unlock the door and we stepped into a quiet long hallway.

"This way."

"Where are you taking me?" I asked, a little unnerved and wondering if I really should be trusting this random New York stranger.

He laughed and said, "I swear, it's just my office. I know it's a bit creepy in this part of the building but trust me."

Somehow I did trust him. I can't explain it, but for some reason, it felt like we had known each other for a long time even though we had only just met.

We came to a vast staircase and climbed two or three flights before finally reaching a hallway with people moving in and out of offices.

Blake showed me into his, and as soon as I stepped in I immediately fell in love with it. The wood was dark and heavy and a massive bookcase filled with old books covered an entire wall.

There was a heavy oak desk in the middle that had piles of papers and specimens in glass jars. A proper mad scientist's office.

He went over to the large windows. "Come and have a look."

What other surprise could this intriguing stranger have in store for me? When I got to the window I looked down. From this point, you could see almost all of Central Park.

"This is your view? It's amazing. You are so lucky."

"I know. It's good, right? Especially when it's snowing."

I looked at him. Who was this man? This was wonderful; more than I expected from anyone, let alone a stranger.

He must have seen the questioning look in my eyes because he caught my gaze and held it.

The chemistry between us was so thick it filled the room.

I barely knew this man, had only been in his company for thirty minutes at the most.

What was happening to me?

CHAPTER 4

I was in a historic New York building with the vastness of Central Park below us. Blake leaned in closer his voice down to a whisper and said, "Want to get closer?"

"Closer to what?" I stepped backwards a little, suddenly afraid he was able to read my thoughts.

"To the park of course."

"Oh, yes of course. I'd love to."

"Okay. But first, we need to make a pit stop." He led the way out the door and back down into the main building.

A pit-stop? I was intrigued afresh, but this man was full of surprises. I liked being surprised so I didn't ask.

Outside, he walked down the museum's front steps and I followed closely behind, noticing that dusk was approaching. "How about we grab some food and have a picnic in the park?"

"That sounds like a perfect idea."

"Great," He led the way to a row of street vendors, got one of everything and made us a sort of street food buffet — pizza slices, a gyro, hot dogs, a couple of bottled waters, and two hot chocolates.

We entered the park and the beauty of it took my breath away.

Most of the trees had lost their leaves and their spiralling bare branches reached high into the sky.

I understood how people could stroll the entire length of this massive space daily.

We sat down on a grassy area near a long avenue of trees. Blake laid out our buffet in front of us.

"That's a lot of food," I joked.

"Yes, well I couldn't decide what your first New York food vendor experience should be, so I got them all.

"Try the pizza first. You have to fold it like this," he said as he picked up a slice and folded it before handing it to me.

I laughed a little and took a bite from the cheesy gooeyness, while he did the same with the other slice.

"Delicious!" I cried after I swallowed my first bite.

"And that's not even the best pizza in town. Okay for a street vendor, but by far not the best. I'm glad you are pleased though."

Before long I was stuffed. I lay down on the grass looking up at the trees to give my full stomach some room to digest. He did the same.

"I am so full," I said.

"Yes, me too," he said.

"We're both full of New York," he joked. I laughed and then he joined in.

Then while we were both laughing and in good spirits, the loveliest thing happened.

CHAPTER 5

While we'd sat chatting on the grass, it had gradually darkened into early evening.

The sky was still a light pink from the setting sun, but also dark blue from the oncoming night. But right then, as if out of nowhere and without ceremony, some of the nearby trees lit up.

Sitting up immediately I gasped.

"That's incredible ... so beautiful."

I looked around and it seemed like the entire park came to life with twinkling lights.

The bare trees all around were decorated with delicate hanging bulb strands. It was so beautiful it almost brought me to tears.

I took it all in, absorbing the magic.

Now it truly felt like Christmas.

I looked at Blake, but he wasn't looking at the lights, he was looking at me. His face was lit from the glow of the nearby trees and I got the feeling he had been watching my reaction the entire time.

"I can't believe this is real," I said.

"Me neither," he replied gently, and again I got the feeling he wasn't talking about the lights.

Then he looked me directly in the eye and leaned in a little closer.

"Madeline, I don't normally do this. Meet a stranger on the steps and take off and spend an afternoon with them. It's been really special, and unusual for me. I just thought I should say something to give you a little insight as to who I am. It's as if I can't separate myself from you…"

My eyes got wide. I had never had a man be so forthright with me. To just put his cards on the table like that. Things like this just didn't happen. At least, not outside of the movies.

Was this guy playing games with me? Did he have something else in mind? Was that statement about not wanting to separate from me just a ploy to get me back to his place or something?

My warmed heart was beginning to turn a little cooler and now I felt very naive.

"I've said too much, I can tell I've made you uncomfortable," he said.

Yet, he had done nothing to make me not trust him, I realised. I was the one planting these negative thoughts in my head. I had only just met him and I was already assuming the worst. The break-up had done a number on me. The experience of being cheated on had scared me more than I had known. I willed myself to stop all the chatter in my head and to just stay in the moment.

"No, I'm fine. I'm sorry, I'm just not used to such honesty," I admitted.

"Right, it was a bit too much. I'm sorry I don't know where that came from."

The awkwardness was broken and everything was well again.

"Let's take a closer look," I said as I stood up. I made my way to the trees and the closer I got the more I realised just how many tiny lights there were.

They twinkled and glowed in the fading daylight. Now, it was beginning to look and feel a lot more like A New York Christmas.

This was that festive magic I had expected from the city. It was all so lovely. My feelings of paranoia and lack of trust began to melt away. The season had that effect on people I supposed.

It made them softer, more trusting, and more open. It was affecting me in that way now. The lights made Blake's eyes now seem a crystal watery grey. Like the sea during a storm.

"I want to show you more; more of the city's festivity, if you'll let me," he said.

"I would love that."

He arched his elbow out and I duly wrapped my arm under his. He then led me down the path.

"Where are we going now?"

"It's a surprise. But I think you will like it."

I grinned. This guy seemed to like surprising me, and I loved being surprised.

I wondered what next he had in store.

CHAPTER 6

We strolled through the park arm in arm, and chatted more about our lives.

Blake told me about his work and what he did at the museum. "I was actually just taking a break from finishing a paper when I was sitting on the steps earlier. I had planned to go back inside and finish. Then I saw you."

"Oh, no I'm so sorry. Had I known I would not have let you stop working for this." I said, feeling guilty.

"It was worth it. I had to take that chance when I saw it. I would forever regret it if I didn't."

My heart fluttered into my throat. His honesty was so disconcerting, yet refreshing too.

He never hesitated; he just blurted out what he was thinking, and I admired that.

Finally we emerged from the park onto Fifth Avenue, the world-famous shopping mecca. I immediately felt a thrill of excitement when I spied the huge giant snowflake hanging above the centre of the street, signalling where we were.

"Come on, this way," Blake urged, leading me further down the avenue.

We came to an imposing building across from the park entrance and slowed our pace when arriving at the front of it. The Bergdorf Goodman department store. I looked up at the windows and squealed with delight. The festive displays were beyond words.

It was an outdoor White Christmas scene. The setting was a winter forest and mannequins wore long sequinned designer gowns in Victorian style.

They were draped in white fur capes that trailed several feet behind them. The background was full of Christmas trees and various branches and shrubs all decorated with artificial snow and glitter, which also covered the ground.

Everything was white and the light reflecting off the scene in the city darkness made the entire window glow.

Even the accessories were white, including the glittering diamond bracelets and necklaces worn by the mannequins. It was a vivid, magical wintery scene and I was completely absorbed in it, trying to take it all in.

So much so that I almost forgot I wasn't alone.

"Do you like it?" Blake asked.

"I love it! It's everything I could have hoped for. This is the exact kind of thing I longed to see," I rambled on.

Blake laughed at my enthusiasm and said, "I'm so glad. I rush by here every year and never really stop to take a closer look. I guess because in the back of my mind, I knew I wanted to share it with someone."

I looked up at him. Every second longer I spent in his company I was falling for this man, and it was scaring me. I watched him look at the window, smiling. I could stare at him forever.

"There's another great one further down the street at Saks if you want to keep going?"

My eyes widened, "Saks?" I repeated in barely a whisper.

Blake chuckled, obviously delighted by my enthusiasm. "You are too cute." Then he looped my arm in his and led me further along the busy street.

We stopped at another street vendor along the way.

"Can't go see the Saks windows without hot chocolate," he insisted.

"But I've already had one today."

"Oh, do you have a chocolate limit or something?" He joked. "It's the holidays. Enjoy yourself. And at Christmas, hot chocolate is *definitely* a New York tradition."

I laughed. "Well, I am a bit cold, and I do like traditions."

CHAPTER 7

Blake bantered with the street vendor a little. He had that effect on people; able to talk to them like they were old friends.

We walked until we came upon the Saks building.

"Wait, hold on," he said as he put one hand over my eyes and one arm around my back to guide me.

This was adorable. He really wanted me to get the full experience. I slowly shuffled my feet as he positioned me in front of the window, then he took his hand away from my eyes and said: "Okay, open your eyes."

I did. It took me a few seconds to process what I was seeing. In the first window was the setting of a Victorian living room, or parlour, as they must have called it then.

There was a Christmas tree in the corner of it and on the wall a sign that read, "Twas the Night Before Christmas."

Blake stood beside me and said. "It's a story, each window is a scene from the story."

My eyes watered over. This was breathtaking.

I stepped closer, completely hypnotised by it.

In the centre of the parlour was a fireplace, and 'stockings hung by the chimney with care.'

The stockings must have been true vintage pieces, with red and green patterns, not the commercial Christmas ones you get now, but actual socks.

The green garland above the fireplace was simple and thin, but also vintage in appearance. A tree was decorated with handmade ornaments, each different from the other and made of wood or paper.

There were a few glass baubles, but not many, as it would have been a luxury to have those during that period.

A small toy train and tracks went around the bottom of the tree skirt while an old wooden vintage train set circled intricately wrapped presents with red, green, and gold paper and velvet ribbon.

There were only a few presents, maybe five in total. Large winged-back chairs were set before the fireplace with a cosy blanket throw across the back.

A small table near the chairs had an old book on it, *Twas The Night Before Christmas*.

I looked at Blake, and smiled, "It's the loveliest thing I've ever seen."

"I'm glad you like it," he said. "Come on, let's see the whole story."

"Wait," I said.

He stopped and looked back at me.

"Thank you, Blake. For all of this."

"It's my pleasure." He put his elbow out for me again and I encircled my arm in his, took a sip of my creamy hot chocolate and continued on.

The next window was the children's bedroom. They were snug in their beds and wore adorable night clothes in a wrought iron bed.

The requisite sugar plum fairies hung from the ceiling, and sprigs of holly from the corners.

The next window had a white powdered rooftop with smokey chimneys, and featuring the man himself.

There was a large sled being driven by Santa Claus, as it landed on the roof. He wore the iconic Victorian dark maroon suit, not the bright red and white one, common today.

He had rosy cheeks and a thick white beard and next to him was a large velvet bag full of intricately wrapped gifts. The reindeer were so lifelike and each one wore jingle bells.

The whole thing was pure Christmas magic.

The store really went out of its way to make this classic festive story come to life, and I was grateful to have the opportunity to see it.

"So, is it all you hoped for so far?" Blake queried.

"It's more than that. I've heard about this kind of thing and have seen pictures, but experiencing it in person doesn't compare."

"I'd love to show you more Christmassy stuff while you are in town. I wish we could keep today going for longer, but I really do have to get back to my project. Would you allow me to walk you home?"

I tried not to sound disappointed that our festive whistle-stop tour was now coming to an end.

CHAPTER 8

We walked back through the length of the park and at one point, Blake gently reached for my hand.

When we came to the other side and exited back onto the street, I felt like we had entered a different world.

I'd almost forgotten that I was in the city because the park had once again made me feel like I was in a fairy tale.

We finally got to Sarah's condo and stepped under the long red awning that covered the path in an archway to the front door.

"This is it," I said.

"Are you free tomorrow night?" Blake asked then. "I'd like to take you to dinner."

"Yes, I would love that," I said, hardly daring to believe it.

"Great. Pick you up here at 7?" Then he looked down at me and continued,

"Madeline, what is happening here? This is so unreal. I've never connected with anyone this instantly."

"I ...I'm not sure."

Then he leaned in and hugged me. A soft gentle hug, because the doorman was watching.

"I'll pick you up tomorrow, OK?" he whispered.

Then we parted ways. He stood there watching until I went inside, feeling like I was walking on air.

Upstairs, I opened the door to the apartment to find Sarah at the kitchen table, piles of paperwork spread out before her. She looked exhausted.

I must have been glowing because as soon as she looked up at me she raised an eyebrow.

"What happened to you? You look almost…hypnotised," she said.

I skipped over to her. "I met someone … a guy."

"What? You've been in New York less than 24 hours and it's the holidays. How?"

We both laughed. Then I told her everything. Of how I had sat in front of the museum at lunchtime and met Blake. I explained the rest without leaving out any details. Sarah was astounded.

"Wait stop," she said. "Let's move onto the couch. I need to get away from this workspace." Then she went into the kitchen and opened a bottle of red wine and brought two glasses to the couch. "Is this guy for real? I almost feel like you made him up. No one is that perfect."

"Yes, he does seem too good to be true, so much in fact that there's a problem."

"Well, that's a relief at least," Sarah laughed.

"I can't help but think he's pulling some kind of trick or something. Maybe he's just trying to get me into bed. He's so romantic and seems so honest. Every time he says something about his feelings for me, I can't enjoy it because I feel like there's some sort of ulterior motive."

Sarah sighed and rolled her eyes. "When you said there was a problem, I thought you meant with your perfect man. But there's no problem there. Just an issue you made up in your head."

I sighed. "Maybe you're right."

"I know I am. Trust me. So, what are you going to wear to dinner tomorrow night?"

My eyes grew wide. I hadn't even thought that far ahead.

"I have no idea."

"Come on, let's see what you brought," Sarah stood up and went into the guest bedroom where I had my stuff.

We threw open the closet and I tried on every outfit I owned. It was a complete fashion show because with it being cold outside, I had to put on every outfit and then put on my coat and boots to see if everything went together.

"I don't like anything I have. I just don't have the right clothes for freezing weather," I groaned.

"Come on, I do," Sarah grabbed the wine and glasses and led me to her room.

We went through the whole thing all over again with her clothes. I tried on every dress she owned. I found a festive red one in a fitted style that went to just above my knees.

It was off the shoulder, with quarter-length sleeves and made of pure silk. This made it elegant, but not over the top; the perfect balance.

Sarah clapped her hands in delight. "That's the one. It's perfect."

CHAPTER 9

❄

The next day, while I spent a lovely morning wandering around Manhattan again, Sarah had a break for lunch so I met her at a little café near her office.

She was on her phone most of the time, still conducting business so I was kind of glad when it was over. I wanted to prepare for tonight anyway.

Around six o'clock, I began to get jitters. What if Blake didn't show up?

I took a deep breath and allowed myself to trust this man. Trust that he would show and not stand me up. I went ahead and got dressed and at seven o'clock sharp, the doorman rang up.

Blake was downstairs waiting for me. I breathed a sigh of relief, grabbed my coat and headed out.

He stood in the lobby and I was taken aback at how I felt as soon as I locked eyes with him.

He stood there, his tall figure towering in the brightly lit lobby. He wore an elegant black suit and his woollen pea coat. He topped it off with a red silk scarf around his neck, the perfect compliment to my dress.

His eyes were wide as he looked me up and down.

"Madeline, you looked stunning," he said greeting me with a light hug.

The doorman held out my coat, offering to help me put it on.

"Allow me," Blake said.

He slid my coat on and then planted a light kiss on my cheek. "Shall we?" he asked, as he offered me his arm.

A black car was waiting for us. I was confused, as I'd thought we would surely be walking.

A few minutes later, I stepped out and nearly gasped out loud. The Plaza Hotel.

A visit there would be a treat for anyone at any time I knew, but at this time of year, it was doubly astounding.

The entrance was beautifully decorated in holly wreaths and delicate lights. It was intricate and elegant, and again had that classic New York feel I'd so longed for.

Blake put his arm around me and said, "You mentioned you wanted an old-fashioned Christmas experience. There's no better place for that than this hotel. It hasn't changed much since it was built in the early nineteen hundreds."

I looked up at him. This was perfect.

Blake flashed a grin, before putting his hand on the small of my back and leading me inside.

The lobby was alive with festive cheer, with several Christmas trees elegantly decorated and buzzing with people enjoying the holidays; everybody beautifully dressed and being fussed over by attentive waiting staff beneath sparkling chandeliers.

I was in complete awe of the glamour. I really did feel like I had stepped back in time.

Even with me in heels, Blake still towered over me. As we stood there in the lobby, surrounded by all this festive beauty, he looked down and then in one unexpected motion he kissed me.

"I'm so sorry, I couldn't help it," he said, pulling away quickly.

I didn't want him to stop, and while I loved his politeness and hesitation, I wanted to keep going.

Right then I forgot all about my ex-boyfriend and any mistrust I had in Blake. It had all vanished in just twenty-four hours.

Walking around New York, and exploring a new world was exactly the kind of thing I needed to get a different perspective of how magical life could be.

Blake and I enjoyed a silver service dinner in the Palm Court; turkey roast and vegetables with brandy and for dessert we shared pudding and a cup of nutmeg.

At the end of the night, we said our goodbyes at the door of Sarah's condo, with no pressure to carry things further. Almost the way old-fashioned courting would've been.

"So, see you tomorrow night?" he suggested. "I was thinking maybe ice-skating this time."

He leaned in and planted another kiss on my lips. Slow and romantic, full of feeling and it made me feel a bit dizzy.

It was like this man really could read my mind.

CHAPTER 10

The next day I went for a daytime walk through the park by myself.

Reliving memories from the time before with Blake, I was in a great mood and I smiled and said hello to every passerby - so much so that eventually people started avoiding the crazy-looking Irish girl.

When I neared the museum I remembered the pretzel stand so I thought I would grab one.

Exiting the park, I crossed the street near the building and suddenly saw Blake sitting on the steps.

With an attractive female alongside him.

I stopped in my tracks, feeling instantly duped as realisation dawned.

Was this what he did all day? Was this his pick-up spot? Did he even work in the museum at all?

I was crestfallen but worse, my heart was breaking again.

I watched as they talked to each other. They seemed very comfortable together and smiled a lot as they chatted, very much like we had only a couple of days before.

I debated whether I should go up to him — to confront him - or should I just let it go, walk away and never talk to him again.

After a few minutes of staring and not knowing what to do, I watched as they both stood up. It was unbelievable, they were going inside.

This *was* his thing! This is what he did.

My despair quickly turned into anger, and I stomped off in their direction. I stood at the bottom of the steps as I watched them disappear into the museum together.

Just then Blake turned in the doorway. He locked eyes with me and smiled in recognition. But I didn't smile back. Instead, my eyes darted immediately to the woman and then back at him.

Turning quickly, I raced down the steps and back into the park. I wanted to disappear as soon as I could in case he was coming after me. I didn't want to hear his pathetic excuses.

I ran all the way home, in disarray. Sarah was at work and I had no one to confide in. Everything suddenly felt grey. Now the cheery Christmas tree in the living room seemed to taunt me.

CHAPTER 11

I fell asleep on the couch and woke up a few hours later.
I looked around in the darkness. It didn't look like Sarah had come home yet.

I checked the time and saw that it was only seven o'clock. It felt so much later. The embarrassment of what had happened earlier flooded back.

Why was I letting this get me down? Yes, I was hurting, but I came to New York to enjoy myself. I wasn't going to let a player destroy my dream trip.

What would I be doing right now if I'd never met Blake? I would probably be ice-skating at Rockefeller Center, under the giant tree.

It was exactly what he'd suggested we do tonight. He knew me well - or I should say he knew well how to woo idiot New York tourists like me.

I pulled myself together and decided to go anyway.

I would put all thoughts of him out of my mind and continue on as if I had never met him.

I washed my face and got changed into a comfortable pair of

jeans and a sweater, perfect for ice skating, then headed downstairs to the lobby where the doorman stopped me.

"Miss," he said. "You have several messages from Mr Blake." He handed me a few small notes.

"Thank you," I said grabbing them and walking out the door.

As soon as I saw a bin on the street, I tossed them inside. I didn't open them. I didn't need to.

CHAPTER 12

❄

Finally, I arrived at Rockefeller Plaza.
I could see the tree as I approached, but getting up close to it was beyond words.

I titled my head back staring up mesmerised at the massive spruce right in the centre of the plaza above the ice-rink.

It was even more glorious in person. There must've been a million lights on it. The entire plaza was decorated for the holiday season; beautiful life-sized angels blowing trumpets, and giant painted nutcracker soldiers lined up all round.

Below on the ice rink, people were skating and full of cheer and laughter, while spectators sipped hot chocolate and ate peppermint fudge.

I sat down on nearby bench and gazed at the tree.

Its magic now seemed to only mock my sadness. I thought of Blake again, wanting to cry.

I was only kidding myself with all these distractions. It wasn't working.

It was then, right in that moment of thinking about him that I heard a familiar voice.

"May I?"

I looked up to see Blake towering over me. He was gesturing at the space on the bench beside me.

I didn't say anything but he sat anyway.

"Madeline, I've been trying to get hold of you all day. The doorman wouldn't let me up no matter how much I pleaded with him. I tried for an hour at least," he said.

I just looked at him and while I willed my heart to harden, I could feel my eyes watering over.

His sincere way of talking was enough to make me crack. I wanted things to be as they were before. I did not trust this man. I don't think I trusted any man at this point.

"Why did you run off like that today?" he asked.

I could barely get the words out. My voice was shaking.

"I watched you, on the steps. Talking to that girl and then I saw you bring her back into the museum, just like we did. Is that what you do to pick up women? It works. It worked on me, I was stupid enough to fall for it, just like the girl today was."

Blake's eyes were wide. At first, I thought they were wide at having been caught. But then he spoke.

"Madeline, that's not what that was — at all," he gasped. "You've got it so wrong, and I'm sorry if what you saw hurt you. That's the last thing I would ever want to do, but if you would just let me explain…"

"I don't see the point in an explanation. I could never tell if you were lying."

"That is true," he said. "Would you like to meet her then?"

"Meet who?" I asked.

"The woman you saw me with earlier. That's the only way I can prove that I'm not lying. She's at my apartment right now," he said.

"What? She's in your apartment?" I repeated outraged at his brazenness.

"Yes, I couldn't make it home for Christmas this year, so she came to the city so that I had some family around."

"Family?"

"Yes. She's my sister."

My heart sank. I couldn't say why, but I believed him.

Now I felt like a complete idiot. I was kicking myself for acting so rashly earlier.

Sarah was right. The problem wasn't this man. It was me. The breakup had left me a paranoid mess.

"I'm so sorry. I feel so stupid," I said.

"It's okay. Don't be. I'm kind of glad it happened."

"What? Why?"

"Because I wasn't sure if you felt anything for me. When we look at each other I can feel a connection, but you haven't said anything…about what you think or how you might feel. But seeing your reaction today … now I know for sure you feel something too. And that I might be more than just your New York Christmas guide."

I sat in silence and processed what he had said. Perhaps I needed this to bring me to that next level.

This entire thing had been such a roller coaster.

"So, we're okay?"

"Yes, we're okay. And I'm sorry," I whispered, feeling stupid again.

He held my shoulders and turned me toward him.

"No need to apologise. I want you to be honest with me. I know this is crazy and we only just met, but I think we might have something here. I knew it when I saw you for the first time. You're the best Christmas present I could have asked for. Maybe this was meant to be."

I looked up at him, my eyes watering over. This dear sweet man was all I could ever hope for and he was pouring his heart out to me. Beneath the most magical Christmas tree in the world.

"Now, I seem to remember I promised you ice skating."

And when a little later Blake took my hand and led me out onto the ice rink, I looked around again at the twinkling lights on the tree and the scene around us, unable to believe that I was actually here and this was really happening.

Everything felt so surreal. And impossibly romantic - almost like something from a movie.

But then the most magical thing of all happened.

Out of nowhere, it began to snow. Small perfect snowflakes fell on our faces and we laughed amongst the beauty of it all.

This New York Christmas was perfect, even better than I had imagined, more than I could have ever dreamed of.

And as Blake leaned down and kissed me, I also knew I wanted to experience it over and over again.

A WEEKEND IN ROME

CHAPTER 1

"Molly?" a voice called up to where the blonde twenty-eight-year-old sat gazing out the window as a dusting of snow fell softly outside.

Molly O'Brien barely noticed the noise. She was captivated by the magic of this first snow – even if it was just flurries - and which she knew would have melted away by the time she and her parents boarded the plane to Italy later that morning.

There was just something about Christmastime – the brisk cold weather, greenery around the hearth, candles and fairy lights, holly and mistletoe – that filled her with such joy she could hardly contain herself. And with everything building to an even more joyous occasion now just a couple of sleeps away, Molly was entranced.

"Love?" her mother's voice came again, this time from just down the hall.

Molly sighed and returned to the suitcase laid open on her childhood bed, folding up the last of her clothes and stuffing them in the remaining spaces.

A long packing list rested nearby. She glanced through it as her mind raced. Forgetting anything for this trip would be disastrous. She couldn't afford to be distracted or unfocused.

A gentle knock came at the door, followed by a creak as it opened. Her mother Helen stood in the doorway.

Just then, Molly was struck by the greyish streaks in her mother's blonde hair; surely they hadn't been there before. But her ever-glamorous mum was getting older. They all were.

However, despite the strands of grey and the faint lines around her lips, Molly couldn't remember a time when Helen looked better. The years agreed with her.

She smiled. "Hey, Mum."

'We're all set to go, love. Have you packed the last of it?"

Molly nodded and took her mother's arm, bringing her over to the window. "Look," she smiled. "Isn't it beautiful?"

Helen sighed. "It is, honey, yes," she said wistfully. "I remember you and Caroline sitting here as young kids for hours just watching the snow fall in winter. We could barely peel you two away for anything. Well, except maybe for a few Jammie Dodgers…"

"Feeling nostalgic?" Molly asked casually. She looked at her mother who had the same dreamy look on her face she herself had. It ran in the family apparently.

Helen shook her head. "Just a bit, maybe," she admitted. "It's hard to see your baby grow up before your eyes. And now, well I suppose I'm just wishing we could have the wedding for you that your father and I always envisioned. I always knew you would get married at this time of year with that love of Christmas of yours, but I never expected that you would do it somewhere else."

"Ah, mum," Molly replied, "we've been through all this a million times already." She was exhausted. Her parents had barely let up with their complaints since, she and her fiancé Ben had announced their intentions to get married in Rome.

Helen put her hands up defensively. "I know, I know," she responded, "and it is of *course* your wedding – yours, and Ben's."

Helen thought back to the little girl playing weddings with her best friend, Caroline. There was always a beautiful red and green bouquet, teddy bears and dolls representing friends and family - and snow boots under an old white costume.

"Mum," Molly said gently. "Look around this room. What do you see?"

Helen looked at the walls of the room that had been Molly's bedroom for most of the last three decades.

Framed posters of the Colosseum, St. Peter's Basilica, and the Trevi Fountain graced the walls.

On the bookshelves were everything from Italian phrasebooks and texts on Roman history, to tomes by Dante Alighieri and Italo Calvino.

Even the wallpaper, though a bit frayed and yellowed now, featured a watermark of the Arch of Constantine.

It was in effect, the most Italian room in all of Ireland.

"I've been dreaming of this forever," Molly continued. "A Christmas wedding in Rome has *always* been the dream. And finally it's coming true."

Molly was as in love with Italy almost as much as she was with her fiancé.

She had studied Italian literature in University College Dublin, and had even taken several Italian cooking classes for fun. While she may no longer be that little girl dressing up teddy bears and 'marrying' her best friend, she was still the woman with Italian posters, books, and maps in her bedroom.

Helen nodded. "I know, love," she said kindly. "And your dad and I want to give you the wedding of your dreams. Even if it happens to be in another country."

She had struggled to come to terms with her daughter's decision, but at this point, there was no turning back. Molly and Ben were getting married in Rome on Christmas Eve - two days from now.

"Girls!" Molly's father Paddy yelled at the two women from the foot of the stairs. "It's time we headed off."

Paddy O'Brien had also been staring out the window at the snow rolling in and wondering how long they would be stuck at Dublin airport because of it.

"We're coming now," Helen called down to him. She turned to Molly. "Ready, sweetheart?" she asked with a smile.

Molly looked through the packing list once more, nodded and pulled her stuffed suitcase off the bed.

She grinned. "Ready as I'll ever be."

CHAPTER 2

"Tell me again why we couldn't fly First Class?"

Patricia Pembrey did *not* like flying steerage – and she certainly did not approve of the sort milling about in Luton Airport just then.

She made a horrified face as an elderly couple slowly walked past her, chewing gum loudly and clicking their canes against the tile floor.

"Because, mother," her son Ben said flatly, "we're going to travel like normal people for once."

He had predicted his mother was going to be a pain, but he had no idea she would be this intolerable. The complaints had started months ago and it looked like they were not ending anytime soon.

"Oh, nonsense, Ben," Patricia said coolly, adjusting the foxtail scarf over her shoulder. "We do travel like normal people, normal for our class." She stuttered, lifting her arms in frustration, "Tell him, James."

Lord James Pembrey, 15th Earl of Daventry, was nonplussed.

"I know, dear," he said pompously. His travel usually included a private boarding area at Heathrow away from the public, waitresses with endless champagne flutes, and takeoffs scheduled around his agenda.

This was too much like roughing it for his liking.

Ben shook his head, completely frustrated with his parents' inability to see past their own wants and needs.

"Look," he said, his brown eyes darting towards the fast food lines. "I'll pop over to Costa and pick us up some coffees. Will that do?"

He loved his parents, and they had given him a wonderful life filled with opportunities many only dreamed of – but they could be such woeful snobs that he sometimes wondered whether he'd been adopted.

He had been so completely different to them that when he'd gone off to university, he'd deliberately chosen not to go to Oxford or Cambridge but instead to University College Dublin – much to his parents' chagrin.

And he was glad that he had; it's where he'd met Molly.

He remembered clearly that first night he'd laid eyes on her at a social in a pub following a big rugby match.

Molly and her friend Caroline had come in, and Molly's large doe eyes met Ben's from across the crowded room.

He was normally confident, but something about her had told him that she wasn't the type that would instantly fawn over him, as so many other girls did once they found out he was bona fide English gentry.

But, unlike in the UK, that kind of thing meant little in Ireland. Part of the reason Ben had shipped out of England in the first place.

He took a deep breath and marched over to talk to her – and promptly knocked a drink off a server's tray and down the front of her top. Horrified, she'd stomped out of the pub with Caroline following at her heels. It was as awful a first encounter as any had ever been.

He counted himself lucky, then, that only two weeks later, they happened to meet again at a college party for Italian & Classical Degree students.

Ben had been invited by a mutual friend after he offered to make a pasta dish his old nanny cooked up for him and his brother every time his parents were off travelling.

Molly had made her way into the kitchen, the smell of the homemade sauce tempting her. When she saw the idiot from the bar, she'd immediately turned on her heel but Ben was faster. He grabbed her arm as she was leaving, apologising the entire way.

She'd looked at the man in the dirty apron, red sauce splattered on his cheeks, with his dark hair, deep brown eyes boring apologetically into hers, and couldn't find a reason to be angry any longer.

They'd ended up talking the whole night through, eventually watching the sun rise over campus.

As he watched her in the glow of the early morning light, the warm sunshine reflecting in her wide blue eyes, Ben knew, even at that early moment, that this was the woman he was going to marry.

On Christmas Eve five years later, he had it all planned out as he took them on a journey of their old college haunts. They'd gotten fish and chips from the chipper they'd always gone to after a night on the town, went for a drink before closing at the pub where they'd had that first run in, and eventually wandered into St Stephen's Green.

With light snowflakes swirling around them, and fairy lights shining amidst the trees above, Molly pushed her bundled-up body closer into his as they sat down on one of the benches.

As she talked about their Christmas plans for the next day, she turned to him expectantly, her eyes shining with excitement.

But Ben was not there, at least not where he had just been sitting. He was down on one knee, and pulled out a little black velvet box, his hands trembling as he searched for the words he had rehearsed for months – before promptly dropping the ring in the snow.

Ben was horrified as he squinted his eyes and searched the

damp snow for the sparkling diamond once belonging to his grandmother.

But Molly only laughed and bent down, easily picking up the antique ring with its beautiful three off-centre diamonds, tears in her eyes.

She brought her red-gloved hand to his face. "Oh, you don't even have to ask," she told him, beaming. "Of course I'll marry you."

There hadn't even been a question of where - or indeed when - to get married. Winter in Rome, at Christmastime.

While Ben had suggested that Molly's family might be more comfortable with a traditional Irish ceremony at home, she wouldn't hear of it.

She also knew Ben too well – particularly, that his family's wealth and prominence embarrassed and irritated him.

Anything traditional would have been dwarfed by the excess and pomposity the Pembreys would no doubt insist on bringing to the table.

So in the end they'd both known that a small, intimate gathering at an historic church in Rome – just family and friends - was exactly what they wanted. The arrangements had taken nearly a year, though they'd had lost of help from a wedding planner in Italy to navigate the details.

And now days before Christmas, Ben found it hard to believe that here he was, ordering coffees at the airport, about to board a plane to Rome to meet his soon-to-be wife.

He grinned and thanked the barista as he picked up the coffees, leaving some change in a small jar next to the register. "Thanks - Merry Christmas."

He returned to their boarding gate to find his mother, daintily dusting off the plastic airport seat with his father's handkerchief.

"Oh, you have *got* to be joking, Mother," he said, rolling his eyes and thrusting a cup her way.

"What?" she inquired innocently. "We'll have to find a reputable dry cleaner once we have landed in Italy. I am not packing this handkerchief in our luggage."

Ben handed his father his coffee and strode away. "Ben?" his father called from behind him, "where are you going now?"

"To find a bar," he grumbled. "I need a stiff drink."

CHAPTER 3

"Caroline!" Molly darted excitedly towards her best friend, her trainers nearly bouncing off the tiled floors of Rome's Da Vinci Airport.

Yes it had been a couple of months since they had last seen each other, as Caroline now lived in Cork, but by Molly's reaction, one would think it had been years.

Caroline Davison giggled and bounded in the opposite direction and the two embraced forcefully, their collective weight tilting to and fro from their exuberance, eventually causing them to almost fall over in a fit of laughing and hugs.

"Oh my God, Molly, you're getting *married!*" Caroline exclaimed, her green eyes sparkling and dark curls bouncing, as she helped her friend to her feet.

"Wait - I'm doing what?" Molly teased, a wicked smile filling her face.

"Grand. Well, we're here now, so to hell with Ben, let's find you a nice Italian Romeo!"

The two laughed hysterically as Molly's parents joined them near the baggage claim.

Helen's arms stretched out towards Caroline, embracing her in a familiar, gentle hug. Caroline gave both O'Briens a kiss on the cheek, wishing them a Happy Christmas.

"How was the flight from Dublin?" she asked.

"The flight was fine," Helen replied. "It's everything since that…"

"*Mum,*" Molly scolded.

"All your mother is saying," Paddy picked up, "is that maybe the natives could be a *bit* more helpful."

"Dad," she groaned, "Italians aren't required to speak English, you know."

"No," Paddy agreed, "but when you go to an airport cafe and order a cup of tea, they should at least have *some* idea what you mean."

"Relax, Mr O'Brien. It's nearly Christmas…though you wouldn't know it here," Caroline said, casting a dubious glance around the airport.

Unlike Cork airport from which she'd flown earlier this morning, she was surprised to find that the festive decor in Italy seemed lacking. While airports back home were usually all holly and ivy and Christmas trees, here, everything seemed a bit more subdued.

Only a few strands of fairy lights and some signs reading *Chiuso per Natale* ("Closed for Christmas") let travellers know that any sort of holiday was imminent.

But perhaps the Italians didn't make such a big deal of it? As it was Caroline's first time in the country and she knew very little about the place, she couldn't be sure.

But no doubt she would soon find out. In any case, her best friend adored the city and was looking forward to not only her wedding, but also showing everyone around.

Molly was about to speak again when a pair of hands covered her eyes and a familiar voice whispered in her ear.

"Guess who?" She grabbed the hands, turned around, and found herself face-to-face with her fiancé. She held Ben's face in her hands, stood on her tiptoes, and kissed him.

"Here comes the groom," Caroline laughed, as Ben then bent over to kiss her cheek.

"Great to see you, Car," he said. "How's life in Cork?"

"Fine as ever, Ben, how are you?"

He opened his mouth to reply, but as he did, came the sound of someone complaining on approach "...and I swear to you, James, if there is no butler service, I won't stay. I simply won't!"

"And I wouldn't hear of it, darling," Ben's father replied. He searched the crowd, finally finding his son in the mix of faces. "There you are. We've been looking for you. We have a driver waiting."

Molly shook hands awkwardly with both Patricia and James Pembrey. She'd met his parents a couple of times over the years, and was well used to their snooty behaviour.

At first, she wasn't sure what to make of them, especially considering Ben was as humble and down-to-earth as they came. Fortunately because they lived in the UK, she and Ben didn't have much to do with them.

"And you remember my parents, Paddy and Helen?" Molly said quickly, while the rest of the wedding party exchanged muted greetings.

Both sets of parents had met briefly after the engagement, but as her working class parents had little in common with English nobility, it had been somewhat … strained.

Caroline watched the whole scene unfold as she waited at carousel belt. After a few more beats of awkward quiet amongst the families, she cleared her throat.

Molly looked to her confusedly, then added, "Oh of course! And Caroline, my best friend and bridesmaid."

Caroline smiled and approached the Pembreys. "Hello there," she greeted, beaming.

She got little in response. Instead the Pembreys, the O'Briens, and Caroline all stood there in complete silence as the conveyer belt clanked and clattered around.

"So," she said, attempting to break the ice, "who's ready for some wine tasting?"

"As long as it's not one of those so-called 'Super Tuscans,'" Patricia groused. "Never had a more overrated wine in my life."

The awkward silence resumed. Caroline smiled tightly and stared down at her feet until she was tapped on the shoulder by a small man with a wiry moustache.

"Scusi?" he said in a heavily accented voice, "You are Miss Davison, yes?"

She nodded. "I am. Can I help you?"

"Can you come with me, please?"

She followed him, perplexed.

"Signorina," the man said once they were away from the crowd, "I am afraid I have some bad news."

"What do you mean, 'bad news?'" she repeated, frowning.

"Your package," he said.

She was puzzled. "My… package?"

"No, scusi, that is not the right word," he apologised. "Sorry, my English, it is not so good. I mean, *luggage*. Your luggage – it did not arrive."

CHAPTER 4

❄

The lobby of the Hotel Marliconi was gloriously opulent, a mix of old-world wood, Italian marble and art deco stained glass.

White stone statues of women with water pitchers stood in a small fountain in the centre of the massive reception room, giving it the extravagant feel of something from a movie, while overhead a magnificent fresco depicted a classic Renaissance scene.

Additional Christmas-themed decor – a tree, nativity scene, and a few red-and-green bows dotted here and there – gave the hotel a somewhat more festive look, though Caroline couldn't help but notice again how much more subdued it was compared to the glitzier stuff back home.

Still, any Christmassy decor paled in comparison to the inherent beauty of the city itself.

Caroline was still reeling from her first sight of the Colosseum on the approach to the city of Rome from the airport. And everywhere she looked were jaw-dropping sights of Renaissance architecture and Italian grandeur.

A gigantic structure of Corinthian columns, fountains, and equestrian sculpture in the centre of the city that Molly pointed out as the Victor Emmanuel monument was awe-inspiring, as was a passing glimpse of the Roman Forum, and the myriad Baroque fountains and pretty piazzas that gave the picturesque city an almost other-worldly feel.

Now she and Molly approached the reception desk arm-in-arm. Molly still seemed jittery, bothered by the absence of Caroline's bridesmaid dress and she thought, a little put out by the fact that her best friend seemed to be the only one in the wedding party impressed by the city sights.

On the way in the taxi, the O'Briens seemed distracted and uncomfortable, and only nodded in passing when Molly pointed out areas of interest and beauty.

For someone who loved Italy as much as her friend, and was so eager to share her great passion for the city she'd chosen as her wedding destination, it was no doubt disappointing.

She rubbed her friend's shoulders reassuringly.

"The dress will come in time, Mol," she soothed, guiding her to the front desk. "Don't worry. It's just a hiccup – nothing to worry about. It wouldn't be a wedding without a little bad luck."

Behind them, Molly's parents gazed around the hotel reception, a little taken aback.

"It's a bit … grand, isn't it?" Helen commented.

"It is," Paddy responded. "I don't mind paying for a nice hotel, but I certainly didn't expect a palace."

At the back of the group, James and Patricia Pembrey shuffled into the lobby, followed by Ben, whose voice echoed off the marble walls as he barked into his phone.

"Mark, this is simply ridiculous," he said testily. "No – no – I don't – listen to me, I don't *care*. This is my *wedding*. You're my brother, my best man. I think it's fair of me to expect you to be here at least … okay." He hung up the phone and shoved it back in his pocket.

"So where's Mark?" Molly asked when Ben caught up with her at reception.

He sighed. "Still back in London working on some kind of 'server issues,'" he said in an irritated voice. "He says he's 'trying' to get away, but it could be well be tomorrow night by the time he arrives." Then he took a deep breath and put his arm around his fiancee. "Look. Let's just get everyone checked in and then we'll all go have a drink and chill out a bit, OK?"

Molly nodded, and turned back to the check in desk. The young Italian woman behind the counter had a bored, almost lackadaisical look on her face as she leaned against the back wall, gazing at her phone.

Ben threw a quick glance towards Molly and called out, "Um, excuse me?"

The woman sighed, put her phone in her pocket, and walked up to her computer.

"Buonasera," she greeted with fake cheeriness, "how can I help you today?"

"Buonasera," Molly replied with a smile. "We'd like to check into our rooms please. There should be four in total, all under the name O'Brien."

The woman typed some info into her computer, and the machine beeped. "I'm sorry," she said, "I have no rooms under that name. Would they be under another?"

"Erm, Pembrey, perhaps?" Ben offered.

She typed the letters in. This time there was no beep, but rather a chime, followed by a look of sheer confusion on the part of the clerk. "I am sorry," she said, not looking particularly apologetic, "I must speak to my manager. One moment, please."

Caroline joined them at the desk. "What's going on?" she inquired.

Molly shrugged. "Dunno," she said. "She just looked really confused and then bounded off."

A few moments later, the clerk returned with a short, bald, mustachioed manager, a grave look on his face. "Buonasera," he greeted them, "are you Signorina O'Brien?"

"I am," she nodded. Ben's parents now huddled close to them, attempting to hear what was going on. "What's the problem?" Molly asked the manager.

"It seems we have a small ... issue," he stated. "Our hotel – it is fully booked, and though we have your reservation, it seems we have sold the rooms."

Molly's jaw nearly hit the ground. "You've done *what?*" she demanded.

"It was a mistake, I assure you, Signorina, and not one that happens at this hotel often." He looked towards the staff member suspiciously, as if she personally were the one to blame.

Molly threw her hands up in the air and walked off. Ben looked to his parents – at which point James stepped in – and he darted after his fiancée.

As he went, he heard his father assume his most pompous, House of Lords voice: "Now see here, sir, this is our son's wedding, and we were assured of having four suites at this hotel. It was *guaranteed*, so do you know what you're going to do? I'll tell you what you are going to do. You will…"

BEN WAS out of earshot when he found Molly at the other end of the lobby, staring out the window towards a picturesque piazza. He went over and put a hand on her shoulder. "Molly, hon," he said consolingly, "it's going to be okay – "

"'Okay?'" she whispered, as she turned to face him. "Ben, *nothing* is okay. First, Caroline's dress doesn't get here, my parents do nothing but complain about the place, your best man isn't even sure he'll make it… and now, they can't find our room reservations. What exactly is okay?"

"That we're here in Rome to be married, like we always wanted."

"Oh, Ben," she cried, tears threatening. "I know that, but …I'm wondering if doing this at Christmas was a mistake. This has been nothing but a disaster so far – and we've only been in the city less than an hour. To say nothing of the fact that it doesn't feel very Christmassy at all."

Ben hugged her close. "Do you trust me?" he asked, a glint in his eye. She looked up at him, wiped her eyes, and nodded. "Then trust me when I say it's going to work itself out. I promise." She sniffled a bit but nodded again.

A few moments later, Patricia and James rejoined the group, along with a handsome Italian man in his late thirties with deep brown eyes, and a smile that immediately sent both Caroline's and Molly's hearts aflutter.

He went straight up to Molly and kissed her on both cheeks. "Signorina," he said, still smiling, in perfect English but with a delicious Italian inflection. "My name is Fabrizio, and I am your coordinator for your stay with us here at the Hotel Marliconi."

He turned to Ben, who held out his hand for a handshake, but Fabrizio leaned in and kissed him on both cheeks as well. "Here in Italy," he explained, "we do not shake hands usually – we are a passionate people. We enjoy intimacy."

Molly's father rolled his eyes. He leaned forward and whispered to his wife, "A handshake will be intimate enough for me, thanks very much." Helen stifled a laugh as the wedding planner introduced himself to the rest of the group.

"Firstly," Fabrizio said after his introductions, "please accept my apologies for the mix-up with your reservations. Signor Pembrey –"

James cleared his throat. "*Lord* Pembrey, actually," he corrected pompously.

" – sorry," Fabrizio apologised, with a twinkle in his eye, "*Lord* Pembrey. We are not yet very certain what happened, but rest assured, we will do everything we can to accommodate you."

Molly brightened immediately. "So we're getting our rooms then?" she asked.

The smile left Fabrizio's face. "Well," he said, immediately causing her face to fall, "that is what we hope. We unfortunately have all of our suites currently occupied. However, we can for now put you in our also beautiful Deluxe Room, and if a suite becomes available, we will of course move you there."

Molly opened her mouth to protest, but Ben took her hand and wrapped it in his.

"It's better than nothing," he said.

"*Fantastico*," Fabrizio said enthusiastically, his smile still in place. "Now, I will call someone to help you with your bags. Perhaps you would like to bathe, relax for a bit. Can we meet at our terrazza restaurant in, say, one hour to discuss plans for your wedding?"

"Sounds good," Ben replied.

"*Eccellente!*" the Italian man grinned. "I will send up the luggage with, maybe, a bottle of wine for each of you? Will that be acceptable?"

Caroline perked up at the words she'd been waiting for. "*God* yes, please," she said. "We could *definitely* use some of that."

CHAPTER 5

❄

*P*atricia rubbed her damp hair with a towel, a scowl on her face.

"Dear God," she complained, "what is this made of, sandpaper?"

James lay on the bed, scanning through Italian broadcasts on the TV. "How was the water pressure, dear?"

"Awful," she frowned. "And the bathroom has some kind of… odd fragrance."

"I think they call that 'soap,' darling."

"This really is intolerable, James," Patricia replied, exasperation in her eyes. "I understood that this hotel would be acceptable to our standards."

James shook his head. "The concierge chap assured me that they're going to get this taken care of, my dear," he told her. "For now, we'll just have to… make do. Though I agree this bedlinen does seem quite garish."

NEXT DOOR, Molly and Caroline opened the bottle of wine that had been delivered to their room a few minutes before.

Molly took a long, deep sip while Caroline kicked off her shoes and put her feet up. "This really isn't so bad, is it?" she asked her.

"It's not," Molly agreed, gazing out the window at the Roman rooftops below. "But I really wanted a suite."

"Oh come on, Mol," Caroline chuckled. "When in Rome - isn't what they say?"

Her friend sighed and sipped her wine. "Is it so wrong to just want this to be perfect?" she asked after a long pause.

"Every bride wants her wedding to be perfect," Caroline said soothingly. "But it very rarely happens that *nothing* goes wrong."

"It just worries me, a little that's all. Like, is *this* how my life with Ben is going to start?"

"You mean, in one of the romantic cities in the world at Christmastime?" Molly took a large swig of her wine. "Nasty."

"Ah, you know what I mean."

"Yes," Caroline nodded – but she smiled teasingly.

"Of course I know what you mean. In your head you're been planning this perfect Italian wedding for most of your life. But you are putting too much pressure on yourself. At the end of a wedding day, is just a *day* – no matter where it is. It's going to be brilliant of course, but don't put *too* much emphasis on it."

"That's easy for you to say," Molly countered, finishing her wine, "seeing as the closest you've come to getting married was when we were four and you and Raggedy Andy were an item—"

She stopped short, realising what she'd just said. She looked over to Caroline, who stared at her, the slight tremor on her friend's lips making it that clear Molly had hurt her.

"Oh, God, Caroline," she began, "I – I don't know – I'm so sorry. That was *literally* the nastiest thing I could've said to you. What is going on with me?"

"It's fine," Caroline said softly.

"No, it's really not," Molly continued. "I'm really – "

"I know, Mol," Caroline said, a half-smile on her face. "Besides, maybe I'll meet a gorgeous, bronzed Italian while I'm here."

"Like Fabrizio?" she teased.

"Ew," Caroline replied, horrified. "He's so…"

"Charming? Handsome? *Dreamy?*"

"…cheesy, I was going to say," Caroline concluded. "The guy is every bad stereotype of every movie set in Italy ever." She finished off her own wine and poured another glass. "Why can't life just be like *Pretty Woman?*" she asked.

Molly looked at her quizzically. "You want to be a prostitute with a weirdly expressive mouth?" she asked, giggling.

"Okay, right, not *Pretty Woman* – the other one – *Runaway Bride?*"

"*Not* the best comparison," Molly said, dissolving in a fit of laughter. Then she sighed and reached for her friend, enveloping her in a tight embrace. "You know I love you, don't you?" she said. "And that I'm proud beyond belief that you're going to be bridesmaid."

"Enough of the Hollywood smaltz," Caroline berated but she was smiling. "Now, drink up. We have a lot of work to do before we meet up again with Fabio this evening."

"Fabrizio," Molly corrected. "*Fabio* is the dude on the cover of romance novels."

"Same difference," her friend grinned.

CHAPTER 6

❄

*A*t seven pm, the wedding party reconvened on the hotel's rooftop terrazza, taking in the extraordinarily beautiful cityscape.

Ancient icons such as the Colosseum, Roman Forum and Pantheon recalled Rome's time as the fearsome hub of the Roman Empire, while catacombs and clandestine churches harked back to the early days of Christianity.

Lording it over the Vatican was St Peter's Basilica, the greatest of the city's monumental basilicas, a towering masterpiece of Renaissance architecture and clearly visible from where they sat.

Paddy had at first been a bit disappointed that there was no Guinness and the only beer available was bottled Peroni, but being able to look out at such a glorious view seemed worth it.

He sat with his wife making small talk with Ben's parents whom he wasn't all that keen on.

"So," he said, a bit awkwardly, "have you been to Italy before?"

"Oh," Patricia said, with something that sounded vaguely like a combination of a forced laugh and a throat-clearing, "*many* times. We used to take Ben and Mark to the Amalfi Coast on holidays when they were little. Stopped a few times here to see the sights and take in the art and culture. But if you're to do anything in Italy, you simply *must* visit Tuscany. The wines..." she nodded towards her half-full glass, "...are much better than *this* swill."

The awkward silence resumed until Ben's father spoke up. "So then, Paddy my good man, what is it that you do again? Forgive me - I've forgotten."

Paddy took a sip of his beer. "Well, I worked in courier delivery for a number of years, mostly delivering packages locally. DHL bought the company a few years back but I still run the delivery service - I just don't have to actually *go* on the deliveries anymore."

James sat upright. "So," he said interestedly, "you used to pull out packages from a van or something like that?"

"Well," Paddy replied, his eyes narrowing somewhat, "it was something *like* that in that the job title was *literally* pulling packages out of a van so... yes."

"I think I need another glass of wine," Patricia interjected, swallowing a large gulp from her glass and hailing the waiter.

MOLLY WAS FEELING CONSIDERABLY HAPPIER after a bath and a few glasses of chianti with Caroline.

She now sat on the hotel's beautiful rooftop terrace curled up on a wicker sofa alongside Ben, munching absentmindedly on some Italian cheeses and grapes, while Caroline relaxed nearby.

"You know," she said, "Santa Maria church is very small. Mum and Dad won't know what hit them when they see how tiny it is."

Ben snickered. "You think *your* parents will be surprised?" he asked. "Mine will simply be livid. I can hear it now: mother getting her nose in a snit, saying things like, 'Huh! It's so dusty in here,' and father with his upright disapproval, wondering where the 'right honourable gentlemen' of Italy are supposed to get married." He exhaled through his nose dramatically. "It's going to be *classic*."

Caroline, seated across from them, giggled. "You two," she smiled. "You're so... so *perfect* together. I'm just... I'm just..."

"Drunk?" Molly suggested, laughing. "We did go through that wine Fabrizio sent to the room awfully quickly."

"Speaking of which," Ben noted, looking at his watch, "where *is* Fabrizio? He's over an hour late."

"Dunno," Caroline said. "Want me to go look for him?"

"Would you mind?" Molly asked gratefully.

She patted her friend on the knee. "I'll be right back," she promised. She got up and made her way towards the lift, heading down to the lobby.

At the desk, she asked the clerk if she'd seen Fabrizio, but he apparently hadn't been around since earlier.

Annoyed, she returned to the lift but as she exited the lobby, she noticed a man sitting by the downstairs bar, flashing a big smile and flirting with the pretty young bartender.

Caroline marched over to him with a full head of steam and tapped him on the shoulder.

"Excuse me," she said, "exactly what do you think you're doing?"

Fabrizio turned to look at her and smiled. "Ah, *Bella*" he greeted energetically, "so wonderful to see you again."

"Don't give me that crap," she said sternly. "We've been waiting upstairs on you for an hour. And I find you sitting down here, drinking and – and – *flirting?*"

Fabrizio took her by the hand. "Signorina," he said, dramatically, "I did not mean to offend. But life is too short to worry about being a little late. Sometimes, we must go where the moment takes us."

Caroline pulled her hand back brusquely. "Well, buddy" she replied her voice terse, "the 'moment' had better take you up there to talk to Molly and Ben about their wedding in short order, or we're going to be finding another planner *and* another hotel."

The Italian put his hands up defensively. "Okay, okay," he said, "but tell me, Signorina… are you more upset that I am late, or more upset that I was speaking with a woman whose beauty is so inferior to yours?"

Caroline blushed slightly but didn't break her icy stare. "Don't think for a second that nonsense is going to work on *me*," she said fiercely. "I've heard all about you swarthy, Italian charmers."

Fabrizio raised an eyebrow. "Swarthy?" he repeated bemusedly.

Caroline continued without breaking stride. "You're all 'passion' and 'fire' and 'embrace your inner blah-blah-blah' for foreign women – and then when you get what you want you never speak to us again. So don't try your tricks on me, mister."

Fabrizio nodded curtly. "Yes, Signorina," he said, his face a picture. "I will no longer comment on the radiance of your beauty, which puts a sunset to shame…"

Caroline rolled her eyes. "If you're done doing… whatever it was you were doing here, I'd appreciate it if you'd come now and talk to my friend about her wedding. She could really use your help."

Fabrizio downed the last of his drink and pushed out his stool from the bar. "After you," he offered.

"Oh, no," she said sarcastically, "I insist – after *you*."

Caroline was pleased with her performance; she'd successfully done exactly what she set out to do, performing her bridesmaid duties well.

But despite herself - and feeling like a bit of an idiot for feeling that way - she couldn't help but admit that there was something about Fabrizio's smile that made her insides tingle.

CHAPTER 7

❄

"I don't think you understand..." Molly said tersely.

They'd been discussing her plans and expectations leading up to the wedding on Christmas Eve, but Fabrizio's nonchalant attitude was now seriously rubbing her up the wrong way.

No matter what she suggested they do, the Italian gave off an air of frustrating carelessness, and resisted giving their days any structure whatsoever.

"We really want to see the sights of Rome - show the wedding guests some of this wonderful city."

"Of course, *Signorina*, of course," he responded gently, again flashing his debonair smile. "But *Roma* – she is not like other cities. She demands a certain... spontaneity. You must listen to her to see where she takes you."

Molly's father had had just about enough. He threw his napkin onto the plate in front of him – still full of small, white *calamari*, which Paddy couldn't bring himself to eat, considering the look of the tentacles – and jabbed a finger at the man sitting across from him.

"Now, listen here lad," he scolded, "I think we have been very patient so far with you. There's a lot we want to see and do while we're here, and I think we have the right to have some sort of plan. For God's sake man, this is our daughter's wedding!"

Helen put a hand on his arm, and he calmed down a bit. "What my husband is trying to say," Molly's mum began, "is that we want to make sure everything about the trip is being taken care of, and right now you aren't reassuring us that it is."

"*Signores*," Fabrizio responded apologetically, "Please, listen. All will be fine. We have the church, we have a priest – Padre Beppe, he is the best – and afterwards, we will have a wonderful dinner here on the terrazza. It is also Christmas, yes? We will drink some wine, eat some delicious Italian food, and have some fun."

Patricia cleared her throat. "I certainly hope so. In the meantime, if you would be so kind as to bring us a bottle of the '67 Conterno Monfortino, we'd like to buy a bottle for the table."

"And perhaps a few packets of crisps as well?" Molly's father added hopefully, as Patricia glared at Paddy as if he was something she'd scraped off the bottom of her shoe.

Fabrizio stood back and bowed his head. "But of course, *signores*. Would anyone like anything else? Caffe? Limoncello?"

"Could we get a pot of tea as well?" Helen inquired. "I could really go for a good strong cup right now."

"Ah," Fabrizio frowned, "I am afraid the hotel will likely not have any tea to speak of. Perhaps a caffe – erm, espresso?"

"Coffee?" Paddy gaped incredulously. "At this hour? Are you mad? We'd be up all night."

Fabrizio eyed Molly's mother. "Perhaps that is a good thing, yes?" he joked.

Caroline snorted and Molly blushed, but Paddy was not amused. "Now, see here lad ..." he insisted, evidently offended.

Fabrizio looked abashed. "I am sorry, signore," he said with a feint towards apologising, "it is only that I am, how you say, hot-blooded and your wife, she is so beautiful. I joke."

"Well, it's not amusing, nor is it appreciated," Paddy replied curtly.

Fabrizio again flashed an apologetic look towards Helen, then he turned to Caroline and winked before walking off to get the drinks.

"WELL …" said Caroline after Fabrizio was out of earshot, "He's a saucy one, isn't he?"

"Very much so," Helen agreed, sipping from a glass of still water on the table. "He just seems so… forward." She sighed and blushed a little. "Though I have to say, it's been a while since a strange man looked at me like that."

"Mum!" Molly was aghast. "Anyway," she said wickedly, "I think he's much more interested in Caroline.

Caught off-guard, Caroline began stammering. "Wha – I – I wasn't – I – that is—" She was completely flustered, and she fought down a fierce burning in her cheeks. "I don't think so," she said finally, attempting to salvage what was left of her pride.

"Methinks the lady doth protest too much," Ben teased.

"Oh come *on*," Caroline protested. "Sure, he's … erm, good-looking… but you know how these Mediterranean men are…"

"*I* don't," Molly said with a grin. "Enlighten us, Caroline since you seem to know it all."

"I've heard the same stories you have," she sighed, looking around the table for support but not getting any. "Oh stop it, you know exactly what I'm talking about. There are stories – legends, really – about Italian men and their dashing good looks and well-cut jaw lines and *gorgeous* accents and – *ahem*—" She noticed she was getting a bit carried away and cleared her throat. "*Anyway*, they're always on the prowl, looking for a foreign girl to make their… conquest."

"Because they're Romans, and they conquer things?" Helen volunteered, with a glint in her eye. "Much like your dad over here."

"Mum!" Molly blurted, horrified afresh at her mother's brazenness, while Caroline and Ben laughed uncontrollably.

Patricia scowled. "My word," she said, disapproval dripping from her voice. "Is this *really* conversation for polite company?"

"Quite so," James agreed as Fabrizio returned with the bottle of wine. He stood up. "I think it's time we turned in for the evening, Patricia," he continued. "We've had... a very long day."

"Oh, come on, Father," Ben pleaded, "don't be that way."

"Was it something I said?" Fabrizio asked, coming back with the wine. When no one responded, or even met his eyes, he understood the implication. "Well, I will not keep bothering you. I shall see you all tomorrow then. *Buona notte.*"

He left again, leaving an air of despondent silence to settle on the rest of the group.

"You know something?" Caroline said, cutting through the rampant awkwardness. "I think I should turn in, too. We have a long day ahead of us tomorrow, and I think I've had enough wine for one night. Would you mind, Mol?"

Molly shrugged. "You're right," she said. She yawned as she got up, only now realising that, despite the abrupt way the Pembreys had exited, there might have been some truth to what they'd said, too.

And she was exhausted, and so disappointed that their Italian trip had started so badly.

Ben's parents were annoyed, her own parents out of their comfort zone, and what with the disinterested wedding planner, missing dress and best man still absent, it seemed nothing had gone right for them so far.

"Night all," she sighed, giving her parents a kiss on the cheek. "Hopefully tomorrow will be a better day."

CHAPTER 8

❄

Ben sat back in his chair, equally deflated.

Here they were, in Molly's favourite city in the world, during her favourite time of the year to get married– and she seemed miserable.

Helen put a hand on his knee, breaking his reverie. "Don't worry about her, love," she said warmly. "She's just nervous about … well, all of it I suppose."

Ben nodded. "Yeah, I know." He smiled at his future mother-in-law and stood to leave. "I'd better turn in, too. I've got a few things I need to take care of before bedtime. Hope you understand." He shook hands with Paddy and kissed Helen on the cheek. "You two have a good night."

Once Ben was gone, Paddy turned to his wife. "So… what do you make of the Pembreys?"

Helen rolled her eyes. "*He* doesn't say much," she began, "which I suppose is a good thing. Whereas *her* …"

Paddy nodded. "I know what you mean," he agreed. "She comes off as a bit … stuck-up, doesn't she?"

"Stuck-up, pretentious, condescending… So unlike Molly. Or

Ben, for that matter." She sipped her wine and sat back, gazing out at the glorious Roman skyline. "Paddy, honestly," she said sadly, "what on God's green earth are we doing here?"

"Supporting Molly," he answered. "She is young, and she's stupid, but she is wholly in love with that boy. And this city for whatever reason." He looked at the plate of *calamari* again, eyeing the tentacles suspiciously, as if they might begin to twitch and move at any second, "Despite that, we owe it to our daughter to give our love and support."

Just then, his phone buzzed, and he pulled it out to take a look.

"Well yes, of course," Helen pressed on, "but a Christmas wedding in Rome? A tiny church? These little—" she picked up a piece of *calamari*, "—*things*, with their tentacles and round heads? Bit of a disaster really…"

"What's that?" Paddy hadn't heard a thing his wife had just said. An email he had just received said that something had gone wrong with a delivery back home. His eyes narrowed towards the phone again as he began typing furiously. "Sorry love, I really have to check in with the office."

"Paddy," Helen chided, "you're in Rome. For your daughter's wedding. For God's sake, ditch the phone for the next forty eight hours at least."

"It'll just be a minute," he insisted. "I promise. I'll be right back." He stood and walked off to talk on the phone.

Helen sat in silence, gazing out over the city skyline.

She sipped her wine quietly for a few minutes, thinking. Paddy had always worked hard, but lately he'd become obsessive. Her husband simply was a workaholic. She'd held out hopes that he could put the phone away while they were here, but the indication already was that he wouldn't.

She waited nearly half an hour like that, watching the city lights from her perch on the *terrazza*.

When Paddy didn't return, she finished the rest of her glass and gave up, sighing deeply.

Once again, the work that was supposed to be easier now that he wasn't making the deliveries ended up being more difficult.

Helen called the lift and returned to her Roman hotel room alone.

CHAPTER 9

The following morning, the sun shone brightly from the small hotel window, waking Helen from her sleep.

Paddy was already downstairs in the lobby sipping the one kind of tea he had managed to get from the kitchen.

She stretched her neck, trying to get the crook out of her neck from the lumpy mattress and quickly got dressed. She could only hope today's adventures in Rome would be nothing like the day before

The rest of the group drank their *caffè e latte* with bread and jam. Paddy could not believe that there was no eggs, rashers or sausages – bacon didn't seem to be in the Italian diet at all.

"What I wouldn't give for some black pudding," he whispered regretfully to his wife as she signed for the bill.

"I'll be hungry in an hour," Helen agreed. "Though I suppose it explains how all these Italians are so slim…"

IN THE LOBBY, the wedding party once again waited for Fabrizio to meet them.

Somewhat unsurprisingly (at least to Caroline), he was nowhere to be seen. She went up to the desk to inquire about their coordinator, but Fabrizio was absent.

Though she wasn't certain the desk clerk had fully understood her, routinely referring to their coordinator as *il capo*, which according to Caroline's iPhone translator app, meant *the boss*.

She chose to keep this from Molly and the others to avoid their stress. Instead, she asked the receptionist for some tour brochures, and arranged for a taxi to be called.

When she finally rejoined the others, she was completely armed with maps and tickets still warm from the hotel's printer.

"Okay," she said as she returned. "Turns out, Fabrizio isn't able to make it this morning, but we've got a whole itinerary here, so don't worry."

Molly opened her mouth to protest, but Caroline kept talking. "So first up, we're going to go check out the Forum of Augustus, followed by the Colosseum. After that, I suggest we get ourselves some lunch near the Piazza di Spagna, and maybe do some shopping, because why not? We're in Rome, so let's do this right. And if we're finished in time, we can go and see Santa Maria, where you two lovebirds—" she motioned towards Ben and Molly with a wide, gaping smile, "—are getting married."

The cars pulled up moments later, not giving anyone a chance to disagree with her last minute plans.

However, Ben held back a little and when they were alone, he asked Caroline intensely, "Where exactly is Fabrizio? I thought he was supposed to meet us here."

She shrugged. "Apparently, the guy is about as reliable as our reservations were," she said. "So I improvised."

"You did all this on the fly this morning?" Ben looked impressed. "That's … incredible. Thank you."

Caroline nodded. "That's what bridesmaids are for. But listen: don't tell Molly about this, okay? She's stressed enough as it is. And with your parents and hers… well, I think you can agree that we have to make this as easy on her as possible."

CHAPTER 10

❄

Incredibly, the weather was sweltering, and not at all the festive picture postcard Molly had been hoping for.

The unseasonable December warmth meant that just in walking around the Forum of Augustus, she found herself sweating profusely, even though all she was wearing were jeans and a t-shirt.

She took a look around, perched on the steps just outside the Temple of Mars Ultor, trying to see it for the first time through her parents' eyes.

She should have felt exhilarated – but instead, she seemed oddly let down. All around were tacky shops selling postcards, shot glasses, t-shirts, official Forum of Augustus chocolates – everyone looking to make a few euros off the tourists who passed through the gates each and every day.

Whatever the Forum might once have been, whatever its relationship to what Rome once was in the days of Caesar Augustus, it just wasn't authentic anymore.

An hour and a half later, as they walked around the Colosseum, she felt little better. Here was *the* place from her posters and textbooks and Roman histories, a building of Italian antiquity that had haunted her dreams since she was a child…

"What do you think Dad?" she asked Paddy who was shuffling along behind her, looking hot and bothered in his red woollen jumper and heavy jeans.

"It's nice, but I thought it would be bigger. I suppose it's kind of a skeleton of the football stadiums back home?'" he said, decidedly unimpressed.

Ben noticed her dejected demeanour and came up behind her, wrapping his arms around her waist.

"Hey," he said, kissing her on the cheek. "Having fun?"

"Actually, no," she replied sullenly. "You know, I've adored this city since I was a little girl, and I loved it when I first came here back in college too, but whatever I'm seeing doesn't seem to at all translate to my parents. I so want them to understand why we chose this wonderful city for our wedding."

"Yes, but what can you do only show them around?" he asked. "Maybe organise some gladiator battles? A few lions?" His eyes twinkled.

"I don't know," she replied glumly. "Maybe they have a point too. To a lot of people, this seems like just another Italian tourist site, something to be catalogued on Instagram photos and Facebook check-ins." She sighed. "Or maybe I'm just stressed or overtired or something."

Ben released his arms and took her hand in his. "Listen, Mol," he said in a low, voice. "It's not about where we are but where we're going. You and me, we're getting married in a couple of days. And I don't care if we're in Dublin or Rome, New York or New Delhi – all I want is you as my wife. This will be great because of you. And because of us. What matters isn't this," he explained, pointing to the ancient ruins surrounding them. "What matters is how we feel about each other now, and when you walk down that aisle on Christmas Eve."

Molly stood on her tiptoes and kissed Ben on the lips. "You know," she said, smiling, "you're very sweet sometimes."

"I do what I can, Mrs. Pembrey," he replied, kissing her again.

She laughed. "I'm not Mrs yet, *Lord* Pembrey."

"Ugh, don't remind me of the title. My mother does enough of that for both of us."

CHAPTER 11

❄

After leaving the Colosseum, the wedding party headed towards Piazza di Spagna.

Molly took their driver's suggestion for a classy, tasteful *ristorante* for lunch, after which they planned to break off and walk around the stores in the area – Gucci, Armani, Prada, and all the other high-end Italian designers with storefronts nearby.

Sitting next to Paddy on the way was a chore for Helen. Once again, her husband spent the whole time on his phone, spitting directions at his assistant, tapping out emails and seeming extremely stressed over what sounded like minor issues.

Bad weather in Dublin had caused a delay on a major shipment, and never once did Paddy look up from the screen, so engrossed was he in trying to fix the unfixable from afar.

A few times, Helen tried to point out some of the sights ("Look, the Opera House. "We *must* remember to come back and walk through this park while we're here"), but to no avail; Paddy was in his own little world, consumed by work as usual.

At the restaurant, Patricia and James insisted on paying, and proceeded to order the most extravagant things on the menu in highly affected (and to Molly's ear - poorly worded) Italian.

Soon, buttered quail arrived on their table, followed by spaghetti with anchovies and squid as their *primi*. The younger ones gamely kept up with the Pembreys, but Paddy and Helen found themselves once again at a loss.

"How are we supposed to eat this stuff?" Paddy whispered.

They tried to munch on what they could, but he felt a cold shudder go down his spine each time his nose even caught wind of an anchovy.

As if that weren't enough, the *secondi* course came out blazing and steaming with a smell that Helen found stomach-churning. "What on earth is that?" she asked Patricia.

"Beef cheeks," Ben's mother said reverently. "They're quite the delicacy - you'll love them."

"Actually," Helen said, "I'm not feeling very well just now…"

"Oh Mum," Molly said, "do you want us to call you a taxi or—"

"No, no," she said, "I think a bit of fresh air might do me good. Paddy, can you…?"

"Of course love," he said. They exited together, a look of disapproved consternation overtaking Patricia's face.

CHAPTER 12

Outside the restaurant, Paddy was famished. "This is all mad stuff, isn't it?" he said glumly as they walked down the cobblestone street. "I'm starving."

"I don't understand why Ben's parents can't just eat normal things," Helen added. "Who in their right mind would eat a cow's cheek when you could have steak or roast?"

"The same people who order for the whole table without asking, I'd say," Paddy joked and the two of them laughed together.

They stopped at a nearby cafe and picked up a couple of cold-cut sandwiches. Without even a passing familiarity with Italian, ordering was difficult, but they were able to point at the meats that they wanted, and it did the trick.

Helen guided Paddy back towards the park she had seen on their way over in the taxi, and Paddy picked up two chocolate gelatos from a shop just outside the entrance.

She felt her heart melt along with the gelato as she walked along on Paddy's arm. It was almost like she was a teenager again, meeting him on a first date.

The park – which turned out to be the famed Pincian Hill, or *Pincio* – could not have been better for a romantic stroll. A beautiful lake surrounded by trees strung with fairy lights, sparkled in the late afternoon sunlight.

Latin columns, street lamps and statues lined the winding paths, where children giggled and played while their doting parents dashed off after them, ensuring they were never completely out of sight.

Helen sighed, taking it all in. It was perfect – exactly the kind of authentic Italian experience Molly was always taking about.

But it didn't last.

Shortly before they were supposed to rejoin the rest of the wedding party, Paddy got yet another phone call from Dublin.

"Paddy," she pleaded, "can't you just ignore it? Felicity and the others can handle it. Isn't that why you employ them in the first place?"

"I'm not just a worker anymore, love," he replied. "I'm the *manager*. If something fails, it's not just a problem for me – every one of our employees could be at risk. This is our busiest time of the year too. I have to take this. Sorry." He walked off a few paces ahead of her.

Helen sighed sadly and continued walking, watching the late winter sun cast magnificent light over the Eternal City in these glorious surrounds, all by herself.

CHAPTER 13

When that evening, the group returned to the Hotel Marliconi, they were greeted by a familiar form with ruffled hair and a winning smile.

Fabrizio was standing by reception and grinning at them.

Caroline was not amused. "Stay here," she told the rest of them. She marched over to the Italian, her jaw set and determined. "Where in God's name have *you* been all day?" she demanded.

"Ah, Signorina Caroline," he said, letting the word roll round on his tongue, "how has your day been so far?"

"How – has – our – day – been?"

"Yes, that is what I asked," he replied pleasantly.

"*I* planned the whole day, Fabrizio," she exploded, jabbing a finger towards his chest. "I did it to keep the bride that *you're* supposed to be working for, sane. I arranged *every*thing. And you helped with *nothing*. I have been improvising all day, because *you* - Mr Wedding Planner can't do your job."

"Ah, signorina," he soothed laconically, "you really must relax. I am sorry you thought I would be here today. I did not mean for you to have such difficulty."

"That's the point, you absolute *arse*," she continued yelling. "Molly and Ben are *paying* for a service, and you're not providing it. I'd fire you right here and now if it was up to me, but I don't have any say in the matter."

"Signorina – Caroline – please, allow me to make it up to you." Fabrizio put his hand around her shoulder. "If you'll go up to the terraza…"

"We've already *done* that. I'm not waiting up there again all night expecting to hear plans, only for you to sit at the bar flirting."

"Please. Come with me. And bring the others, too. I will go now – meet me up there as soon as you can, yes?"

Caroline sighed angrily. "I swear to God, Fabrizio, if this turns into another one of your 'let's-meet-ups' where we wait for an hour for you to show your face…"

"I promise you, it will not," he said solemnly. Then he bowed and headed upstairs without another word.

Caroline gathered the others and headed to the lift.

On the way up, she was stuck with the endless prattle of Patricia Pembrey, who was having a very one-sided conversation with Helen O'Brien.

"Yes, the Dolce & Gabbana store was fine, but Prada was incredibly disappointing. 'So many shoes, so little time,' I thought, but really, it was about fifty variations on the same shoe. And the handbags? Pssh. Nothing worth mentioning. Now, of *course* I walked out with a new pair," she slapped a shopping bag, "but I wasn't particularly impressed, at any rate. Now Gucci, on the other hand, was something special. I simply *had* to pick up a few scarfs, and then a shirt to go with them and before I knew it, I was so weighed down with clothes that I could hardly move! It was—"

The ding of the lift cut Patricia off, much to the others' relief.

They exited and were immediately shocked: there, in front of them was a table set up with seven places, along with twinkling wine glasses, and that perfect late evening view of St. Peter's Basilica below.

Candles on the table and fairy lights strung overhead completed the scene of romantic Italian serenity.

"Did you...?" Ben asked Caroline, pointing at the table.

She shook her head. "No, I – I had no idea," she said in wonder, glancing over at a beaming Fabrizio, who held out a chair for Molly.

"Come, come," he said. "Pembreys, O'Briens, and the beautiful Signorina Caroline, come! Sit! Eat!"

He pointed at the salad set out in little bowls on the table. "Here we have salad with lettuce, onion, green pepper, tomatoes, and crumbled gorgonzola cheese. We will pair this with a sweet vermouth *aperitivo*. Please, enjoy."

Caroline couldn't believe it. She had been raging at Fabrizio all day long, but here, he had outdone himself. This was beautiful, and she could tell by Molly's face that it was a lot more like her Italian dream.

When she saw him head back to the kitchen, she excused herself and followed him. "Fabrizio," she called when she was far enough away that the others couldn't hear her.

He turned and smiled. "Ah, Signorina Caroline. Is there something not to your liking?"

She shook her head. "No, I have to say... I did not expect this at all. The lights, the food, the wine, the view... It's fantastic. Molly and Ben are thrilled. But I have to know... when I was yelling at you before, downstairs, why didn't you tell me you had this planned?"

His smile grew wider. "Because then, I wouldn't have the opportunity to speak with you now," he said, laying the charm on even more thickly.

Caroline blushed slightly. "Well, I think I owe you an apology. This is truly wonderful. You've done a very good job."

He nodded. "Now, if you will excuse me, signorina, I must get back to the kitchen to bring out the *primera*."

"Can I ask what we're having?" she asked.

"And what kind of surprise would that be?" he winked.

She watched him walk away, thinking to herself, *Okay, so maybe he's not completely cheesy.*

And even if he is, maybe that's not so bad...

CHAPTER 14

True to his word, Fabrizio's presentation was superb.

The *primera* of pasticcio al forno, "a traditional Christmas pasta bake," according to their host, delighted the guests. Layers of rigatoni, ground lamb, tomato sauce, and generous helpings of cheese were a welcome way to replenish after a day of sightseeing.

The tender slices of veal and delicious roasted potatoes that comprised the *secondi* were an absolute delight, too. When Helen O'Brien raised a faint objection to eating veal, Fabrizio noted that, "little animals are the sacrificial victims of the Italian lust for meat at Christmas. It is… tradition."

One bite later, Helen's moral qualms melted away like the meat in her mouth.

So delicious was everything that no one seemed to notice just how much wine was being consumed.

This was partly Fabrizio's doing: rather than leaving a bottle of wine for the table, he insisted on pairing different wines with each course.

By the time dessert rolled around, everyone had had more than their share of delicious Barberas, Sangioveses and Vermentinos.

It was after Fabrizio brought out a delightful-looking *zuppa inglese* that things started going downhill.

The festive dessert, made of rum, jam, pastry cream, whipped cream and fruit, reminded Paddy of sherry trifle, easily his favourite dessert.

He hadn't been particularly impressed by the wines nor the *limoncello* Fabrizio had foisted upon the table, but this – this was a rare slice of home, and Paddy was simply delighted.

"Nothing beats a good trifle," he said, his mouth watering.

Patricia shot him a look. "Trifle?" she repeated, amusedly. "How... *quaint*."

"Now, don't get me wrong," Paddy continued between mouthfuls of *zuppe*, "it's nothing compared to my Helen's here. No one does it better. But this isn't half bad at all."

"I can't say I've ever had trifle before," James mused.

Patricia nodded. "Of course you haven't, dear," she said haughtily. "It's a rather ... common dessert, no flair or artistry needed."

Helen's gaze shot up. "Really ..." she said decidedly unimpressed.

"Oh darling," Patricia insisted, "that wasn't meant to be insulting."

"Good," Helen replied flatly. "Because it certainly sounded like that."

Patricia wasn't finished. "I just think," she continued, "it speaks to a certain... *kind*."

"Mother..." Ben interjected warily.

"No Ben," Patricia continued, holding up a hand to silence him, "I am tired of having to hold my tongue. You are asking me to be something that I simply am not. And I also resent being told that I have to pretend to think this....Italian charade... is all okay when it simply is *not*."

Ben shook his head apologetically at Molly. "Father," he motioned towards Patricia, "couldn't you..."

James merely looked down as his wife continued on. "Ben," she said, softening as she gazed concernedly at her son, "this can't truly be what you want - a hush-hush ceremony in a tiny church in a foreign country? You are entitled to so much *more*. You are the son of a lord, and heir to an important title. One day, you will be the 16th Earl of Daventry. Our family has certain *standards* to uphold. And however pleasant this young lady," she motioned towards Molly, "might be, I simply do not believe she understands what inheriting such a title might mean. Of course, I cannot blame her for that. Manners are taught as much as they are learned."

"Now, you hold on!" Helen exploded, shocking everyone at the table as she stood angrily. "I don't know who you think you are to insult my daughter and my family the way you have, Patricia, but this is *truly* beyond the pale. Your so-called English *title* does not bring with it the opportunity to look down your nose at *any*one's manners, at least not with the way you yourself are acting."

Helen's breathing increased in rapidity, and she felt her heart race in her chest. She glanced at her daughter, who looked on the verge of tears, and took a deep breath before continuing in a more relaxed tone.

"For Molly's sake, I am going to assume that you simply have had too much wine tonight, and it has loosened your tongue. I can be far more forgiving of an obnoxious drunk than I can the nasty person you are showing yourself to be this evening. I think we should leave now, before I say something I myself might *truly* regret. Paddy?"

Paddy looked at Molly, then to Ben, and finally stood and joined his wife.

"I – good evening," he said simply as Helen stormed off.

Molly stared at Patricia, who seemed unconcerned by their exit.

"Molly, dear," she said with a put-on smile, "I hope you know this had nothing to do with you…"

The bride-to-be looked shocked. She looked at Patricia quizzically. "Nothing… to do… with me?" she repeated.

"Of course not," Patricia shook her head. "We simply want the best for our son that's all."

Molly's jaw hit the floor. "So... what you're saying is... I'm *not* the best for Ben." She looked at her fiance, who said nothing. "How... *dare* you...!"

"See. Like mother, like daughter," Patricia muttered under her breath.

"And *you*," she exploded, turning on Ben. "That you could just *sit* there while this... *woman* insults me, insults my mother and my father while all we're here in Rome - for our wedding?"

"I – I don't—"

Molly narrowed her eyes. "You know what, Ben?" she snapped. "You can keep your titles, and your Lordship and your stuck-up parents. I can't be with someone who cares so much about a title and so little for his wife-to-be."

With that, she spun on her heel and walked off.

Caroline jumped up to chase after her – but before doing so, she turned to the Pembreys. "You're just... I can't even ..." she muttered before going after her friend.

Ben sat at the table in stunned silence. His mother sipped on her limoncello, a satisfied look on her face, while his father continued to stare off into the distance. "See Ben, this isn't—"

"Mother," he said quietly, "can you *please* give it a rest for once?"

"I'm only saying..."

"Not. Now."

"All right, all right," Patricia responded. "But at some point, you're going to have to face facts, Ben: that girl is simply all wrong for us. And her family is —"

"*Mother*," Ben interjected hotly. "That is *enough*. You have been rude, pretentious, and condescending, particularly towards the O'Briens. And now, you've ruined the one thing that has made me happier than anything ever has. I want to *marry* Molly. I'm *going* to marry Molly - here in Rome on Christmas Eve. And there is simply nothing you can say or do that's going to stop me." He stood up and angrily tossed his napkin on the table. "Molly however, might well be a different story."

CHAPTER 15

❄

Tears streamed down Molly's face as she wound her way through the cobblestone streets and back alleys of the beloved city of her dreams.

The sun had set on Rome, and everywhere she looked, shops were closing up, their darkened windows displaying clothes of red and green and large, intricately decorated signs proclaiming, BUON NATALE.

It was too much to take. What had she been thinking, bringing her and Ben's families here?

Since she was a little girl, all she'd ever dreamed about was a romantic Christmas wedding in Rome.

She knew the place so well she felt almost like an honorary Roman. She knew the sites by heart, knew the history of the city and the empire that bore its name, the names of the great men and women who had made this the single most legendary Italian city in the world.

And one of the most important things she'd planned for her wedding day was bringing the guests to the Trevi Fountain after the ceremony, to carry out the famed tradition of throwing coins in the fountain.

A WEEKEND IN ROME

But would any of her guests truly want to return to Rome? And more to the point, after this trip, would Molly want to?

She passed by the Pantheon, its columns illuminated by a row of Christmas trees lit up along the piazza in front.

It was beautiful and looked so magically festive in such glorious surrounds, but for once, failed to lift her spirits.

She continued walking, eventually crossing the Tiber and coming up on Vatican City.

St. Peter's Basilica glowed in the sun's fading light.

I'm usually so entranced by this, she thought glumly. *What's wrong with me?*

But she knew exactly what was wrong: Ben. Why hadn't he stood up to his parents back there? How could he let his mother say such things about her family – and to her?

She could never have imagined sitting idly by while Paddy or Helen said similar things about Ben.

How can we recover from this? she wondered as she found herself walking past the Castel Sant'Angelo.

She knew the answer to this, too: maybe they couldn't. This was *it*.

She was in her city of her dreams, at her favourite time of the year…supposedly to marry the man of her dreams, and now everything was ruined.

All because of stuck-up Patricia Pembrey and her penchant for wine and haughtiness.

Molly saw a tram coming and decided to escape for a while.

She bought a ticket and jumped randomly on the departing #19 and took a seat in the back.

She gazed longingly out the window, watching her beloved Eternal City passing by, wishing for something – anything – to give her that familiar burst of inspiration.

It wasn't forthcoming. Everywhere she seemed to look now, she saw commercialism, tourist traps, and big-city trappings.

There was no magic here anymore, she decided sadly; it was like just any another city.

The accents might be different, the language more melodic-sounding, and the skin tones a bit darker, but a city was still a city. Her parents were right; she should have just got married back home.

Married. She cringed. Was she still getting married? She loved Ben, certainly – but she simply couldn't handle his mother being the way she was. And if he wouldn't stand up to Patricia, stand up *for* his new wife, his new family, this simply was not to be.

She shook her head, and got off the tram to unfamiliar surroundings. The sign designated this area Piazza Buenos Aires, but she was pretty sure she'd never been here before.

She wasn't sure how long she'd been travelling, nor exactly where she was either. She shrugged and trudged on dejectedly.

That was when she saw it.

It wasn't quite a clock tower – there was no clock on it – but it nonetheless rang out, a bell tower dressed up in its festive finest, beautiful brown Tuscan architecture housing tresses that seemed to stretch up into the sky.

Molly walked towards the structure, entranced.

Suddenly, as the tower rose in front of her, she came upon an archway, lit up with fairy lights, a face in the centre almost gazing down upon her, beckoning her to enter. Where was this?

Balconies like something out of *Romeo and Juliet* adorned buildings that almost looked like miniature castles. Cars, apartments, trees, and green grassy areas were all smashed up against each other in a thoroughly confusing fashion.

The entire area was decorated with white fairy lights, while multicoloured bulbs hung from the tent coverings of pop-up cafes along the street.

She heard a rhythmic beating from somewhere nearby: a drum circle, replete with locals dancing in time had apparently sprung up in a nearby park.

The winter wind blew chilly now, but no one seemed to care.

Molly turned around in full circle, in awe of what she had just stumbled upon. She closed her eyes and breathed in deeply, taking it all in. *This* was the magic of Rome she knew.

It wasn't in the historical sites or the typical trappings of the ancient city she'd shown her parents – it was *here*, in *this* place, wherever it was, with these people, obviously locals, dancing and singing and being festive. The lifeblood.

She grinned as she found herself swaying to the beat, smiles of joy now replacing tears of heartbreak and frustration.

This was *her* Rome.

CHAPTER 16

"Well, where *is* she?" Ben demanded, breathing heavily and sounding more than a little panicked, as he paced his hotel room.

"I've tried phoning her, asked around the hotel – I even asked that dopey desk clerk if she had seen her. Nothing. No one knows where Molly went."

Caroline poured a glass of water and handed it to him. "Calm down," she said soothingly. "I'm sure she'll turn up. She was really annoyed by your mum. She probably just needs to blow off some steam. This is the city of her dreams, isn't it?"

When he looked even glummer at this, Caroline put a hand on his shoulder.

"Ben," she continued, "Molly's a big girl. She can take care of herself. Look, maybe we should talk about something else, help get your mind off things."

"Like what?" he asked.

"Like, what in God's name is wrong with your parents?"

Ben shook his head disappointedly. "I don't even know where to begin. My mother can be—"

"A heinous she-witch?" Caroline offered.

"—difficult. Hell, she's difficult in the *best* of times, let alone when she's had a few…"

"But we're here for your *wedding*," Caroline pressed. "What does she have against Helen and Paddy? And what was all that rubbish about dessert - and that whole trifle thing? I love trifle myself."

Ben sighed. "It's just …" he ventured, "my mother has always had issues with 'new' money."

Caroline cocked her head. "What do you mean, 'new' money?"

"Like, money that hasn't been inherited. Self-made wealth."

"Well, Paddy's hardly *wealthy*. I mean, he and Helen are reasonably well-off, I suppose, but nothing like—"

"Me?" Ben offered.

"Well, I wasn't going to say it, but your father *is* a member of the House of Lords…"

"*He* may be, but *I* don't want to be."

Caroline threw up her arms, exasperated with Ben's naivety. "Oh come, *on*, Ben!" she exclaimed. "You of all people *know* that's not how this works. When your dad passes away, that's it: *you* become the Earl of Coventry—"

"Daventry."

"—whatever. The point is, that English nobility stuff means nothing to the likes of us. We don't do gentry in Ireland as you know. And then for your mum to go around pretending like she's… I don't know, the Queen of England or whatever, is a bit much."

"I get that," Ben nodded. "But what's that got to do with *me*? Why would Molly be mad at *me* for how my parents act? She knows I don't agree with their values *or* their attitudes."

"Because, Ben, you didn't stand up for Molly or her parents back there! You're like a turtle: when confronted, you went right back into your shell. And if I know Molly, all she wanted was to hear you put your parents in their place."

"But I did," Ben insisted. "After you all left, I lit into them. Told them they'd better get used to the idea of Molly being around, because I'm *going* to marry her."

"Great," Caroline told him, "but does *she* know that?"

"She knows me," he replied. "She should know that about me."

"Molly's not a psychic, Ben," Caroline told him. "All she saw was you kowtowing to your mother's nastiness - and with only a day to go till your wedding. I'd imagine *that*, more than anything, is what set her off."

Ben slumped down in a chair. "I just don't know what to do Caroline," he said sadly. "If the wedding is called off —"

"That," she insisted, "won't happen." She grabbed her coat and headed towards the door. "Look," she told him, "I'll head out and see if I can find her, talk her round. You just stay there, and keep in touch."

Ben nodded glumly, and Caroline went back out to the hallway … where she collided straight with none other than Fabrizio.

CHAPTER 17

"Signorina Caroline," he said happily, "I am so happy to find you. Everyone left so quickly..."

She stared at him impatiently, waiting for him to explain what he was doing outside her room.

It was then that she noticed the clothing bag hung over his arm. "I bring good news: your dress has arrived. The wedding is saved!"

Caroline chuckled ironically as Fabrizio handed the bag to her. "Well," she said, "thanks anyway, but we're no longer sure at this point if there's actually going to *be* a wedding."

"What do you mean?" he asked, looking shocked.

She sighed. "Well," she explained, "everybody left because there was a big row over dinner between Ben's parents and Molly's, and it ended with Molly walking out on Ben."

"Oh no," he replied concernedly. "So where is she now?"

"That's the thing," Caroline said. "I'm heading out now to try and find her. She took off, and no one seems to know where she is."

"And you are going to, what, walk around *Roma* after dark calling out her name until you find her?"

Caroline shrugged. "She can't have gone far," she replied.

Fabrizio shook his head. "Of course she can. There are trains, buses, trams, taxis – she could be halfway to *Napoli* by now."

Caroline's face fell. "Oh God, Fabrizio," she said, panic rising in her voice, "you don't think she would do that, do you?"

"I do not know," he answered. "She is your friend, after all. You know her best."

Caroline nodded. "Right, right," she said. "Okay, let's see... where would she go?"

"Perhaps something related to the wedding?" Fabrizio ventured. "Maybe the church or to the *Fontana di Trevi* to think."

"At this point, I think the wedding is the last thing she wants to think about. You didn't see her, Fabrizio. She was very upset. She ran off before I even had the chance to to talk her."

Fabrizio nodded. "Okay, I have an idea. Go, leave your dress in your room, and meet me downstairs in a few minutes. We will drive in my car to a few places I know. Perhaps we will be lucky."

Caroline stared at him again – only this time, it was in admiration. "Fabrizio, that's very kind of you... I'm..."

"I know," he said, flashing her his increasingly charming smile. "I will see you downstairs."

CHAPTER 18

A few minutes later, she stood outside the hotel, craning her neck to see where Fabrizio might be. Several cars passed by, but there was no indication any of them was being driven by the handsome Italian.

Her attention was struck moments later by a gorgeous yellow Lamborghini, sleek and stylish and very cool.

Boy, she thought to herself, *nice to have the money to afford one of those babies.*

The Lamborghini turned into the hotel turnabout, and the horn honked towards her. She squinted to see the driver.

It was Fabrizio. "Of *course*," she murmured.

He opened the door for her – opening it not out but *up*, which made her stand back.

"Come," he motioned.

The interior of the car was even more luxurious than she'd imagined. Gorgeous cream and black leather seats, a smooth, crisp dash, top-of-the-line stereo system… it was almost too much, and she said so.

"What," she teased, "you couldn't do well enough with a *moder-*

ately expensive car? You have to go with the one that costs as much as a house?"

He smiled. "My job," he explained, "causes me to have to drive quite a bit. I like... style when I do so."

"And you can afford this?"

"I can afford many things."

"How is that possible?" She herself had worked at a hotel before. Even at a luxury one like the Hotel Marliconi.

"The hotel at which you are staying," he said matter-of-factly, "is my main source of income."

"There's no way you can afford a Lamborghini on an event specialist's salary."

He looked over at her quizzically. "*Signora*," he said, "I am many things, but I am no event specialist."

"What are you talking about?" she asked, frowning. "Molly has been working with you for months now."

Fabrizio shook his head. "No," he said, "Molly was working with our event specialist, yes, but he is no longer employed with us. I fired him last week."

"What do you mean, *you* fired him? Are you his manager or something?"

"You mean... the Pembreys did not tell you?"

"Ben's parents? What did they not tell me, exactly?"

"The Hotel Marliconi," he said. "It is my hotel."

Caroline felt a shock ripple through her entire body. "Wait – *your* hotel? So that would make you..."

He looked at her and once again flashed his smile. "Fabrizio Marliconi. At your service."

CHAPTER 19

"Wait, wait, wait," Caroline stammered as the car sped off. "This doesn't make any sense. Why would the owner of a luxury hotel be helping out a tiny wedding party like ours?"

"Lady Pembrey," he responded, "is an old family friend. Her mother and mine went to the same university in England. Cambridge. She asked me to step in to help with the wedding."

Caroline sat there in stunned silence. There was no way – there was simply no *way* that that horrible, vile, bigoted woman had stepped in and saved the day.

After all the complaining, the negativity and those awful things she'd said to the O'Briens... could Patricia really not be as terrible as everyone had thought?

A little while later, her thoughts were interrupted by the car jerking to a sudden stop.

"There," Fabrizio called out, pointing to a girl dancing in the middle of a nearby side street.

It was Molly.

Caroline jumped out of the car and ran straight over to her best friend. "Molly Rose O'Brien," she called out. "What on earth do you think you're doing?"

Molly just smiled, looking almost giddy.

"Caroline!" she cooed. "Oh, I'm so glad you're here. How did you – " She stopped when she saw Fabrizio standing by his car.

"Long story," Caroline said curtly. "Where have you been? We had no idea where you'd gone. Ben's been worried sick about you – literally."

Molly squeezed Caroline's hand in hers as they walked back towards Fabrizio's car. "I went exploring," she explained. "I hopped on a tram, got off completely randomly, and I kind of just stumbled upon this place. I have no idea where we are, but – Caroline, isn't it wonderful? *This* is what Rome is all about - this was the city I wanted you to see."

Molly was beaming with an enthusiasm Caroline hadn't seen since their arrival.

She took a look around her for the first time. She had to admit, this area, wherever they were, had a certain authentic charm to it, possessing more of a true Italian feel to it than other more heavily commercialised areas of the city.

"Fabrizio," she asked when they returned to the car, "where exactly are we?"

"Il Quartiere Coppedè," he said. "The Coppedè district. It is well-known for being more… erm… I am not sure of the English word… *svariato*… than any other district in Roma."

"It's wonderful," Molly said dreamily. "But now I think maybe it's time for me to get back."

"To your groom I hope?" Fabrizio inquired.

Molly nodded. "Yes, I suppose so." She turned to Caroline. "Is there any way I can have Ben's parents banned from the ceremony?"

Caroline squeezed her friend's hand again. "I don't think so love," she smiled. "But, listen… just leave everything to me. They'll be on their best behaviour, I promise."

"Fabrizio held open the car door. "After you, ladies," he said.

When they reached the hotel, Molly gave Caroline another hug. "Listen," she said, "I'm going to talk to Ben. I think we have some things to work out."

"You've only got a few hours left 'til your wedding, remember?" Caroline said. "Do talk to him. Explain it all, but don't forget that you love him – and he loves you."

Molly waved to Fabrizio as she walked away.

"Thanks for the lift," she called.

"My pleasure," he smiled, waving back.

ONCE MOLLY WAS GONE, Caroline went over to the Italian and kissed him on the cheek.

"You might just have saved the day, Fabrizio," she whispered. "Thank you for your help."

She turned to walk away, but he grabbed her arm and pulled her back towards him.

"*Signorina*," he said, his dark eyes boring intensely into hers. "Caroline. I do these things for you because I find you fascinating. I do not normally meet women like you," he continued.

Caroline trembled slightly despite herself. "Women like me?" she scoffed shakily. "You hardly know me."

"Few women are willing to speak their minds the way you do," he told her. "You are fearless and brave. You will tell people what you think whether they want to hear it or not. I… admire that."

With that, he took her face in his large, olive-skinned hands, and brushed her hair off her face.

A moment passed between them that felt to Caroline like an eternity.

"I'm telling you, Fabrizio," she said quickly, "I'm not—"

She didn't get the opportunity to finish, because she suddenly found his face against hers, her lips locked with his.

It was the kind of kiss that made a person weak in the knees, long and serious, blissful and playful – and when it was over, left an impression.

One hell of an impression.

Caroline's eyes were still closed when he broke away. "Fabrizio —" she murmured, momentarily awestruck.

"You see, *signorina*?" he asked.

Caroline opened her eyes, realising what had just happened, and shook her head. "No," she insisted quietly.

"No?"

"No," she repeated. "No, no, *no*. I'm – I'm *so* not doing – this can't – " She began to back away from him.

"Caroline," he pleaded, more intently.

"No, Fabrizio, look, thank you for helping me find Molly, but I – I have to – to go." She walked backwards away from him unsteadily, almost in a daze. "I'm – I'm sorry. I— "

Caroline didn't say another word, but instead, turned her back on him and picked up speed until she was almost running to the lift, her mind racing.

Oh God, she thought, *What in the world have I just done?*

CHAPTER 20

❄

Ben was watching *Sky News* – Italy's Finance Minister was caught up in some sort of scandalous affair – when a knock came at his door.

He jumped out of bed, knocking over a less-than-sturdy nightstand (and taking down a lamp with it) in the process.

He cursed mildly over his stubbed toe and hobbled over to the door to reveal an absolute shock.

"Mother …" he said, irritably.

Patricia held her expression neutral, but he noted a slight smudge in her usually impeccably applied mascara. She'd been crying.

"Ben darling," she greeted, her voice wavering ever-so-slightly, "may I come in?"

He didn't answer, but left the door open and headed back into the room. Patricia followed, swallowing hard.

"I'd offer you a drink," Ben said coldly, "but I'm pretty certain you've already had quite enough."

She chuckled a little. "I suppose I should've stopped after that first bottle of wine."

"Mother, I don't give a damn how much wine you drank," he scolded her. "What you did – the way you acted – it was—"

"—unforgivable," she finished for him, nodding. "I know, dear. I know. I was only…"

"You were *only* thinking about yourself," he snapped. Patricia stayed silent and looked to the ground. "Is there something you needed?" he asked.

She shook her head. "I just – I want you to under—" she stifled a small heave in her chest before continuing, "—to understand all that comes with being the Earl of Daventry. Because it won't be—"

"Oh for God's sake, mother!" Ben yelled. "I don't care about being the Earl of Daventry, or the rank, or the title, or any of that. I care about *Molly!*"

He ran his fingers through his hair and paced a bit around the room. "Do you know what Caroline is doing now?" he demanded. Patricia shook her head. "She's wandering around the streets of Rome, hoping that maybe, somehow, she'll run into Molly, or Molly will answer her phone. And the reason I'm not out there with her is I'm afraid that seeing *me* will only make things worse. And you know what I have to thank for that? The damned Lord and Lady Pembrey! You, and your stuck-up, closed-minded, pretentious nonsense that makes you think that because you married Father, you're somehow entitled to better treatment than your so-called social inferiors."

At this, Patricia broke. She knew her son was right; he had every right and every reason to be upset with her. But more than anything else, she also knew *she* was right.

"Ben," she said, choking back a sob, "I know the title means nothing to you. But it doesn't mean nothing to everyone. In fact, it means a great deal. It imparts status and power – not for me – I grew up without it, obviously – but for your children. The only time I've ever invoked the title has been to help *you*."

Ben looked her in the eye, his blazing fiercely. "I never *asked* for that, Mother," he said darkly.

"You never *had* to," she insisted. "You are my *son*. Perhaps… perhaps when you have children of your own, you'll understand."

"If I have children," he said, "it's going to be with Molly. I only hope she can forgive me for not standing up to you sooner."

"Oh Ben," Patricia remarked, "I'm not concerned with whether or not you have children with Molly or – or – bloody Princess Beatrice!"

Ben arched an eyebrow. "Wha— why would I ever have children with— what?"

Patricia shook her head. "Never mind. The *point*, my dear, is that you can marry whomever you want – but you must choose carefully, because what you stand to inherit affects not only you but your children and your children's children." She fumbled with her fingers a bit before continuing, obviously searching for the right words to convey her feelings. "Do you remember Digadoo?"

"Digadoo?" Ben chuckled. "Sounds like a really awful kids' TV show."

"Digadoo," Patricia explained, "was your imaginary pony. When you were about three, you were absolutely *obsessed* with ponies, and you said you wanted one. When your father and I told you you'd have to wait 'til you were older, you invented this pony of your own, Digadoo. He was your friend, your confidante – and apparently, he could fly, too."

"Right."

"You and Digadoo were the best of friends for about a year. You'd do *everything* together. You even had me set a place at the dinner table every night for him."

"So whatever happened to him?'" Ben asked.

"Well, after about a year or so, we realised that you were still serious about this pony, so we got you riding lessons at the club."

"I remember *that*," he said. "But I don't remember Digadoo."

"That's because you don't need to, darling," Patricia said. "Digadoo faded into your memory the way imaginary friends are supposed to, and got replaced by reality. And the reality we were able to provide you with was far better than any fantasy you might have had."

"I don't recall the horse being able to fly," Ben said softly.

"No, but do you recall the fun you had?"

He nodded. "But that's hardly the point, Mother," he elaborated. "Money, wealth, power – they're all fine and well, but you can't buy happiness. And I can't remember, but I presume I was very happy with Digadoo."

Patricia shrugged. "You may have been," she admitted, "but you were three. You would have been happy with a bowl of custard and a few ladyfingers. Children can't appreciate what their parents can offer them. It's for the parents to provide the opportunities. And the Earlship provides more opportunities, opens more doors, than you can possibly imagine."

"That may be, Mother," Ben agreed, "but that doesn't excuse how you spoke to the O'Briens. And it doesn't excuse how you treated Molly. She's a wonderful person, mother. If you'd only get past your own ludicrous biases, you'd see that."

"She might be," Patricia replied. "She could be the loveliest girl who's ever lived. But I just don't know that the... the societal *manners* she and her parents have shown is compatible with giving your children, my grandchildren, the very best of lives."

"God, Mother!" Ben complained. "This isn't a Jane Austen novel. Manners and discipline and polite society? It's all nonsense. To say nothing of the fact that none of that gentry stuff even exists in Ireland. The only thing that's important is how we treat each other. That's what all the sermons at all the masses we attended when I was a boy said. *Do unto others* and all that. It doesn't matter if Molly wanted to get married in a foreign city, or that her parents tell saucy in-jokes. They are good people. They are kind people. And they deserve far better than how you've treated them." Incensed afresh, Ben rose and opened the door. "I think it's best if you leave now."

"Ben," she pleaded, panic overtaking her face, "I wish you would only try to understand. I'm not against Molly or her parents. I simply want what's best for you."

"What's best for me, Mother," he responded flatly, "is to be happy. And the only way that's going to happen is if Molly comes back tonight, safe and sound, and we get married in this city tomorrow. You and Father can come or not come to the ceremony – that's entirely up to you – but if Molly will still have me, we're getting married tomorrow."

Patricia nodded curtly and left the room without saying another word.

BEN CLOSED the door behind her and collapsed against the door. He knew his mother cared – the fact that she'd remembered an imaginary friend he'd forgotten like Digadoo was proof of that – but her haughtiness and closed-mindedness were simply unforgivable.

He was startled to attention rather quickly by a brusque rapping on the door. He stood, straightened his shirt, and began opening the door. Patricia, it appeared, had more to say. "Okay, look," he began, "I need you to hear me loud and clear: what you think at this point is imma— *oh.*"

It wasn't his mother standing in the doorway. Instead, it was a vision from heaven itself, an angel sent to guide him home. It was Molly, and she was grinning lopsidedly at her fiancee.

"Hey there, handsome," she said in her best American drawl. "Wanna get hitched?"

CHAPTER 21

Ben took Molly into his arms and kissed her. "Where on earth have you been?" he asked. "I'm so sorry."

Molly smiled. "I went looking for something," she said. "I needed – I don't know – I needed to remember that Rome was the same city I knew and loved, I needed it to calm and heal me in the way it always did. And I needed to think."

"About my mother?" Ben asked warily. "Look, I need you to know – whatever she thinks, you are the woman I—"

Molly was shaking her head rapidly. "No, no, no," she insisted. "Not about your mum. About *me*." She took a deep breath before continuing. "Ben, I've been unfair to you," she began.

"No, you—"

"Please," she insisted, "let me get this out." She straightened her dress in front of her and continued, her voice barely above a whisper. "I've been very unfair to you and everyone. I wanted this wedding in Italy at Christmas. I pushed ahead with it despite what our families - both our parents wanted. And I tried to force my dream, my perfect vision of Rome on everyone.

And before you say anything, I know we both agreed on this, and that at the time it suited *both* of us. But if I'm being honest, you've given me everything I've wanted, while I haven't really given much back."

"That's not true," Ben argued. "Molly, you've been more than fair. Putting up with Mother – and Father – isn't even the half of it. Everything's seems to have gone wrong since we got here, and—"

"It's all gone wrong *because* of me, trying to make everything perfect. And when I walked out on dinner—"

"—which you had every right to do…"

"Perhaps," Molly admitted. "But it was still poor form. And after all your parents have done …"

A confused look overtook Ben's face. "What are you talking about?" he asked.

"It's okay," she said patiently. "Caroline told me all about what your mum and dad did. About how the wedding planner I hired messed everything up, and how Fabrizio is the owner of the hotel…"

"He's *what?*" Ben gasped.

Molly titled her head curiously. "Wait…" she said, putting two and two together. "You didn't know?"

"Know what?"

"That your mum asked for Fabrizio's help because she's old friends with his mum."

Ben sat down, mystified. "I – I honestly had no idea," he murmured. He looked up at Molly. "Mother was just in here. I read her the riot act because of how she'd acted. I… I had no idea she'd done that." He shook his head, recalling the conversation. "But that still doesn't excuse what she said to you and your folks."

"No, it doesn't," Molly agreed. "But Ben, whatever your mum said while she was drinking, I don't know if that means she actually *believes* it. She just wants the best for you, I suppose."

"*You* are the best for me," he said, standing and taking her in his arms.

"So then, you do still want to marry me?" she asked.

"Only if you still want to marry me," he said, adding, "and marry *into* my family."

Molly half-smiled. "I think I can make do," she mused. "Besides, we'll only have to see them occasionally. Every other Christmas or so."

Ben nodded. "If that, even," he said. "We could always move somewhere they'd never come, like—"

"—Naples?" Molly joked.

Ben laughed and kissed her. "I love you, Signorina O'Brien," he said, his heart filling up.

"And I love you, Lord Pembrey," she teased.

"Don't call me that," he insisted.

"I think I will actually," she said, smiling and holding him close.

CHAPTER 22

❄

Helen stood in her room, staring out the window at the glorious Roman skyline lit up against the darkness.

Behind her, Paddy sat on a chair, his laptop open in front of him and his ear glued to his mobile phone.

It seemed yet another shipment was running late, and rather than trusting that everything would be taken care of, as the others had been, he seemed to think he could will the packages to their destinations in time for Christmas by sheer thought.

"No, Felicity," Paddy said, irritation rising in his voice. "N-no— no— look, just get it done, all right? Now, where are we with the Jefferson Electronics account?" He typed a few notes on his computer, continuing back-and-forth with his assistant over the other end of the phone.

Helen had heard enough. "Paddy," she called soothingly, turning back to him. "We have barely hours until our daughter's wedding. Don't you think you can give the phone a rest? Can't someone else handle it?"

Paddy covered the receiver with his hand. "What?" he asked her, squinting towards her form. "What did you say, love?"

"Nothing," Helen sighed. "Nothing at all." She resumed looking out the window. Why couldn't she get him to put down the phone for more than a few minutes at a time? He hadn't always been this way. Only when DHL had taken over the business did his penchant for working constantly become an issue.

Here they were in one of the most beautiful cities in the word two days before Christmas, their daughter's relationship was in crisis, and all he could think about was computer part deliveries.

Helen stared across at the Vatican and St Peter's Basilica, silently wishing for a miracle.

CHAPTER 23

*I*n the room next door, things were only slightly less frosty. "I simply don't know what more to say to him," Patricia told her husband.

"Perhaps you shouldn't say anything," he counselled her. "Ben's a grown man. He needs to make his own choices, questionable though we may think them."

"But James," she whined insistently, "the O'Briens are… so…"

"Oh, they're all right, Patricia," he scolded her. "Paddy is a decent sort, and Helen is quite charming."

"But they're so… so…"

"Ordinary?"

"Yes!" Patricia exclaimed. "How can Ben settle for that when he can do so much better?"

"Do you even know your son?" James asked her. "He's far more comfortable with them than he ever was with us. He skipped out on Cambridge for Dublin, for God's sake. Let's let him make his own decisions. And I won't have any more of these hostilities. You will go and apologise to Molly and her parents."

"You can't be serious."

"Of course I'm serious," he said sternly. "This wedding is going to happen whether we want it to or not, Patricia, and I would prefer that we make the best of it, wouldn't you?"

Patricia sighed. "You're right, of course," she said resignedly. "All right. Tomorrow, over breakfast… I will… apologise."

"You know why I adore you, my dear?"

"Why's that?"

"Because you have more sense than any woman I've ever known."

"Tell that to your son," Patricia muttered.

"I plan to," James said, grinning and taking her into his arms.

CHAPTER 24

Caroline paced around her room. What had she just done? This was exactly what she'd wanted to avoid – what she'd *tried* to avoid. Now, not only was it obvious Fabrizio was interested, but it turned out he was handsome *and* wealthy.

Good God, she thought to herself, *could I possibly be any more of a cliche?*

She was still pacing when Molly walked in, a smile plastered to her face.

"Caroline," she cooed, "I have to thank you. You've really gone above and beyond. Again." She went over to her friend, oblivious to her distress, and hugged her. She broke the embrace, however, when she noticed her face. "What's wrong?" she asked.

Caroline shook her head. "I can't even begin…" she said exasperatedly. "I'm just… I'm an idiot, that's what."

"You're not," cried Molly. "What are you talking about?"

"Oh," Caroline said, a note of sarcasm in her voice, "you have *no* idea, Mol. I've just been making, you know, fantastic decisions since I got here. Flirt with the suave Italian host? Check. Have a combative but strangely endearing relationship with him? Check.

Find out he's loaded? Check. Snog him in the lobby of his hotel? Check. Make a total gobshite of myse—"

"Hang on," Molly cut in, putting her hands up in a *stop* motion. "What's all this about snogging? And are you talking about Fabrizio?"

"It's not like I even *wanted* to," Caroline said manically as if Molly hadn't interjected. "I mean, yeah, I'd thought about it a bit, but he was so – I mean, he was just *there*, but then he'd been so sweet as to help me find you, and that smile – oh, that smile – but *no*. I can't be the stupid tourist on holiday who falls for the first Italian who gives her the glad eye. I mean, he's Roman. He'll flirt with anything that moves, probably charm the pants off them, too…"

"Caroline," Molly said, putting her hands on her friend's shoulders, "Get a grip. Are you trying to tell me something happened between you and my wedding planner?"

Caroline finally snapped out of her fit and looked at her best friend. "Your wedding planner …oh my God, Molly," she said with a half-smile, "you're getting *married* tomorrow…you are still getting married tomorrow, aren't you?"

Molly nodded. "Ben and I had a chat," she said. "Though really, a lot has been my fault too. But now, back to this… what happened with Fabrizio?"

Caroline pursed her lips and let out a long puff of air.

"Well, when you left to talk to Ben," she explained, "I thanked him, and I might have kissed him on the cheek. But only friendly-like," she added quickly. "And then… he twirled me into his arms, ran his hands through my hair… and … kissed me."

Molly positively beamed. "Oh my *God*, Caroline," she cried. "That's *so* romantic."

"It's not!" Caroline retorted. "It's cheesy and obvious and – and – *stupid*! It's exactly the cliche I wanted to avoid coming here."

Molly shook her head. "Oh come *on*," she told her friend. "Don't be ridiculous. He's *very* good-looking. And for the love of God, he owns the hotel. At the very least, you'd be able to come back to Rome any time you wanted and stay for free…"

"You see?" Caroline said, a wry smile coming to her lips. "This is why I never tell you anything. You always have to go from a simple kiss to a lifelong romance."

"It worked for Ben and me."

"Did not."

"Fair point. But *seriously*, if you were ever going to take a chance on love, now's the time to do it. I mean really, what is the worst that could happen?"

That question made Caroline pause. What *was* the worst that could happen? Certainly, things could be worse than a holiday romance with a handsome, rich Italian who owned a hotel and drove a fancy car, and at Christmastime no less.

Still…

"Honestly?" she finally replied. "I think I'd lose some respect for myself."

"Whatever for?" Molly asked, incredulous.

Caroline sighed deeply. "I'm… I'm not like you, Mol," she explained. "I don't go all passionate about things and fall head-over-heels. Not that there's anything wrong with that, but it's just not my style. And I never, ever wanted to be a cliche. I absolutely *hate* that holiday romance nonsense."

"Okay," Molly assented, "but I want you to think about this: why do you think they become cliches in the first place?"

"What?"

"All those films and books with broad-chested, impossibly handsome men on the covers… They might be sensationalised fantasy, but in the end, do you think those cliches just sort of happened, like they were just created out of thin air? No way. They were inspired by things that really happened, or that we always *wanted* to happen.

A woman gets swept off her feet by a gorgeous, rich suitor in a romantic Italian city… what in the world is wrong with you that you *wouldn't* just jump on that ride and see where it takes you?"

Caroline was dumbstruck. She hadn't really thought of it that way. It wasn't just a matter of not wanting to be a cliche, she realised – it was her own pride that she'd been riding for last few days.

Fabrizio was a fantasy of sorts: impossibly handsome, incredibly wealthy, and rather sweet. And yet, here she was, pushing him away, just so, what, she could prove a point to herself? She had to admit, that seemed really…

"Stupid," Caroline said finally.

"What's that?" Molly asked.

"*Me*," she continued. "*I'm* stupid. Molly, I've been an absolute idiot. This lovely man has been throwing himself at me, and I've pushed him away. What is wrong with me?"

Molly laughed at that. "There's nothing wrong with you, honey," she reassured her. "You're just as human as the rest of us. And sometimes, that means we do stupid things. But it's nothing that can't be fixed. You just need the opportunity."

"What kind of opportunity?"

"Well," Molly said, beaming, "I hear there's this big celebration tomorrow…"

CHAPTER 25

❆

"Paddy?" Helen called from the bathroom the following morning. "Love, can you bring me another towel?" She waited a few moments before calling her husband again. "Paddy? Are you there?"

Helen stepped out of the bathroom wrapped in a towel, a plume of steam trailing her. She rounded the corner into the bedroom to see where her husband was – only to find him barking orders into the phone.

Again.

"Felicity," he said sternly, "we need to – well no, I – don't make – well just go over it again then."

"*Paddy O'Brien!*" Helen thundered.

"I'm going to have to call you back," he said sheepishly into the phone before hanging it up. "Something wrong, pet?" he asked, turning to his wife.

Helen's face was red with fury. "Paddy," she said, her voice so low he had to strain to hear her, "today is your daughter's wedding day. It is a day for celebrating. For God's sake, Paddy, it's Christmas Eve! No one should even be at the office today."

"I hate to break it to you, love," Paddy replied patiently, "but today is the busiest day of the year for us. I can't just abandon them."

"Oh, you can too," she snapped. "I swear, if I see you on that phone *once* between now and the end of today, I'll break the damned phone – or your neck – or both."

"Yes, mammy," he chortled. He fixed his eyes directly on his wife. "Helen," he said, rising from his seat and approaching her, "I've never left Felicity in charge before. She's nervous, and I'm nervous, and we both just need everything to go smoothly."

"I realise that," she responded, "but the least your family can expect today is your undivided attention. Besides," she continued with a wink, "I'm going to need all the support I can get if I'm to deal with that – that – *woman*."

Paddy embraced his wife, who attempted to pull away. "Paddy, don't," she chuckled, "I'm all wet."

"I don't care," he replied. "We'll just have to be wet together, then."

"That's not *all* we can be together..." Helen said suggestively. "But for now," she added, kissing him on the nose, "I have to do my hair." With that, she returned to the bathroom mirror and turned on the hair dryer.

She left it on as she returned to the room to grab her hairbrush – only to find Paddy back on the phone again, barking orders.

Helen sighed, rolled her eyes, and went back to fixing her hair.

CHAPTER 26

Down the hall, Ben was practically screaming into his own phone.

"What do you *mean*, 'I forgot my suit?' Why did you not just wear it on the plane? … No, Mark, I don't. Just… just stop off somewhere and buy one. It is Italy after all, home of well-cut suits. Yes. Okay. Half-eleven. I'll see you there."

He hung up the phone and ran his hands through his hair. Once again, his idiot brother was throwing a monkey wrench into the best-laid plans.

How could Mark *possibly* have forgotten his suit? He was the *best man*. It was the one thing he was asked to bring. He wasn't even responsible for the rings. He – that was –

A sudden panic came to Ben's mind. *Oh God*, he thought, *what did I do with the rings?*

He first checked the room safe, but he didn't even remember using it, and sure enough, they weren't there.

Neither were they in or under the bed, in the bathroom, or on the desk.

He eyed his suitcase and, in a moment of pure hysteria, grabbed the entire case and attempted to flip it upside-down over his head.

Unfortunately, being less than coordinated on even his best day, he tripped on the suitcase table and went tumbling forward, knocking the side of his head on the edge of the cabinet and sending clothes and toiletries flying every which way.

He cursed loudly and stood, noticing a sharp pain at his temple. He went to look in the mirror for what he already presumed was there – and sure enough, a long trail of cut skin and blood streaked down the side of his face.

What a start to your wedding day...

He had just begun to clean up the blood with a washcloth and some soap when a knock came at the door. He opened it to find, much to his surprise, his father standing outside. The chipper look on James' face turned to horror when he saw his son's face – and astonishment when he saw the state of the room.

"Good Lord, Ben," James said, shocked, "what in heaven's name happened in here?"

"I – er—" his son stammered, "I couldn't find the rings. And I kind of – you know – panicked."

To his utter surprise, James burst out laughing. "Ben, old boy," he said, the sounds of his laughter echoing off the tiles in the bathroom. He was laughing so hard, he couldn't even get the next sentence out, so instead, he reached into his pocket and pulled out a small, black velvet box and opened it. Inside were two gold bands.

Ben closed his eyes in exasperation with himself. "Oh," he said slowly, "I... am such... an *idiot*..."

James shook his head and handed the box to his son. "Nonsense, my boy," he said, "you're just nervous. As you should be. Today's a big day."

"One you don't approve of," Ben said glumly.

"Now, whatever gave you that idea?"

"Oh, I don't know," Ben replied sarcastically. "How about *everything* that happened yesterday?"

"You mean, that business with your mother? Ben, your mother is the love of my life, but she and I are by no means a single mind.

Believe it or not, she's really just trying to help. And she's scared. She's losing her baby boy after all."

"What? But you've still got Mark."

"Mark is… a sweet boy. But you know as well as I do, he's incomparably stupid."

Now it was Ben's turn to laugh. "He is, isn't he?"

"Absolutely," James responded. "But Ben: your mother may have her faults, but she is also immeasurably sensible. And her worry isn't so much that Molly won't be good for the title; it's that she won't be good for *you*. All we want is to see you happy."

"But don't you see? I *am* happy."

"I know, son. I know."

"So why these shenanigans then, Father?" Ben asked. "Why allow Mother to treat the O'Briens like her inferiors?"

"Your mother is going to apologise to them this morning. Most of what happened was because of the wine. Your mother's tongue was loosened, and she made some very poor choices with what was being said. I seem to remember something similar happening a few Christmases ago."

"That business with the McGanns?"

"Precisely right," James agreed. "What started it all was your mother making an ill-advised comment on Lady McGann's – erm – *ample* posterior."

"Oh God."

"You have no idea. It took six dinners between me and that insufferable Earl of Cheshunt to get things back on track. 'Your mother has a history of saying ill-timed, ill-advised things. But she isn't bad by any stretch. In fact, she quite often has a very lucid understanding of the situation. And her worry in this case is that through your association with Molly – and the O'Briens generally – you will forget about the title, and hurt your children's chances at the finest things you always had access to."

"I never *wanted* access, Father," Ben insisted.

"I know that, but that's hardly the point. Don't you want the best for your children, whenever you may have them?"

"Of course I do."

"Well, that's all we ever wanted for you, too."

Ben closed his eyes and exhaled deeply. "I know, Father. And I appreciate it – *all* of it."

"Right then," James said, ready to change the subject. "Let's get you cleaned up and ready. It's not every day a future Earl of Daventry gets married in Rome."

CHAPTER 27

"What do you think?" Molly asked Caroline as she came out of the bathroom.

Caroline clasped her hands against her face. Her best friend looked stunning beyond belief.

The dress was perfectly form-fitting, gleaming white like falling snow, with a stripe of red and green around it for a suitably festive feel.

Her silver high heeled shoes sparkled with tiny crystals, while red beads looked like holly berries expertly threaded throughout her elegant blonde chignon,.

"Molly," Caroline said, awestruck, "you look like a Christmas princess."

Behind her, a knock came at the door, which Caroline answered.

Helen walked in, grinning ear to ear. "Caroline, you look gorgeous this morning," she said – before she laid eyes on her only daughter. "Oh," she said, stopping dead in her tracks. "Oh – oh *my*... " Tears came to her eyes and she dabbed at them with a handkerchief and strode up to the younger woman. "Oh *Molly*," she said, now sobbing as she hugged her daughter. "Oh my little girl, my beautiful little girl…"

"Mum," Molly laughed through her own tears. "Stop, you're going to leave streaks on my dress."

Helen sniffled and pulled away. "Oh, I'm sorry," she said, laughing too. "I'm just… my goodness, Molly, you look so beautiful."

"I do, don't I?" Molly said immodestly and all three women laughed again.

Caroline went into the bathroom and came out with three glasses and a bottle. "Okay, girls," she giggled. "I got this downstairs earlier. It's grappa, not champagne, but same thing, I think."

Caroline poured three glasses and Helen raised a toast. "To my Molly," she said. "May your perfect winter wedding in Rome live up to all your dreams and be a delight …"

"…and may all your Christmases be white," Caroline rhymed wickedly.

The three women collapsed in a fit of laughter so cacophonous that they didn't hear the knock coming from the door, nor the creak as it opened.

Suddenly, Caroline straightened up, quickly followed by the others.

"I'm so sorry," Patricia said quietly, "the door was open a crack, and I didn't know if you could—" When her eyes caught sight of Molly, she smiled. "My word, dear," she said sincerely, "you look absolutely ravishing."

"Thanks," Molly said flatly.

"Caroline, I don't suppose…" Patricia said, motioning towards the door.

"Yeah… I'm – er – going to see if I can find some more – erm – ice," Caroline winced as she looked apologetically towards Molly and Helen. "I'll be back in a few."

Once the door was closed, Patricia inhaled deeply. "You're probably wondering why I'm here," she began.

"You could say that," said Helen coldly. "Though honestly, I'm wondering why I'd care, too."

"Right enough," Patricia conceded. "Molly, I should start with you. I was entirely out of line with what I said last night. I had far too much wine and far too loose a tongue, and I pushed my concern for Ben way, way too far. I apologise."

Molly nodded but said nothing.

"And Helen," Patricia continued, turning to the younger woman, "I—"

"Save it," she cut her off. "I don't want or need your apology."

"Mum," Molly said gently, "let her speak."

"No, love," Helen's iciness continued. "There is much I can abide, but Patricia, you aren't just a snob or a lush. You're mean-spirited. You think so much of yourself and your titles and your family, but you have no regard for those who don't share your obsession with nobility. You are conceited and self-interested, and I have no use for any of that. Particularly when it comes to the way you hurt my daughter."

Patricia swallowed her pride and pressed on. "Helen, I realise what I did. I know it's too late to take back, and I wish that I could, because it isn't something I actually believe."

"Oh it's not, is it?" Helen charged, her anger rising. "Come on, Patricia. Let's be honest here. Because of this English nobility business, you think yourself and James as being *better* than Paddy and me. You don't think Molly here is worthy of Ben. Isn't that right?"

"Do I think we're *better* than you?" Patricia repeated. "No, I don't think we're better than you, Helen. But do I think Molly is worthy of Ben? Of course not." Helen's eyes flashed, but Patricia continued, "We're being honest, here aren't we? So tell me – honestly – do you think Ben worthy of Molly?"

The words hit Helen like a stone into still water. She liked Ben; she thought him a nice boy and a fine catch, but was he *worthy* of marrying Helen's only daughter?

"No," she admitted quietly. "No, Patricia, you're right. I don't think he is, and I probably never could."

Patricia smiled warmly. "You see?" she asked, a kindred kindness in her voice neither Helen nor Molly had ever heard before. "We have at least that much in common." She eyed the bottle sitting on the table and poured three glasses quickly. "Whatever the case, dears, I would like to propose a toast: to new beginnings. May we all have the opportunity to wipe the slate clean and start today anew – as friends."

Slowly, Helen took up her glass, never taking her eyes off of Patricia. The two women clinked glasses and drank down the grappa, not noticing that Molly simply was watching them, not having her own.

"Oh *God*," Patricia winced. "That is simply *dreadful*!"

"Isn't it?" Helen laughed. "Disgusting. Ought to be outlawed."

"I need wine. Or champagne."

"Or both," Helen added.

Molly smiled. "Why don't you two go head out and find yourselves a drink then? And if you could, open the door carefully; I'm sure Caroline is right outside with her ear pressed against it."

With that, Helen and Patricia left, and to Molly's delight, they were talking.

Perhaps there was hope after all.

CHAPTER 28

❄

"You can't be serious," Helen said to Fabrizio as he led her, Caroline, Patricia, and Molly to Santa Maria, a tiny church close to the Trevi fountain, "This is a *church?*"

From the outside, it wasn't much to look at; indeed, Helen would have walked right past it on any other day, thinking it an apartment or maybe a small hotel.

But a church?

"Wait till you see it, Mum," Molly responded cheerily. "It's absolutely *perfect*."

Helen and Patricia exchanged skeptical glances – but those looks began to melt the second they stepped into the building.

The inside of Santa Maria was as far from its nondescript exterior as could possibly be.

It was certainly tiny – just a single row of wooden pews extended in front of the altar – but it was adorned in magnificent Italian opulence.

Paintings of the Virgin Mary and the crucifixion hung in ornately woven golden frames along the sides of the entrance. Renaissance-era archways held up walls reaching to the sky.

And most impressively, a large fresco, painted on the ceiling, showed the Assumption of Mary in vibrant colours that stood with even the great Sistine Chapel as a Renaissance masterpiece.

Molly had seen the church before, but to be getting married in it was beyond her wildest dreams.

"See, Mum?" she laughed at her mother's gaping mouth. "I told you this would be great."

"Well," Patricia told her, "I have to admit, Molly, that I was indeed a bit worried about this when Ben told me how tiny the church would be— oh my!"

Patricia was surprised by a man dressed all in black, standing quietly and solemnly in the back of the church next to the Advent wreath. It took her only a moment to realise he was the priest. "Beg your pardon, Father," she said apologetically.

The priest waved his hand as if to say, *don't worry about it*, and summoned the four women and their companion to him.

His face was serene, but it suddenly became quite expressive, a smile breaking out across his wide face. "*Buongiorno! Buongiorno!*" he said excitedly, "*e Buon Natale!*"

"*Buon Natale, Padre,*" Fabrizio replied. "*È tutto pronto per il matrimonio di oggi?*"

"Please, Fabrizio," the priest said happily, "For respect of our guests, let us speak in English." He went straight up to Molly. "And you, I imagine, must be our beautiful bride."

She smiled. "I am," she said happily.

"Wonderful. *Wonderful!* Well. I am Padre Giuseppe Mazzolo, but please, call me Padre Beppe."

"Padre Beppe," she cooed, "I'd like to introduce my mum Helen, my best friend Caroline, and my fiance's mother Patricia."

Padre Beppe seemed absolutely tickled. "It is so good to see you. We so rarely get to have non-local weddings here. This is very exciting for me."

"For us, too," Helen replied.

"I am certain," Padre Beppe said. "So," he continued, slapping his hands together, "We have a little sanctuary in the back where you can get prepared and so that your husband does not see you before we start. Since there is only a small congregation today, I have done away with much of the boring stuff. We will make this very *bam-bam-bam,* quick and painless, yes?"

The women laughed.

"That sounds ... perfect, Padre," Molly said, gulping a little.

"Well," Fabrizio told the group, "it seems you have everything you need here. I must go and prepare something for the groom, and then bring the men over here. I will see you ladies shortly." He turned to walk out the front of the church.

Molly nodded in her bridesmaid's direction and then jerked her head towards Fabrizio.

Caroline took her meaning. "Excuse me just one moment," she said, "There's something I need to, just really fast..." With that, she hiked up the bottom of her dress and shuffled down the aisle quickly. "Fabrizio," she called. "Wait up a second, would you?"

Fabrizio paused and turned around on the steps outside the church. Caroline joined him outside and caught her breath. "Is everything okay, *signorina*?" he asked.

Caroline took a deep breath before starting. "Look," she said, "I wanted to explain myself. About last night..."

"Ah," he said, holding up a hand, "there is no need. I realise I overstepped."

"No, Fabrizio," she said, slightly abashed. "That's not what I meant at all. I was ... I've never been very good at romance. I've always been... guarded. Especially when it comes to something spontaneous like this."

"But how could one live without spontaneity?" he asked sincerely.

Caroline shrugged. "I guess I just like to have a plan," she replied. "Or at least an exit strategy. I don't just go on flings. And I certainly don't just fall for random strange men."

"Fall for?" he repeated bemusedly.

"Yeah. That's not me. I'm not the kind to fall head-over-heels for a guy I've only just met. And yet..."

Fabrizio grinned. "And yet," he said quietly, "you find yourself... falling for me?"

Caroline looked down at her shoes, feeling stupid. "Yeah," she whispered, feeling her face go hot like she was a teenager.

Fabrizio placed his index finger under her chin and lifted her head up to face him. "Caroline," he said, "I do not know where this path will lead us. But I do know one thing: if I did not at least follow the path as far as I can, I would regret it the rest of my life. Is this what you feel?"

She nodded.

"Then perhaps we should take the journey together," Fabrizio said. And with that, he leaned in and kissed her.

After what seemed like an eternity (but more likely was only a few seconds), he broke away. "I am very sorry," he said, "but I really do have to go. But I will return soon. And afterwards we can spend a bit more time together, yes?"

"I'd like that," Caroline smiled. "But yeah, go. Go get the groom."

Fabrizio nodded and went off as Caroline returned to the church a huge smile on her face.

Inside the sanctuary, Molly cast her a furtive glance. "So...?" she inquired.

Caroline shrugged. "So... what, Mol?"

"Oh come *on!*" Molly nearly exploded. "What's the story with your Italian gigolo?"

Caroline only smiled in response.

CHAPTER 29

An hour later, Ben stood outside the church with the other men – including, finally, his errant brother Mark.

"Ready to do this, big brother?" he asked, a glint in his eye.

Ben, visibly nervous, nodded tentatively and wiped the sweat from his palms onto his suit pants. "I could use a drink," he said.

James laughed. "So could I, son," his father said, "but there'll be plenty of time for that soon enough. Shall we head in? Paddy?" He turned to the bride's father.

"—and I don't care if they have to work 'til all hours of the morning, Felicity," Paddy spat into the phone, "I want that delivery there before their kids come down for Christmas morning." He held up a finger to ask the others to wait a moment. "No— No— Yes. Yes. All right, just heading off for Molly's wedding now, I'll call again later."

He hung up the phone to find all four of the other men with exasperated expressions. "Sorry, lads," he apologised, "couldn't be helped. Christmas and all."

"Okay then," Fabrizio said at last, "I think we are all ready then. Shall we?" He motioned towards the door, holding it open as the men went in.

Ben, Mark, and James took their places in front of the altar, while Paddy stayed back to await his daughter.

Molly surprised him by coming in behind him, unnoticed. His eyes fell to her dress first, then her face, and he found himself overcome with emotion.

"My God, Molly," he said, "You are a vision. I—" He wiped away a tear streaming down his cheek.

She collapsed in his arms. "Oh Daddy," she sniffed.

"I know, love," he said, patting her back. "I love you, Mol. More than anything in this world. And all this ..." he gestured to the church and the beautiful Italian surroundings "you were right, this is perfect."

Molly wiped the tears from her eyes. "Okay," she said, straightening her dress. "Are you ready?"

"No," he replied honestly. "Are you?"

She nodded slowly. "Yeah," she said, sniffling away another sob. "Yeah, I am. Let's do this."

"Rightio," Paddy replied. He offered her his elbow, and, arm-in-arm, he and Molly began the procession up the aisle of Santa Maria.

CHAPTER 30

❄

The priest called the service together and blessed them. "We are gathered here," he began, "on this nativity of the Lord's birth, to celebrate that special union between Ben and Molly. The readings today will focus on God's love, but we must not forget that love from on high is manifested so well in these two wonderful young people."

Molly and Ben smiled at each other as the priest continued the ceremony in Italian, as arranged.

They continued smiling through the readings, and even through the homily (though what the priest was saying barely registered for their guests).

Following the declaration of consent, Molly held her breath as they prepared their vows.

Ben went first, watching Molly intently, never breaking his gaze as he took her hand in his and spoke in perfect Italian: "I, Ben, take you Molly..."

Molly felt weak. Ben had been so good about all this, so determined to make this the perfect Italian Christmas wedding for her – and she felt she was going to break down at any moment.

She swallowed hard before beginning. "I take you, Ben, to be my husband .."

Ben smiled from ear to ear as the priest requested the rings, reassuring Molly that everything was going to be okay. She felt filled up, her heart rising as James handed Ben the rings.

Without warning, she heard a *clink! clink! clink!*, the sound of metal rolling down the steps of the altar and into the aisle. Ben groaned and Mark began to laugh.

He had dropped the rings.

He ran down the aisle after them, muttering to himself as he did. Molly couldn't help but laugh aloud. Whatever the case, whatever came next, *this* was her husband, the man she loved so dearly. He was strong, and he was brave – and sometimes, he was a complete klutz.

After finally catching the rings, Ben rushed back up to the altar. "Sorry," he lamented.

Padre Beppe laughed. "You would be amazed at how often that happens," he reassured.

"Really?" Ben asked, heartened.

"No," the priest quipped. "It has never happened before. Not once."

Ben groaned, but everyone else laughed.

"Okay, now, where were we?" Padre Beppe asked. "Ah yes… Ben, please place the ring on Molly's finger – carefully this time – and repeat after me …"

There were several more prayers in Italian, but Ben and Molly were in such a daze that they barely noticed anything until the priest announced, "Ben, you may now kiss the bride."

Ben took his new wife in his arms and gazed at her lovingly. He mouthed, *We did it*, and she nodded tearfully.

He then kissed her with a passion she'd never known before. She enveloped him, wrapping her arms around him. As they finally broke the kiss, he looked her in the eyes again.

"I love you, Molly," he said.

"I love you too," she replied before adding with a mischievous smile, "Lord Pembrey."

CHAPTER 31

A little while later, the wedding party were out on the streets of Rome, everyone beaming at them.

"Okay," Molly called out to them, "time to make a wish."

Fabrizio nodded. "Does everyone have coins with them?" he asked the group. "I have some cents here if needed."

"Not sure Mark has any cents,'" Ben joked.

"That's a really awful joke," his brother mocked him.

"About as awful as your suit," Ben noted, appraising the royal blue and white pinstripes of Mark's jacket, which he clearly hadn't picked up in the Piazza de Spagna. "Did you think you were up for a role as a backup dancer for Lady Gaga or something?"

"That's funny," Mark jibed back, "as I assumed you were yourself going to be a guest star on *Boring Old Married Guys*."

As they rounded the corner, not far from the church to the beautiful baroque structure that was the Fontana di Trevi, they were surprised to find the area relatively quiet.

"It's because it is Christmas Eve," Fabrizio explained. "Not as many tourists now, and locals stay home. You have a perfect opportunity."

"Okay," Molly announced excitedly, "Now, according to legend, if you want to return to Rome, you have to throw a coin with your right hand over your left shoulder. Ready?"

The group turned their backs to the fountain, coins in hand. Just as they were getting ready to toss them in, however, Paddy's phone rang.

He reached into his pocket to answer it. "Hello?" he asked. "Oh, hiya, Felicity…"

Helen scowled and set her jaw. "That's it," she grunted. "I've had it." She grabbed the phone from him and said into the receiver, "Felicity, stop calling and go home. Happy Christmas."

She then took her husband's phone in her right hand and promptly tossed it over her left shoulder and into the fountain.

"Helen!" Paddy exploded. "That's my *phone*!"

"It *was* your phone, love," she said tenderly.

"But – but – I *needed* that!"

"And we need *you*, Paddy. It's time to give up the damned phone calls. It's Molly's wedding day. And it's Christmas!" Seeing the look of consternation on his face, she softened even more. "Tell you what, love: if we get back in a few days and the business is gone, I'll make you a trifle."

Paddy stared hard at her – and then a resigned smile spread across his face. "I'm sorry I've been ignoring you, love. I've been under an awful lot of stress lately…"

"I know pet," she replied. "But it's time to let it go. We're in this beautiful city on our daughter's wedding day - on Christmas Eve. And I don't know about you but I have every intention of coming back here. "

She reached for her husband and pulled his face in for a kiss.

"*AHEM!*" Molly cleared her throat loudly to catch her parent's attention. "Now, if you two lovebirds don't mind …?"

"Go ahead honey," her mother replied, smiling.

"Okay," Molly said again. "One – two – three!"

Eight pennies flew through the air in perfect unison, and clinked against the stone edifice before falling into the water.

Ben grabbed Molly by the hand and kissed her. Helen wrapped herself around Paddy, as Patricia and James grasped hands.

Fabrizio enveloped Caroline in a passionate embrace, while poor Mark just stood by, embarrassingly kicking at a stone on the ground.

Suddenly, as they all stood there, little white flakes began to appear – at first just a dusting falling softly, then more and more until they were pouring out of the sky.

"Snow in Rome?" Molly gasped delightedly. "But how…?"

Ben just smiled. "Merry Christmas, darling," he said to her. Seeing the confused look on her face, he continued, "I talked to Fabrizio, and he called in a favour from a friend who runs a ski resort up north. I wanted to make sure your dream Christmas wedding was perfect in every way."

Sure enough as Molly looked around, she spotted the snow machine a few yards away tucked behind a Fiat, shooting snow into the late evening sky.

"It's… it's perfect, Ben," she cried, hugging him close.

"All right, everybody," Fabrizio called out, "I think we are ready to head back to the hotel. In about ninety minutes, we'll begin dinner on the terrazza. I have reserved it specially just for you. I look forward to seeing you all there."

As the others made their way back to the hotel, Caroline hung back a minute. She nudged Fabrizio with her elbow. "You've really played a blinder on this, Fabrizio," she complimented. "I don't know how we could ever thank you."

He arched an eyebrow. "*I* know how you could," he said.

"How?"

"Come back to me, Caroline."

"What?"

He kissed her, a kiss full of meaning and promise. "I do not want this to be, as you said, just a 'fling,'" he explained. "I enjoy your company. I enjoy everything about you, Caroline. I want to enjoy you more. I want the legend of the Fontana di Trevi to work its magic and bring you back to me."

Her eyes widened. "I just… I don't know, Fabrizio. We've only just met—"

"—so let's continue meeting!" he said excitedly. "I do not make this offer lightly, Caroline. I make it only because I want to see more of you and…"

"…and see where this is going," she finished for him. "No, I get it. I do. And…" She watched her best friend and new husband walking away. Molly and Ben looked so happy, so contented, so perfect together. "Oh, what the hell," she said. "I don't know, maybe it's the romance of Italy, or the snow on Christmas Eve …"

Caroline pulled her handsome Italian down by the collar and kissed him passionately.

Sometimes, being part of a cliche was a very good thing.

CHRISTMAS BENEATH THE STARS

EXCERPT

Cosy up with a short excerpt of another heartwarming festive romance from the Irish Times #1 bestselling author - airing now in the US as a Christmas movie on UpTV!

CHAPTER 1

*H*annah Reid loved Christmas.

She loved the cheery feeling in the atmosphere, the twinkling, festive lights and most of all, the sense that at this magical time of the year, anything was possible.

She couldn't add frost or snow to the list though; a born and bred Californian, Hannah wasn't familiar with more traditional wintery Christmas weather.

Yet.

Andy Williams' warm vocals filled the buds in her ears as she reclined in her seat and peered out the window of the aircraft to an ocean of darkness and lights below.

It would be her first holiday season away from home. Her first ever white Christmas.

It was indeed the most wonderful time of the year ...

Hannah hummed the cheery festive tune and glanced down at the cover of the magazine on her lap, a broad smile spreading across her face.

It still felt like a dream.

Discover Wild, one of the biggest wildlife magazines in the country, was sending *her* - Hannah - on assignment.

She ran her hand over the cover shot of a tigress and her cub as they nuzzled together.

It was an amazing photo, one she would have killed to have taken herself.

"Soon," she mused. *Soon it could be my stuff on the cover. All I have to do is get one perfect shot and I'm on my way to a permanent gig with Discover Wild.*

She hugged the magazine to her chest and closed her eyes, relaxing back against the soft leather seat.

IT FELT LIKE JUST A MOMENT, but when Hannah woke it was to the sound of the pilot announcing their descent into Anchorage.

She sat up immediately and looked out the window.

Everything was white!

She'd never seen anything so beautiful. The mountains surrounding the airport were blanketed in thick snow, and a light dusting covered everything else.

She could see the men on the tarmac clearing away the snow, as half a dozen planes in every size - large Boeings to small Cessnas - lay waiting, along with a row of buses to the side.

She wondered which one of those would be taking her to the holiday village she'd chosen as her accommodation while here.

'Nestled deep in the Alaskan wilderness, Christmas World is a true holiday fairytale if ever there was one.

Set amidst lush forest on the South banks of the Yukon River, escape to a magical land where Santa comes to visit every year, and you can find a helpful elf around every corner. Immerse yourself in our idyllic winter paradise and enjoy a Christmas you will never forget ...'

Hannah couldn't wait to experience the true, out-and-out winter wonderland the online description promised.

Now, the flight was on the ground, but no one was moving. There was a backup of some sort, and passengers were asked to stay on the plane while it was resolved.

Hannah wasn't too bothered; they'd arrived half an hour early in any case, which meant she still had plenty of time before her transfer.

She preoccupied herself with her phone and more online information and picturesque photographs of Christmas World.

The resort homepage featured a group of happy smiling visitors, with various green-and-red-clad elves in their midst.

In the background, picture-perfect buildings akin to colourful gingerbread houses dusted with snow framed a traditional town square. It was exactly the kind of Christmas experience Hannah had always dreamed about as a child.

She couldn't *wait* to be there.

CHAPTER 2

❄

*O*ver an hour later, Hannah was still waiting.
In Anchorage International Airport with forty or so other travellers.

Their Christmas World transfer - the so-called 'Magical Christmas Caravan' was late ... *very* late.

"You can't be serious," a fellow airline passenger commented nearby. "How much longer are we supposed to wait? Are they going to compensate us for this debacle? It is the resort's transport after all," the disgruntled woman asked.

She was surrounded by three miserable-looking children, while her sullen husband stood in a long line of people trying to find out what was going on.

Hannah had noticed the family on the plane earlier, but now she was getting a better look at them. They were exactly the type of people you'd expect to find on such a jaunt; happy family, blonde-haired and blue-eyed, with their cute-as-a-button kids giddy with excitement about a trip of a lifetime to see Santa.

More decidedly *un*happy faces surrounded the resort's airport help desk at the moment, but there were plenty of content ones to be found elsewhere too.

A father with his son excitedly perched on top of his shoulders. A serene mother with her sleeping child, and an elderly couple holding hands while they waited for their connection.

It was everything the holidays should be about, Hannah thought; family and loved ones together at the most magical time of the year.

She had been in plenty of airports, but there was something about this one that appealed to her photographer's eye.

The nearby pillars were like pieces of art, almost abstract; though she didn't really know much about art except what she did or didn't like. These were adorned from top to bottom with garlands and white lights. While elsewhere in the terminal, festive wreaths hung on hooks and there were lots and lots of fresh-smelling pine trees.

And of course, then there was the view....

Hannah had taken countless pictures in her life, some to pay the bills and many more for fun. She'd taken portraits, and even the occasional wedding when things were slow between wildlife jobs, but there was something about the outdoors that she loved most of all.

She'd spent her entire life in it after all, had hiked the Quarry trail in Auburn so many times she felt she knew it by heart. Same for the Recreational River, Blue Heron Trail and the Simpson-Reed Trail, and that was just California.

She'd zigzagged her way across America with her collection of trusty Nikon SLR cameras, but she'd never ventured this far north.

The furthest she'd been was Alberta for a wildlife safari last summer. It was those photos that had opened the door to her current opportunity.

And the reason she was in this snowy picture perfect wonderland right now.

. . .

An hour or so later, and Hannah was peering out the window of Christmas World's transfer coach as Anchorage melted away in a sea of white.

Fresh snow had begun to fall half an hour before, which almost made up for the exorbitant wait.

But at least they were on their way now, and soon Hannah would have a warm lodge, a toasty fire and the most magical Christmas experience awaiting her.

She wondered if there really would be fresh roasted chestnuts available as advertised, and what kind of activities there would be for guests to enjoy when they arrived.

The website listed things like dog-sledding and carolling, plus places to get hot chocolate, Christmas cookies, and a myriad other festive treats.

All of which sounded amazing, especially since she was tired and in sore need of some holiday cheer after such a long travel day.

She imagined the resort town as something like from the movie, *It's A Wonderful Life,* with that close-knit community feel throughout.

Yes, she was here primarily for a career opportunity, but she'd be lying if she said there wasn't the element of living out a fantasy white Christmas too.

Hannah turned back to the window. The snow was falling harder now, and the smile wouldn't leave her face.

She was about to have the best Christmas ever; she could feel it.

It's like Christmas morning. The faster you sleep, the faster it arrives. Isn't that what Mom and Dad always said?

And she couldn't wait for it to begin.

End of Excerpt

Christmas Beneath the Stars is out now in print and ebook.

ABOUT THE AUTHOR

International #1 and USA Today bestselling author Melissa Hill lives in County Wicklow, Ireland.

Her page-turning contemporary stories are published worldwide, translated into 25 different languages and are regular chart-toppers in Ireland and internationally.

A movie adaptation of SOMETHING FROM TIFFANY'S - a Reese Witherspoon x Hello Sunshine production - is airing now on Prime Video worldwide.

THE CHARM BRACELET and A GIFT TO REMEMBER (plus sequel) were also adapted for screen by Hallmark Channel, and multiple other projects based on her work are currently in development for film and TV.

www.melissahill.info

Printed in Great Britain
by Amazon